THE GREAT LETTER E

A NOVEL BY

Sandra Schor

NORTH POINT PRESS
San Francisco   1990

LIBRARY OF CONGRESS CATALOGING-IN-PUBLICATION DATA
Schor, Sandra.
  The great letter E : a novel / by Sandra Schor.
    p.   cm.
  ISBN 0-86547-397-8
  I. Title.
  PS3569.C52818G74   1989   89-3417
  813'.54—dc20

FOR JOE AND
FOR MARK J. MARKHAM

THE GREAT LETTER E

CHAPTER *1*

So help me, I am an hour too late. The episode is over, yet my mind keeps altering its strategies, as if the rabbi were still before me, frowning, gesturing, cautioning. I lean my head against the couch arm and surprise myself: in the fever of reimagining my case, I doze off on the couch.

Marilyn must have been home awhile, since I find her raincoat drying in the bathroom when I get up to take a leak. She has already taken off her wet shoes and slipped into her puffy satin scuffs and is padding about straightening up. Standing at the bathroom sink I hear her banging kitchen chairs and rustling newspapers to let me know she now has things to do when she gets home from work. As if all those years with me were not work. Bob Donahue, that sporting little go-getter, splashing designer eyewear all over the Upper East Side—and installing Marilyn as consultant! Get lost is what she's saying, which means down to the basement study, Glassman. We speak only about financial obligations for the week, Michael, and the bar mitzvah looming ahead of us. We are theoretical and polite. We theorize that I'll sleep downstairs until after Michael's big day and then split. Will it kill us to give the kid what he wants—a last memento of family happiness? So we take our meals together as a front, though it's clear Michael is on to us. Out of cowardice or embarrassment or simply the desire not to lose his bar mitzvah in the swamp of our marriage, we fake it. Maybe it's his adolescent savvy, maybe it's dumb luck, but for some reason, he never backs us into an open discussion. For him it's wolfing down dinner, prolonged silences, and a panicky getaway to homework. I descend to the basement. Marilyn washes up. During the first month, Michael appeared every evening like a lighthouse, beaming a loving "Good night" in all directions; but he doesn't do that anymore.

"I've had it up to here," Marilyn says, standing over me, her flattened palm jutting out at her neck, as I make the mistake of resettling myself on the couch for ten more minutes before dinner. Out of Michael's earshot, she whispers fiercely, her *s*'s steaming like radiators, "I met Dolores Gutman at Gristede's. She said she had just left you. 'The rabbi's angina is acting up,' she says, as though it were my fault. I tell you, get off their backs, Barry." With a swift karate chop across her neck she shows me again up to where she's had it. "Oh, Barry, haven't you argued with them enough? Can't you shut *up*?"

"Anything in the mail?" I say coolly.

"Uncle Nathan has declined."

"He's all the way out in Sheepshead Bay in a wheelchair—"

"But is Gertrude in a wheelchair? or Rita Gans? or Cousin Elliot? They've all declined, along with a dozen others. Whoever heard of tucking a message about atheism into a bar mitzvah invitation?"

I pick up the enclosure that came back with one of the refused invitations. Marilyn, honey—I plead with her silently—my fearful, phobic Marilyn whom I taught to love little dogs and cats and stroke the brown rumps of horses under their police blankets on Fordham Road. Novalis called Spinoza a *Gott betrunkener Mann*. That means "drunk on God"! Is that so damaging? And begin to read.

"Since the Torah does not represent revelation but the high thought of reasonable people, we are pleased to honor a few of our most reasonable family and friends—men and women—by calling them to the Torah. Please say the following when called upon: Blessed art thou God or Nature, in whose extended greatness we all dwell. Our ancestors gave us the Torah as a record of high thinking and a testament to the divine intellect of which we partake. Just as we do not envy a lion its courage nor a tree its height, so we foresee a life for Michael commensurate with his own nature. Amen."

I am as temperate when I read it as when I wrote it, but Marilyn cannot bear to listen. It is one of those moments when her huge chocolate eyes glaze and her disdain of my position is excessive. We have a history of great moments between us. Now they are all empties, and I want with all my heart to cart them away and turn them into cash. Once the tension of the bar mitzvah is behind us, I intend to get on with my life. Enough retrospection. Enough nostalgia. I need a new communion, a fresh start. Grabbing the day's response cards, Marilyn escapes to the kitchen. From across the street the drone of a buzz-saw is grinding up the silence where she stood. For eleven years, after his shift at the firehouse, Ed Hoddeson has cut wood. "What about the Hoddesons?" I yell into Marilyn. "Did they RSVP?"

"All seven of them are coming."

"Michael told me if Deirdre Hoddeson comes to his bar mitzvah, *he* won't."

Marilyn moans. Another contretemps, another wind about to knock us into each other on a street corner. I steady myself with a sip of club soda. Deirdre Hoddeson, menacing my son Michael because all of her secondary sex characteristics (and several of her primary ones) are, at thirteen, in wondrous operation. Thirteen-year-old Michael of the soprano voice, still taken for his mother by telephone callers—"Hello, Marilyn, is that you?" and Michael humiliated beyond speech, thrusting the phone at her in disgust. Barely five foot one, he lifts weights before breakfast, his interest in body-building traceable to a certain morning when Marilyn revealed at breakfast that Deirdre's periods had started. I sensed the ice-cold alarm with which Michael had received this information: continued to spoon Wheatena into his mouth, expression a blank, cereal and cheeks the same pale zero color. Said not a word. Left the table.

"Where's your tact?" I demanded.

"When a boy grows up without a sister, too many mysteries make girls untouchables. Periods are routine stuff. Undergrown thirteen-year-old boys are surrounded by towering thirteen-year-old women. But what do *you* know?"

Thirteen! I could scarcely recall the sensitive little beast I was, always recuperating from one or another of my little forays. I remember seducing my sister Frannie's thirteen-year-old friend Elise into Frannie's bedroom, and as Frannie groped "Für Elise" on the piano in the parlor, I groped for her in the bed. The next day, terrified that Elise would expect to talk to me in the lunchroom, I complained loudly of swollen glands and stayed home from school with a flannel compress around my neck, all feelings of superiority fast slipping into mirage.

"Michael has to be told what other boys see on their sisters."

"Deirdre is at least five foot eight, for Chrissake!"

Marilyn's failure to intuit Michael's needs has become a routine sadness to me. For example, *I* know that his primary need is to grow. (Didn't I hang from my mother's bedroom doorway, stretching a full seven-eighths of an inch in two years?)

Now Marilyn reappears from the kitchen on her way to the bedroom. "Deirdre is the girl Michael loves to hate," she says, not in the best spirit, passing her fingers through her luxuriant dark hair, pulling at it by its roots.

So things are not 100 percent in my little family, with my kid rattling around the house measuring his biceps at 6 A.M., netting his mother and me one additional waking hour in which to be estranged, and a bar mitzvah ready to take off like a train out of Grand Central Station, all doors closed, no getting off.

I should have explained that God is not like anybody we know. Not like Henry Kissinger, or Mother Theresa, or Rabbi Akiba, or Spinoza. God is unimaginable! Perfect and complete as a carrot. God needs nothing, no flattery, no songs of praise, no bargains. I should have said, "Listen, all I want is to get rid of God as king, God as ruler, God as the big negotiator in the sky. I want Michael to say God is infinite, God is necessary, and *only* God is necessary."

Instead, the rabbi walked all over me.

At last all the comebacks come to me: quotations from Spinoza like tiny keys rapidly unlocking my "position," pointed man-to-man retaliations to Mordecai Mayberg and a few to Dolores Gutman—he, wretched as a bar mitzvah boy, she, *presidentka* of our synagogue, cool, aloof, face and body like a Gupta goddess.

"It is God *or* Nature, rabbi," I should have said, "not God *and* Nature, not even God *of* Nature."

As civilly as I could, I pointed out to Mordecai that to know things philosophically is to know them in eternity, and that although October 17 was the official date of my son's bar mitzvah, nothing on *my* calendar was ever more than tentative. *Couldn't* they cooperate? If they changed the wording—just two or three lines!—I would be satisfied. I never meant it as a threat.

A glass of club soda burbles on the end table. The pleasure of gas in my stomach unbubbles the whole repressed little ritual: Mayberg shrinking into a corner, his eyes filling up (I saw real tears). "Don't threaten us, Barry. You know you're like a yeshiva buddy to me. Who else in this congregation can I talk to? Pritzker? Steinman?" and, whispering behind the back of his hand, "*el presidentka*? You think they're curious about God? They come to be big shots, to schmooze, to grow old like their fathers and mothers—God knows why they come! *You're* the one I look forward to seeing. *You're* the one who's got it! I'm always telling Dvora, 'Barry Glassman has got it!' "

"What, rabbi? What have I got?"

"A gene for God!" He brushed gently at the fatigue on his eyelids. "But lately—"

"Don't hand me that 'lately' crap. We've always had our differences, Mordecai."

"Michael deserves a traditional bar mitzvah. He's one of our sharpest kids. Rational inquisitiveness he gets from you, okay—but from Marilyn he gets another side, a normative side. You think I don't remember Marilyn's parents, very *heimish*, traditional people, they should rest in peace?"

"What the hell kind of doubletalk is *normative*—?"

"*You're* accusing *me* of doubletalk? You should hear yourself. Spinoza isn't doubletalk? Reason isn't doubletalk? You could do with a little traditional doubletalk. It's good for the nerves."

"Mordecai, you're misconstruing my purpose—"

"Our most learned cosmologists go beyond reason to a simple, single force separate from the universe. At MIT they are making the leap to a mystical beginning. Don't you read the *Times* on Tuesdays? In the science section, they're tracking God. They see Something—God?—easing a world into being." And I trying to hold onto my footing as I was being eased out by Dolores, handed my raincoat and umbrella, listening to the rain behind the rabbi's drapes, and still clutching the edge of the rabbi's desk: "Of course, rabbi. God is the substance of the universe. I agree. But it's God's intellect we partake of. That's why reason is everything. It's the whole story. Through reason we come to know God, and that knowledge, dear Dolores Gutman, dearest rabbi, is blessed happiness."

I have said this to them three times in the last month, driving home to Bayside in the long September afternoons immediately after the shop closes, appearing casually at sundown as the mourners gather for their nightly kaddish. I stand around. I joke with the regulars. I get counted among the ten necessary for the start of prayers. As the mourners pray, they put me in the mood: I hum along, thinking about what is true and worthwhile in the universe. Then immediately after the last kaddish, as the congregants are rushing to go home for supper, pocketing yarmulkes and packing away books, I move in on the rabbi, following him into his office.

"Modern science is mystical, not philosophic." The rabbi paced feverishly. "Scientists are stargazers like the rest of us." But finally all he produced was a mild ridicule. "Barry, you pray like the rest of the infidels: 'Oh God, there is no God.'"

"Who said there is no God?"

"Glassman," he reached both hands toward me; his voice grew sweet as a mother's, "you are denying that God is king of the universe."

"Oh, rabbi! All I am saying is that God *is* the universe."

I was trying my best for a balanced argument. We had always enjoyed our discussions languorously. I spoke softly. "Just *think* about the difference." I tried to smile. "Put your *mind* on it." Instinctively, I turned to Dolores Gutman, silhouetted like a Balinese puppet in the rabbi's illuminated study, her dark eyes lustrous under the fluorescent lights that also caught the long swoop of nose and the curve of heavy breast under her white silk shirt. Maybe the rabbi would understand my position, but Dolores? I couldn't afford to sound like a crank. Papers and books lay everywhere, in heaps on the desk, in chairs, trailing down from the draped window ledges, and spilling onto the floor. The deep mahogany of the bookshelves shone. I took out a mint Lifesaver and stuck it to my tongue. This was a pleasant room, disordered with my kind of bookish chaos. All those seductive Hebrew volumes, lovelier to behold than a meal or a good-looking Middle Eastern woman. And on the wall, like an eye chart, a magnificently framed diploma in English and in Hebrew, vividly hand lettered in waves of black ink, with a huge, coal black aleph. I envied my friend Mayberg this sublime cave, even his pacing back and forth, his luminous aleph. I valued his confusion. He knew I had spoken up for him at the last board meeting when Steinman swaggered in late and smugly proposed we support the rabbi's anti-intellectual fervor by dispensing with his sermons. Afterward Mordecai squeezed my hand and told me privately what an asshole Steinman was. But many in the congregation were confused by Dr. Steinman's proposal. A rabbi with no sermons? Who needs him? A new fissure of doubt spread among the congregants.

Hadn't Professor Winning always said it, half-consoling, half-mocking our flustered attempts to follow the Spinoza geometry? "Our confusion is part of our perfection." How he misled me into believing I could be a philosopher, praising me after class for my methodical readings of the *Ethics*, for espousing the system with less confusion than anyone else—or so I thought. Then the B+ in "Spinoza," and a glowing recommendation went to Yale in behalf of Lorenzo Levi, the orthodox son of an Italian Jewish mathematician from Sunnyside. Who could forget those ice-cream silk shirts, those blazing eyes, and the tiny scars on his wrists, barely perceptible under the rubber bands he arranged there for emergencies? But he wrote like an angel! I swore then to out-Spinoza Spinoza and out-Levi Levi. Levi and his rubber bands went to Yale and I to the New York School of Optometry. Eventually, they dropped his fellowship: a suicidal Orthodox Jew was the wrong risk for a philosophy department. I finished with honors. Why then do I still see pudgy Lorenzo Levi riveted to my dream of boola-boola and all that crap, while all I have is a drafty optometry shop, lit with a capital *E*, among the crazies on Eighth Avenue?

"You are a marginal Jew, Barry Glassman, only marginal," the rabbi said balefully, the rainy wind rattling the windows of his study. Thus my moment with the rabbi belonged to eternity, or would have had I not noticed that his glasses were ill-fitting, marking time by sliding down his nose and causing him to swat them back up with the bent knuckle of his index finger as he walked. "For your own sake, I will not take you seriously." Dolores Gutman's expression darkened. "Barry," she said malignantly, "think of what you're doing to Marilyn and Michael. Let's get out of here now," she said, opening my umbrella and leading me out to our cars, parked side by side in the rainswept Temple lot. "I have to get to Gristede's before it closes." The rain drummed overhead on the umbrella as we huddled beneath it and walked. "Come to your senses," she whispered, as I pulled the umbrella closed and climbed into my car with it. The rain poured off the hood of her raincoat and ran off the tip of her nose. But she stood until I pulled away. "For God's sake, Barry," she yelled through the downpour, "it's only a bar mitzvah."

CHAPTER 2

Although business is no better than usual, I'm busier since Marilyn and I agreed to separate. How long can I have Feliz taking over her jobs, doubling as benchman and optician, knocking out five or six pairs of glasses a day, while I examine eyes and prescribe lenses? And both of us with bookkeeping now, dusting stock, ordering supplies. Marilyn used to go about her chores shivering on days like this, but now she has heat and wall-to-wall carpeting. Bob Donahue's shop is a palace. My woolen socks itch. Certainly, the rain last night hasn't helped; to avoid coughing in Mrs. Mateo's face, I turn my head as I tell her to look where I point my pencil. "Look here, Mrs. Mateo. Now here." Who wants to be fitted for glasses with a side of TB?

Awful business, the passions: how we allow them to obstruct our vision of the universe! Today, because Michael misunderstands me, I grind plastic lenses for Mrs. Mateo, who requested glass; because on his tough little shoulders he carries the embarrassment of my visits to the rabbi, I get distracted. He has been taking it all in. Marilyn and I let off a little steam, but Michael? He merely stuffs dinner into his mouth and makes himself scarce. Maybe I'm blowing this up out of proportion. Maybe Michael is being tolerant. Even Mrs. Mateo tolerates my error. I expected a good dressing-down. I expected to be told how valuable her time is, what a stupid, clumsy doctor I am. But she picks up her briefcase and crosses Eighth Avenue into Mithra's Luncheonette, recrossing with a container of steaming coffee. Sips it, waits. Feliz all the while is putting his apron on and setting the machinery in motion, flicking switches with extravagant pressure, smacking his forehead. "*Glass*. Is not a difficult word! You have cotton in your ears. We do two times what the whole world does once." I snap the plastic lenses out of the frame and a peevish Feliz regrinds the prescription in glass, using a photosensitive lens that deepens from light beige to a darker beige. After forty minutes, in the tips of my fingers (with Feliz nearby grunting something in Spanish to the customer, who discourages him with a wave of her hand), I feel her temples relax, so hopeful is she of these supple new glasses, and she thanks me portentously in her Puerto Rican English, showing for the first time a tremor of animation, a slit of a smile, ignoring Feliz. Out of her briefcase she removes a checkbook and writes a check.

Turning about with her new glasses on, she reads the posters of beautiful women in eyeglasses around the walls, mouthing the words: *Soft contact lenses may be right for you*; and *Are your eyes telling you that you need bifocals?* "Maybe I need bifocals," she says. "Since the accident, the left eye is blinkin' like crazy."

Her solemnity is very moving. "Were you badly hurt?"

She appears to be waking up, slowly, as if from hypnosis.

"Was it a car accident?"

She takes off her glasses and holds on to the counter. "Three weeks ago, Hector, my husband, is jackin' up a van, is takin' off the tires, is stretchin' out underneath when somethin' slips, the van is rollin' off the support—" she waves me away with a flutter of hands; "he is crush to death."

True misfortune arouses moral horror even in the disinterested. Thus, Spinoza. But what can I *say* to comfort her? Moral horror is no admission to grief.

A tall, skinny youth in thick, steel-rimmed eyeglasses is next.

Feliz does the preliminary workup on the young man. I lead him into one of the curtained examining rooms.

He is seated before the Phoroptor, clutching his eyeglasses in both hands, the lenses small and heavy as whiskey glasses. I switch off the lights and slide various lenses into the refractor, running through my routine. The *E* of the eye chart lights up like a mysterious monogram.

While I work, my mind compiles a list of the possible donors of the great letter *E*:

> Eye
> Ear
> Egypt
> Einstein
> Element
> Elohim
> Existentialism
> Empiricism
> Ethics
> Effort
> Eros
> Enigma
> Espinosa (Despinosa, Spinoza)
> and Elise Edelman, Eighth grade

I do not miss a beat. "Tell me which is better, this? or this?"

He tilts his head away. "The first."

"This? or this?"

"The second."

"Can you read the bottom line?"

"*x v f*—"

"Go on—"

"It's too small."

"Does this make it clearer?"

"Yes."

"This?"

"Hey, slow down!"

"Clear-er?" I repeat, though I am working at my habitual pace.

"No."

"This? or this?"

"Let's have that again."

"This? or—"

He is flustered now. "*x v t*. I made a mistake."

"No problem. This? or this?"

"It's the second one—. Wait, the first."

Of course, when a patient isn't sure, we're at the stopping point. Every few minutes the fellow says, "That bastard, I'm as blind as my old man."

In this unknown father's defense, I tell the son it's not necessarily genetic, anyone can have a corneal astigmatism. "But you'll see better with contact lenses," I say.

"Okay. Then make them blue."

"We don't tint a correction for a high astigmatism." I tell him to come back Friday for a fitting.

"Fuck Friday! I can't wait till Friday."

"We don't stock that lens," I say.

"Don't give me that! I wanted to be used to them by Friday. Shit on 'don't stock'!"

He is outraged, mimicking me, yanking open the curtain.

"Late Thursday, then. Listen," I pop a Lifesaver into my mouth, "you need a custom lens that corrects for a 50 percent astigmatism. We don't stock that lens."

"*We don't stock that lens*," he sasses under his breath and bolts for the door, slamming it so hard that the display of sunglasses rattles and comes crashing to the counter. Feliz's cat dives under the counter for cover.

The universe compensates for itself; patient, tragic Mrs. Mateo for the shitty young man who cannot wait. What the hell has he got to do on Friday? Kill his old man? See his parole officer? Get bar mitzvahed?

Feliz, who has been watching the confrontation, screams after him, "You bastard! Come back here," and, runner that he is, sprints toward the door after the departing customer. "He owes us for the examination," he says, flying past me.

I race after Feliz out onto Eighth Avenue, flinching—the glare, the noise—! suddenly registering the impertinent "us." "Forget it, Feliz," I shout. Garment workers steering racks of ladies' suits, walkers lugging huge radios in their arms. "Let him go!" I can't go any further or the crazies will walk away with the shop. "*Feliz!*"

Regretfully, he gives up the chase. He shoves me as he passes into the store, moody now, his face hot and crimson. "Excuse me, Barry, but you are *wrong*. That money is ours. We earned it."

I glance at him with a tolerance I haven't felt for Feliz lately. He is so sincere, always dragging in accusations, ethical problems, his own proprietary ambitions that lead us nowhere. "The fellow was taken unawares. He had no rules ready," I explain with an air of detachment, "except *blame the old man*. He expected x and got y. Feliz, you have to be ready with behavior to meet any crisis. It's best to let him—"

A sad little smile slides across Feliz's mouth. "You are too soft, Barry. Your customers walk all over you."

By the time Bob Donahue opens the door of the shop, I have counseled myself for a couple of hours. I am thinking seriously about starting over, moving out of the house altogether, finding my own apartment, toughening up the standards in the shop, getting rid of Feliz, whose opinions of *my* effectiveness have begun to interfere with *his*. His outbursts vie with his servility as his least endearing trait. Donahue's arrival takes me unawares. Consideration. Respect. Living through the questions before attempting the answers. But this is not the era of Leibniz, Descartes, Newton, Huygens— why the hell has Upper East Side Donahue navigated all the way to the West Side?

I think I am ready for him. I ask Feliz to take over while Bob and I go into the back room. The bottle of Scotch I keep hidden away among the trays of lenses is down and uncorked, and my two shot glasses, a bit crusty around the rims, are washed.

"Cheers!" we say, and pour it down.

Donahue drifts over to the wall of drawers holding our stock of frames, absently pulling out trays and sliding them back into place. "I'm not going to beat about the bush," he says, his back toward me. I can tell from the broad shoulders of his trench coat that he is stylishly dressed, though I had not noticed it when he came in. As he turns, I remember what a scrubbed dandy he is, what an outcropping of elegance from his deprived Catholic boyhood in a tiny, child-ridden walk-up on Rochambeau around the corner from ours in the Bronx. "I've come to talk about Marilyn."

"I appreciate your concern, but—"

"Not so fast. Your wife didn't send me."

"Then why get involved? Awful business between a husband and a wife.

Did I ever interfere between you and Agnes? Look, our problems didn't happen overnight."

"They never do."

"What makes *you* believe—"

He takes a step toward me. "Listen, Agnes couldn't keep up with the changes. She *couldn't*—"

I caution Bob to keep his voice down. I don't want Feliz in on this conversation.

"Look, Donahue, if you want to play matchmaker, forget it. There's not a chance in a million that Marilyn and I will make it after this."

I allow a moment of silence.

Bob has lowered his chin into one polished hand. When he glances up, a look of such realization appears in his eyes that I am obliged to appeal to him directly. "Bob, I haven't had a good night's sleep in years. I've got this miserable cough. My kid won't talk to me, and his bar mitzvah is only two weeks away. Marilyn has been out of touch with my life for months. Could be years. You don't know the half of it. Why do you look so goddamned surprised that it's not going to work?"

A momentary superiority heartens me. Donahue has come to *me*, taken a bus to the West Side without a trace of good humor, the corners of his mouth caught in an unfriendly firmness, casting his entire face in an unsatisfied expression, as if the questioning and the conferring were at best a half-truth that stood among us out of some old and all but forgotten alliance. He seems to me nothing more than a squirrel, gathering necessary food while the corners of his mouth twitter a bit. I pity him his surprise, his unequal elegance, which seems out of place with the slight sweat from the bus ride that glows on his cheeks.

"It's decent of you to come," I begin again, but Donahue reaches out and clutches my arm. "Oh, man, have you got the picture wrong!" A wave of his delicate after-shave makes me feel faint.

"Drop it, Bob. Neither of us ought to go through this with the other. It's embarrassing. Marilyn really has a kind of contempt for me. Maybe I deserve it, but I don't have to live with it."

Donahue has one hand in his pocket, the other cutting the stuffy backroom air as if to reveal something by its continual effort. "You're forcing me to spell it out, you dumb bastard," he says, angry. Imagine! *He*'s angry with *me*. "Marilyn and I have been seeing each other for quite some time."

He has put together a machine, and he is steering me into its jaws. Quite some time. Two weeks, I think. Six weeks? The last month has left me an eccentric, it is true, and I go bitterly over my descent into the basement as Marilyn has risen to the heights of Bob Donahue's triumph, his high-rise condominium, the incongruity of their burgeoning affair abruptly disadvantaging me. Six weeks, I think!

Or is it longer? "How long?" I ask quietly.

Donahue looks away.

"Come on, you son of a bitch. Lay it on the line." Louder: "How *long*?"

"A year and a half. Almost two."

"Get away from me," I breathe. "Don't you have any respect?" I recall the slow breaking down of our dedication, my tending the bills, writing the checks, her steadfast dinners, her reupholstering, and scheduling dentist appointments for my upper periodontal inflammation, even as these were deceptions, even as our bonding declined into a bankruptcy we both recognized as mediocrity, as lifelessness, the hand writing checks without a tremor of consent or luxury, laundry losing its sparkle, talk dwindling into gray silences, the house gray as mice, as I suspected nothing, nothing beyond the philosophic deprivation that I thought was sweeping me away from sunlight and ethics like an ocean of ideas that tosses a soul as if it were a rowboat. All the while he is fucking her, stroking her clitoris with the flat of that same hand that chops and chops at the back-room stuffiness, listening to her as she confesses my inadequacies, my bookish unconcern for the poor dying quiver of her sex.

A fit of coughing seizes me. Feliz rushes back to see if I am all right. Donahue pours water into his own glass. Years ago we went partners on a pair of roller skates and each with a foot on a skate and a foot pushing the asphalt, we sailed our way down Bainbridge Avenue, later touching our scraped and oozing knees as a blood sign of our partnership. Now I cannot bring myself to sip water from his glass. I knock it over. The Scotch I have just had has brought on a paroxysm in my lungs.

You! God! Is this the future that you have so carefully withheld from me? Is this the unseen part of the whole perfect universe? Only my stubborn ignorance keeps me from embracing the fact, this preposterous idea, this news

about Marilyn and this low-life, this scum as *my* truth: the future is as un-
alterably fixed as the past.

"I thought you knew," Donahue says. "Why do you think she came to
work for me?"

It seems a reasonable question, but the clever little fucker has overwhelmed me. Nothing in my quiet, methodical system can match the dazzle of the question, love beckoning her through an optometrical come-on,
ah, the better to see you with, my dear, the better the seduction, why not
work at the elbow of the beloved and cherish each other's high-pressure
savvy, in a shop shimmering with glass and mirrors and carpets an inch
thick, and in a twilit condo on the thirty-first floor above a jeweled and glit-
tering New York, plummet to the impulses of a huge new passion, why not
come to work for him?

I cannot answer. The machine won't be shut down. It grinds and snaps
long after the innocent material is fed into it. It destroys anything. Victims
sucked into moving parts. Crushed. Asphyxiated.

"You'd better go, you prick," I manage to say, holding my head in my
hands, eyes pressed into my palms. I cannot look at him or at the sordidness
of my shop. Condemnation hurtles through my mind, but it is all directed
at him. To Marilyn I am as loyal as a mandarin duck flying desperately next
to his mate until his wings drop off. Heavy slow footsteps. The door of the
shop opens. Closes. When I look up, I am alone in the back room, the bottle
of Scotch still out, still uncorked, the overturned glass nearby. Shelves of our
inventory close in on me as the sample eyeglass frames stapled to each box
glare down like wall-eyed faces. I take off the frames I wear and wipe the
wetness out of my eyes and the sweat from the bridge of my nose. For
professional reasons I wear glasses, though the lenses are ordinary glass.
Now I look through my twenty-twenty vision, but the clutter in the room
blurs. I pour myself another Scotch and swallow it, gasping, certain I shall
within half an hour be dead of a coughing seizure. Do not dwell on death.
For the next half hour, think only of life, of inner wisdom. Live through the
next thirty minutes with every cell. Think of Michael and the joy of your
lives together. There is no time for penitence.

But the drink brings me to my senses. I restore my glasses to the bridge
of my nose: the clutter has a sparkling clarity. Marilyn, you bitch, running
out to screw Donahue in your secret time at the Vision Centre. The cat wan-

ders in; it leaps onto my lap, and I stroke the little body, remembering when I persuaded Marilyn to extend her hand and for the first time in her life caress a neighbor's cat. Timidly, my hand lay under hers, then slipped away, resting on her knee; she held one limp hand aloft, and I recited to her that all our consciousnesses move toward God, hers, mine, the cat's, all things unchanging. Then again her forearm rested on mine: I felt the slight delay, the vague tremor—was it ceremony or sex?—I whispered to her common sense, talked to her personality, "How brave you are. He's not going to hurt you. Feel the fur. Touch the nice pussy. He likes it." I had to admit I sounded a lot like Professor Winning. Her fingers quivered, the small pink nails with pale moons edging forward, she spoke grudgingly of her willingness, then of her terror of being scratched, but when the tips of her fingers reached the fur, the shoulders of the animal drooped instantly at her touch, the back arched, the purring rose in its profound contentment. She stroked and stroked, and I could feel her draining the cat's erotic pleasure through her fingertips down, down into her excited body. When the cat fled into our neighbor's apartment, and we were on our way to her house, she clung to me, rubbed the back of her hand, the palm of her hand, up and down my bare summer forearm, the triumph of her moment sweeping her toward other triumphs. Like two cats we stole into her empty apartment, and we kept on stroking each other's arms, thighs, our soft bellies, tickling the palms of our childish hands as we hurried to slip into each other's pants for the first time, knowing her mother would be home from work in half an hour.

Feliz attempts to comfort me. He has heard everything Donahue has said. Every salacious word in two languages now stinks up the air. He throws his arms around, corks the Scotch, opens a bottle of 7-Up and makes me drink it. He calls me his physician, his dear physician, says however that I sound bronchial, I must go to the clinic today, he will take me, we will shut up the shop and together we will go for X rays. He throws his coat over my shoulders, runs out in shirt sleeves, and comes back with hot minestrone. He locks the front door and sits next to me, coaxing me to eat the soup. "You are a good person," he says over and over, spooning soup into my mouth. "You are the best person I ever meet. Your wife, your son, your friends"— he pinches his fingers—"they are worth nothing in comparison with you. Now do not speak. Be a ghost and say nothing. The hot soup will take away your nervousness. I stay with you, Barry. Feliz is your friend."

My code of conduct shifts now to make room for Feliz as steadfast friend, Feliz whom I was ready to can half an hour ago, Feliz the gossip and master meddler in two languages. I am the student Spinoza walking in Amsterdam in the 1650s, the thickness of my cape blunting the thrust of a fellow-student's knife.

Someone is rattling the front door. "Sit here," Feliz whispers and runs to unlock the door for the customer. I hear a disturbance. Unwilling to lose a sale, I pull myself together and step into the shop. Two short stocky women with strong Spanish accents, a mother and grown daughter, need to have glasses made. Feliz is in the midst of barring their way, telling them we are closing up, when, assuring him we can complete these two examinations before we leave, I take each woman in turn into the examining room, first testing the elder woman's intraocular pressure. Difficult to tell whether she is tensed up or borderline glaucoma. I urge her to see an ophthalmologist, try to sell the younger woman contact lenses, and end by making my usual workaday sale—cheapest frames, plastic lenses, ready by Friday, pay cash, more Spanish. I open the front door and, still wearing Feliz's coat over my white lab coat, my shoulder blades stabbing sharply against the starched weight, I step into the fresh evening air. The mother and daughter, after lengthy encouragement from a highly professional Feliz, pass me in the street without a word.

The sky is closing, and the avenue is filling with people. Five forty-five P.M. I am astonished that I am willing to stand there amid all the human suffering I feel. A paralytic in a self-driven wheelchair, a pell-mell kind of confusion widening his eyes, flings himself across Eighth Avenue. Though it is not yet the first of October, I raise the collar of Feliz's coat in a chilly salute.

I am recovering out there on the sidewalk amid the snakes and hyenas of the West Side, many of them wired to their own zooey music. The air and speed of the street, like invisible ultraviolet rays, slowly kill off dangerous images of Donahue. My code of conduct formulates itself, except for one question: Does Michael know? Obsessed with this question, I yield myself to it rather than to the answer, for the questioner has greater insight than the answerer. It is probably a given that Michael should know; my obsession with the question is grounded in intuition. Michael eventually will know whatever I know, what all men know of the eternal, limited by finite reason. Does the paralytic know less about suffering than Rabbi Mayberg? than Immanuel Winning? than Spinoza? God is utterly and equally remote from all of us—and yet he runs through us like lymph. The mind is a thinking thing. Swearing that I am okay, I return to send Feliz home. I lock up for the night, coming a shade closer to understanding why, if God is perfect, there should need to be an Eighth Avenue at all.

CHAPTER **3**

Marilyn has already gone on her morning walk. I arise, an utterly dislikeable man. It's Sunday. We made love last night in the basement—who can explain it?—before and during Michael's return from a school dance, Marilyn hollering advice through the shut door to eat the chocolate cake in the fridge as we labored nostalgically over each other's genitals. The bed was without improvisation, more and more docudrama: we were relentless about reenacting our best sexual repertory, always with Michael brushing audibly against the shut door to the basement, banging the refrigerator in the kitchen, or clomping back and forth in the hall between bedrooms like a warship positioning itself in the locks of a canal; but Donahue is the big playboy's yacht stuck in the canal. We keep trying to ram it loose, to free up the canal for the three of us. Nothing wrong with trying, is there? I am unable to forget, I tell her, mindful that Substance is the cause of all modifications that come out of it. I give Marilyn all her positive attributes, the quick funny smile, the do-able competence in the kitchen daring unrepeatable soups with cinnamon and curry and a good veal stock, the excessive respect for dogs and cats, and always the grin of love for Michael. Her clear skin is like a girl's, though lately she has tooth troubles and her jaw seems slightly underslung. Her one personal extravagance has always been fancy nighties and backless satin bedroom slippers with ostrich feather toes on a small satin heel, totally belying the sensible English walking shoes she wears to work. See those slim, tanned legs as she pulls off her panty hose the minute she comes in from work. Barely inside the door, she would sigh with pleasure, rolling the panty hose down over her ankles and off. Last night I fell asleep as of old with my hand slipped between the damp contours of her bare thighs. No, nothing wrong with trying the old rituals, until we realize that a jammed canal requires a new technology.

Bernard Baruch made me proud to be his namesake, sharing the Hebrew name Baruch, used for Torah readings, burials, Hebrew school, and the naming of a child. Baruch College makes me proud, since I am its graduate. But Baruch Spinoza is my teacher and master: from him I learn that our knowledge is partial, we are partially free, partially in ignorance. From him I learn to exist without bitterness and pride. I am what I am, or, in Jehovah's words, I am that I am. I will not complain that I am an optometrist and not an ophthalmologist; that the pathology of that tremulous organism is too specialized for me; that I have one five-foot soprano son and not three six-foot baritones; and have been cuckolded by a lifelong friend. Quests and accommodations are my destiny, as is my unfailing study of the Infinite. But I am no Spinoza! My B + intellect fails me at crucial moments, most recently as I work my tail off on refraction formulas. Just yesterday morning what a rainbow that was! Walling myself into work and away from the disappointments of marriage, I stepped out into the driveway for a breath of early air, and there it was! I immediately thought of Marilyn and the wonders of another chance. Between the blue and the violet, a deep, sheer, diaphanous streak, a blazing indigo—and then it vanished. Which compound in our polluted city produced that soft and spiritual blue baffled me. God, what a color! But even Spinoza surrendered to the vastness of Nature and recognized that he owed his defects to the fragmentary vision of man, even he had limits to what he knew, had to live in a finite house, sleep in a bed, work in a rectangle of a room covered with glass dust, at a wooden lens-grinding machine, until his lungs failed. Amsterdam in the seventeenth century. A malodorous place at the brink of new thought. The new philosophies, after Descartes, were in the smelly air, in the cold chrome light that swept across the Waterlooplein on an October night. Ten years ago I dragged Marilyn to Holland (she wanted Spain and the Alhambra!) and we toured the sacred places where Spinoza lived, studied, died. Oh, if only life were so simple as to begin at birth!

Michael and I, arriving together in the kitchen for Sunday breakfast, stand before the open refrigerator, peering in. He is in his sleep uniform—gray sweatpants, an orange crush T-shirt, feet still bare, thick dark hair like his mother's falling into his eyes. (Mine is Glassman hair, reddish and sparse.)

"What time did you get to bed?" I say.

"I saw the last half of *Saturday Night Live*. And after that some reruns of the 1936 Olympics. They showed Hitler in the stands. He's a ringer for Uncle Nathan."

Michael's light eyes swim toward me with the utmost candor. "I would have called you to watch the pole vaulting, but I thought you were asleep."

Michael sits and eats granola, reaching out periodically to pour more milk, then more granola, into his bowl. He is ignoring me, but his indirectness has landed in my throat. I am having trouble swallowing. In my embarrassment, I stare off to the side of Michael's head, about sixteen inches away from the epicenter of his eyes. When he turns in my direction, I level my glance. "What is it, Michael?"

"You're giving Mom a real hard time."

"You think so?" I am speaking softly. What can he know about an ethical universe?

He nods. "And me, too."

"That's not my intent."

"Then quit bothering the rabbi about my bar mitzvah. All I want is to get it over with. I don't want you to make up a new service. I've got this one down cold."

"But people make up their own wedding services all the time. Remember Aunt Frannie and Uncle Alan's? Frannie wrote the whole thing herself, except for the part about the laws of Moses and the state of California. It was so matter-of-fact, the way she worked in her previous marriage."

"What's wrong with the bar mitzvah everybody does?"

I pause.

"You don't believe in God, do you, Dad? Grandma told me always to pray to God, no matter what Daddy says. She used to say, 'Listen to Daddy about soccer and eyeglasses and to Mommy about money and God.' "

That self-styled *rebbitzen*, what did she know about God? Did she ever teach Marilyn about God? "Michael, come on. What else would I believe in? People roam around the planet with two problems: one, life hands them a few tough breaks and they think they know it all; and two, they confuse selfishness with true self-preservation. Some day you'll read the works of a great thinker, Baruch Spinoza."

Michael has had enough of me. He bends his face low into the cereal and shovels it in. But the truth is he is still listening.

The color in his cheeks is conspicuously rising. Finally, he is picking at a thread of orange T-shirt, then fidgeting with the sack of granola from the health food store, and as I reach out to touch his arm, emphasizing a point about unity, tears stream from his eyes. He slams the bag across the table. He is shrieking at me, swallowing in huge gulps. "Look at who's talking about unity. Spinoza is an asshole. Why can't you just lay *off* ?"

God is neither underachiever nor overachiever. He is maker and made, dreamer and dreamed. It is as impossible to conceive of God not acting as rain not falling or ice without a shape. Whatever God is able to create is already realized. In God's infinite intellect, there is nothing that does not exist in reality. The universe is his achievement, every ant and pebble precise and necessary.

I know what it is necessary to do, and I'm free to do it. But do I do it? A week has passed since my confrontation with Donahue. I sleep fitfully. Dreams come; I am in a Bronx forest, a deep Bavarian glade with the Jerome Avenue El rattling by. It is day—but no, a glimpse of sky reveals it is night. Stars hang over the El. "Baruch, Baruch," comes the nasal voice of my dead mother one night. I awoke, calling back to the dream, "Mama, Mama. God is not transcendent, doesn't hover over the Bronx zoo. He is betrayer and betrayed. He *is* the earth, the zoo, the gum balls fallen like stars from the trees of Kossuth Street. Remember how the Bronx wind blew up Kossuth Street? Blessed Mama, angelic Father of sacred memory, Blessed Baruch."

In my suburban Bayside garden the caved-in cornstalks are God, the dried and stunted ears, the Octobering earth itself. It is impossible to conceive of God looking out for me more than for Donahue or the corn seed. The eye of God is like an empty nostril. To be all-seeing is to see without eyes. To be God is to exist without having been created. God's spirit cannot be incarnated in a seed nor in a man, any more than a cow can reside in a Camembert. In my dream I heard my mother's shy, vulgar voice, booming at me from dingy St. Clare's Hospital on Ninth Avenue, "Baruch, please go to shul, say kaddish for me, *do* it. . . . Forgive all my restlessness. Darling, remember."

The news about Marilyn and Donahue has strangely compelled me to get closer to her. I have my overworked philosophy to put aside and she has Donahue. We meet on more even terms than we have in a long time, and for a few days it works. She begins to talk, announcing that our lives have gone out of control, tells me why she is attracted to Donahue. "He is such a real-ist," she says matter-of-factly. "He's like oxygen after I've been suffocating inside a philosophy book for twenty years. I need fun, money, pretty clothes. I need spontaneity. Freedom!" (Spinoza, the architect of human freedom, imprisons her—from that illiterate fascist Donahue she gets freedom!) "Donahue is all impulse," she concludes. I push her heavy brown hair aside, hold her close to me, and impulsively kiss her, lightly wetting the rim of her ear with my tongue. She allows it, though I suspect we are patronizing each other in some mean, destructive way. Still, she presses herself to me, and I pull her down on me, again in my basement study, the bare light bulb swing-ing from the moment her head has bumped into it. Again we hear Michael come in, this time from band practice and pizza afterward, excessively noisy to let us know he is in the house, but I am in such need that I sanction no in-terruptions (Marilyn yells to him news of lasagna in the fridge), the two of us hurrying through our lovemaking, cherishing the fearful moment as if the Nazis were on our step and could be heard hammering at our door, and she a little ahead of me and pulling away just as I am coming, soaking her belly, her slip, the insides of her thighs.

It ended badly.

So for days I keep to myself. The bar mitzvah is two weeks away and I have not returned to continue my debate with Dolores and the rabbi. In-stead I have become a Marrano. I have gone underground, my Spinozistic thinking haunting my heart as Yiddishkeit haunts the very blood of the Jewish pretender. Wasn't it a Marrano who was Alphonso VI's aide-de-camp when he stormed Toledo? A Marrano physician at the court of Emanuel I in Portugal secretly consulted Maimonides and Rashi for Jewish remedies with which to dazzle the court. I imagine myself healing my mar-riage as I once healed the infanta with an ancient recipe for oil of mustard, and with hot bricks (and a *mishebayrach* on my lips). Oh, if Marilyn only had boils on her neck (I am an ace at boils, and warts lift away at my touch)! In fact, I am obsessed with healing, picking up Michael's new suit—a double-breasted navy blue that makes him look at least 5′3″—and Marilyn's new outfit, a winter white suit that sets off her dark good looks. As they glide through the kitchen in their new clothes, I compliment them. I express my pride; I say, how lucky can you get? I have my best gray suit cleaned and pressed and buy a new pair of black shoes. I stay out of their way, healing from a distance. I go to the shop and put in my routine days. Marilyn goes to Donahue's Vision Centre, and I have to do her work of controlling the crazies who come in off the street—perverts who crave the feel of someone's hands on their face, others at the brink of blindness, for terror of sightlessness haunts even the most degenerate and least moral of us. A windy fall day brings in all the losers, a homeless cinder inflaming the eye, premonitions of blindness smashing inside their blood vessels like the ocean at Rockaway. Motherly assurances and the distraction of slipping on the latest in frames by Porsche were among Marilyn's daily wiles. Once in a blue moon she made a sale. Now, Feliz and I do the mothering.

But my whole life is a lie. I see myself on the beautifully tiled floors of a Spanish patio, sunk to my knees and crying, "How long, O Lord, how long?" I am a soul unlisted in the universe.

Life becomes a duty. Twenty times a day I am slain spiritually, because no one speaks for the soul. The fires of the auto-da-fé are burning my insides, but there is no one to console me. And when Marilyn and I sit down to eat, we are ashamed before each other's eyes. Marilyn, feeling the strain, but keeping silent, wants nothing to erupt before the bar mitzvah. I find no consolation in concealment, but I do it for Michael's sake. Yet we show a prosperous face. The family is intact. One evening after dinner, for example, Marilyn loads the dishwasher and I linger at the kitchen calendar. It's only 8 P.M. but she has already x-ed out all of October 14. Three days to go. Marilyn deals only in trifles, in a new teapot with a spring spout, while the great spirit boiling in *me* has no vent, no mechanism, until I am sick of it, sick of the cruelty of my own rational churning, weary, embarrassed by it, by being a pretender, though when the phone rings I have to envy her easy connection with whoever it is. She is still one of the girls, interpreting my enclosure with the invitations in the most casual terms: "Oh, *that*! You know Barry is eccentric about things like that. Ignore it," and while she talks, in good faith, setting a bowl of chilled grapes in front of me.

The poet wrote, "Good-bye Mantilla, my homeland, good-bye Spain / for the lion is taking me from you in a storm."

Is anything worth losing Marilyn for?

Let me answer that question:

(1) Miracles are natural events, the immediate causes of which we do not know. I do not really know why, for example, she has stuck it out with me for twenty years. Were she to find her way back to me, my behavior might also appear miraculous, since the cause of my tenderness toward her goes beyond the current ability of my reason to demonstrate. For Spinoza does not say that what cannot be demonstrated by reason is absurd; only what is *contrary* to reason! Meanwhile I have scooped out a nest in the basement amid journals, calculators, notebooks, and discarded crutches. Sometimes that place is like Lourdes or Ste. Anne de Beaupré, and I, one of the crippled, having surrendered my last crutch (Marilyn), must crawl on the powdery floor until I am healed.

Will reason fit under my arm like a crutch and get me moving again?

(2) If one can say that Marilyn is doting, superstitious, lazy, then she has a thousand virtues, but imagination is not one of them. A woman of *imaginatio* might have recognized me as a man of science, but Marilyn is no prophet. Like Donahue, she is moody and impulsive; she sees only the Aquascutum trench coat in front of her nose, missing the neon *E*'s pointing on either side to Eternity.

To Espinosa, Error is not a failure of the understanding but a deficit in the imagination. The wife who cannot imagine her man in a Bayside hammock reading the *Ethics* under the fumes of the Long Island Expressway lacks a way to identify Error. But you will say I expect too much of Marilyn. Not at all. I know what a quick study she is.

(3) Each of us has the sense that we belong to something. Each of us desires a bond with what is imperishable. And what is imperishable is a patch of garden, mulch, the eternally sprouting seed.

(4) Giving up my philosophy to win Marilyn back would be like waging nuclear war to save a front tooth.

(5) If all things have been made for one another and any individual thing

is knowable only as it relates to the whole universe, why not freely substitute another "Marilyn" for this one? Eight years ago, I almost did. We had hit an impasse. We had just moved to Bayside. Michael was adjusting poorly to the new kindergarten. I admit Marilyn had her hands full. I was working two jobs, looking for a shop to buy, and writing my note for the *Spinoza Quarterly*. I gave twelve months of evenings to it, filled five copybooks, suffered night sweats while the new house went without shelves and dead-bolt door locks. Mirrors and pictures leaned against the walls waiting to be hung. I argued that since we can have an idea of an idea, we can examine an idea without its object. Marilyn had the idea we would be robbed of all our objects. I sent in one hundred and twenty pages. They printed three-quarters of a page, next to the last in the issue, the last page being paid personals.

In six months Marilyn had turned to ice. In a year I was preparing the text of my own personal: "Quiet, modest Spinozist (Jewish by birth) seeks the company of philosophic female. Leibnizians and left-handed need not apply." (I hate Leibniz, that plagiarist of Spinoza, and I have a theory about the sinister incompatibility of left- and right-handed lovers, stemming from Roman law.) One night Marilyn took Michael and slipped away, but her father, my untiring debater, came to my rescue: "Does he beat you? Does he starve you? Does he insult you?" By the time they came back I was composing a letter to a "Red-headed violinist. Afternoons. Manhattan." Michael did better in first grade.

But we each put on that rift and wore it like a wedding band. It forbade substitutions.

(6) Goethe, a disciple of Spinoza, might have given us a break; the bastard knew the "boundless selflessness" in every sentence of the *Ethics*, how tough it is to slog through it, and finally how exalted to resign oneself to the "great laws of existence," instead of trying to make it through life with the help of "trivial consolations" (a wife!).

Heine said all our modern philosophers see through the glasses Baruch Spinoza ground. Marilyn! Be a philosopher like the rest of us. Put on those glasses and have a look!

(7) Nature's goal is not the comfort or convenience of human beings. Marilyn knows this. She is not a spoiled woman. Who could give up such a woman?

So I reason, nostalgic for debates in behalf of reason. Because I have no outlet, I bang into the furniture. My keys drop, and I go through red lights. My bones seem to vibrate even as I lie in bed at night or get out of my car and stand in the driveway, as if an engine had been left running. Reminders of my failure are everywhere, in the rabbi's two-fisted handclasp as we arrive at Temple, and Dolores Gutman's triumph as she leans over me in the first pew: "I'm so *glad* the day has come," she says, her bosom soft and vulnerable. Even as the congregants behind me chant the prayers, I make my silent adjustments, substituting songs and poems from the secular "Supplemental Readings." Pressing next to me in her white outfit, Marilyn is glowering, since I am obviously in the wrong section of the prayer book. I select a poem written by a Jewish poet of Spain:

> Let man remember all the days of his life
> He moves at the grave's request.
> He goes a little journey every day
> And thinks he is at rest;
> Like someone lying on board a ship
> Which flies at the wind's behest.

When I am called up to bless the reading of the Torah, I recite what is expected of me, flying at the wind's behest. "Blessed art Thou, O Lord our God, King of the universe, who hast chosen us from all peoples, and hast given us Thy Torah. Blessed art Thou, O Lord, giver of the Torah." Israel's election! The chosen people! King of the universe! Giver of the Torah! Preposterous, mean-spirited, self-glorifying myths, and here am I, too compromised to call the lie. Since no grandparents survive, I am the link with tradition. I gaze also at the frontier, facing the unknown decisions a man has to make. And in spite of my anxiety, or maybe because of it, I am moved by the moment and cherish it. My son. Oh my son!

A still, small Yom Kippur voice in me clamors to be heard: *Barry, don't rock the boat.*

When it is Michael's turn to go up, the memory of my own bar mitzvah day descends upon me. My Torah reading that week was Isaac's would-be sacrifice by Abraham. Oh, the craziness of that story. I felt such betrayal because the mysterious bar mitzvah lottery had landed *this* fateful portion on *my* Sabbath. My own dear and saintly father sat next to me. The strain of eyeing him sidelong was giving me a headache. Was he ready to lead me up the mountain to sacrifice? And at the last minute would a goat appear, baa-baa-ing its way down the aisle to the front of the synagogue onto the *bimah*? It was all so nerve-wracking. I had never been so hot, never in such proximity to death. Upstairs among the women, I could see my mother mouthing the words and gesturing at me, index fingers pointing east, "Face front." But I could not surrender my search, stretching, scanning the filled sanctuary, guarding my father out of the corner of my eye. And, exactly behind my eyeball, my head throbbed and pounded. People packed the synagogue, and I couldn't make out a goat anywhere, no matter how I craned my neck. Soon the rabbi's voice grew resonant, magnificent, bellowing inside my eyes, and I passed out in my pew, slumped against my father's shoulder in a cold faint. I awoke to a hubbub among the men, and an old woman who had descended with her smelling salts from the women's balcony hovered over me, spitting over her shoulder lest an evil decree had befallen me on my bar mitzvah day. They stood me up; and marched me to the *bimah*. I went on with the service, my voice barely a squeak, but resolute, and more in love with my father than ever, for he stood next to me throughout the service with his angelic, empty hand consoling my shoulder.

Now turning my head, I see the synagogue filling with the faces of friends, neighbors, and relatives, ranked and exhibited in the pews.

I make the mistake of reaching for Marilyn's hand—for old times' sake. She glares right through me; it is a look of dread and dislike, counterfeiting the holy moment; and withholds her hand. Healthy, triumphant Marilyn bypasses me as a cool vein bypasses an overheated, erratically pumping heart. Of course, I should have known, but my philosophic temperament beats on. Though I try to suppress my disappointment, it is crushing the holy moment of Michael's ascendance. Now is she satisfied? She has finally done it! I have been underground for weeks, and is this to be my reward? The heat of a Middle Eastern desert is spreading between us like an arsonist's fire.

Michael reads with great assurance. His dark hair falls into his eyes, but he chants unerringly. He is well rehearsed. Almost at the end, his voice drops to a baritone, and he manfully chants the conclusion in a voice unmistakably male. When it is over, his eyes flash in our direction, but they do not rest on me. I am aware that Marilyn receives his look with a broad and loving smile. In her white wool outfit and benign face, she looks like a nun. He presses his lower lip over the upper, as he has done since he was a baby to camouflage his satisfaction. How that tiny, intimate gesture unhinges me. Tears stand in my eyes. God, how I love that kid! Only Rabbi Mayberg glances in my direction, his eyes kind and with not a gleam of irony. I am a father, too, they say, honestly, willingly. Is Mordecai to be my only comfort? Men coming down from the *bimah* press my hand. I nod anyway in Michael's direction. The cantor is singing; the ark opens, the congregation rises, but my heart is bereft. There, there is my son holding the Torah scrolls and here is my estranged wife, beaming, singing lustily, and I, in the midst of their great happiness, suffering on the other side of the heat. And where the hell is Donahue at this moment? Has he had the decency to stay away? I know an invitation went out to him long before our meeting in the shop, Marilyn routinely inscribing his address as if he were a cousin or an in-law. But is he here?

By the time the receiving line has ended, the party is about to begin. Ah! Glassman! Look alive! See the lovely ballroom festooned with flowers, tables covered in navy blue, and sparkling with white napery, gleaming silver, shimmering water goblets. I know it is a modest party as these things go, but Marilyn has done a good job: we have always had an eye for class, and this is a small, classy affair. Marilyn is, in fact, a frugal woman. A certain dark Renaissance beauty, by her own devices, is still hers, though on Sunday mornings she dips the silky dark hairs of her mustache into peroxide. She never takes taxis, preferring to hike up and down the length of Manhattan in her blunt-heeled shoes, lunging into them as if time has attached her more permanently to the city and its sidewalks. Our tastes have grown up together—modestly but agreeably. What I spend on books, she spends on clothes, and neither of us has a taste for expensive consumer goods. For the bar mitzvah, as for everything else in our lives, we are governed by a budget; until lately we have always been sensible about money, always finding nonetheless something elegant in a world that outspends us, a tidbit of marzipan, a shred of pâté, like enlightened dogs who live on the scraps of a rich man's cuisine.

But to my horror I am attending this affair as if I were a widower. Wonderful smells of sautéed liver and water chestnuts come off trays being circulated in and out, but I have lost my appetite. Marilyn sits next to me like an office associate, an assistant lens-grinder in the shop. I cannot eat. I do not talk.

Only Mayberg makes conversation—about his headstrong youngest daughter, who is training with the American Ballet. "It's hell," he says of a dancer's life. But I am sitting in my own hell and decide to leave my assigned table. Stick it out, I say to myself. Michael will never forgive you if you take off for home at this moment. Oh, but how tempting it is. Slip away through the stainless steel kitchen doors. Scratch this appointment from your calendar. Go for a drive in the mountains. Look at the leaves turn color.

Instead, I make my way—alone—to the other tables to greet our guests.

The room is not large, and the number of tables has been kept to a minimum. I am surprised to see Uncle Nathan after all, who claps me vigorously on the back. He does look like Hitler, though a gray-faced and defeated Hitler, Hitler after the bunker, immediately after the cyanide capsule. Of course, it is the still black twitch of a mustache that creates the resemblance, and a certain brutality in the eyes, a blunt understanding of beginnings and ends. Uncle Nathan's cyanide is the diuretics and heart regulators, the liquor-free, no-salt diet he is on. He turns to the woman at his left, then to me. "Barry, I want you to meet my driver. Do you remember Enid Moscow?"

I extend my hand. I don't remember her at all, though at first glance she resembles my old high-school math teacher, Mrs. Winston, in her rumpled tweed suit and white sweater. Nathan sees I am ready to leave. With a gentle hand, he detains me. "Do you remember Cousin Harris Mintz? Never without a deck of cards on him—, the one who disappeared?"

"Sure. He was going to be a chef—"

Just then we all elevate our wine glasses as Cousin Loretta Salinger, a thin widow caressing a bottle of wine, makes a toast.

"To Michael's wedding!"

We all drink.

I intercept Nathan's glass and gently lower his arm. "She's Harris's sister," he says, extending his lips for a sip.

"Oh, Enid *Mintz*." After a moment: "I don't suppose there's been any news—It's been a long time."

"Believe it or not," she says, "a detective is still on the case. It was twenty years last August."

"To absent family," I say, raising my glass again.

She looks up in surprise. "And didn't your mother die around that time—though I must have been away at college. For the life of me, I don't remember coming home for any funeral."

"My mother was a confusion of scientific principles and black magic. She insisted on cremation. Then she made me swear to recite the kaddish after her for a year."

A line of thirteen-year-olds has surrounded the table, swaying their arms in time to a song, Michael an inconspicuous member of the circle. Do I imagine that he is sticking his tongue out? His face is turned before I can be sure.

"Barry had a wonderful mother," Nathan says, as the kids charge off to another table. "She practically raised me when our mother died. She was a highly intelligent woman, a scientist at heart. She could have gotten a prize, the way she grew things in her dining room—peppers, parsley. And the dill—it grew tall against the windows, like beautiful green lace. And the fragrance of it lifted your spirit the minute you came into the house! God, I can still smell it. And she could rewire lamps and irons and fix electrical outlets, and when she bought a new outfit, she always dyed a plain white blouse to exactly the right shade to go with it. Even if it took five or six tries, she came out with exactly the color she wanted. Everybody loved that little artist! *Liebe* Leah. I miss her!"

"Nathan, take off the rose-colored glasses. She was more like Napoleon, or Robert E. Lee. Maybe like Isaac Newton," I say, uncomfortable that Loretta and her widowed sister-in-law Claire are so attentive. "Once she showed me how light breaks into color. Was I five, six? She pricked a hole in a window shade, placed a prism in front of the hole, and allowed a ray of sunlight to strike the prism. At first it was pinkish, the color of a lox, and then it exploded across a bedsheet she had hung on the wall behind. She was ecstatic because she had all the colors of the rainbow to give me! All of them." Another lifetime has annexed my being.

The waitress arrives with a steaming tureen of soup.

"Barry, maybe you'll find time to look over my finances. I'm a little worried—"

"Nathan," I whisper into his ear, "put your napkin up and eat your soup. We'll get together," I say loudly, and I hug Nathan to my chest.

Reluctant to return to Marilyn's table, I scan the ballroom, spot a few of my optometrist cronies, and glide over in their direction.

It is fair Stan Gunn. "Stan, the man! How are ya? Cathy!" I bend over to kiss his wife.

Several optometrists are at this table. Albie Rashkin and Herm Gluck; only that fuck-off Donahue, rich and overeager, is conspicuously absent, having had the good sense to stay home. His shares of the burgeoning "Vision Centres" is worth, they say, close to a million dollars. Along the way up he dumped his childhood sweetheart, simple little red-haired Agnes, who played video games while she waited for him to come home. I've known him and Agnes all my life. We'd go to a bar mitzvah a week when we were thirteen, though their nuns didn't like it. He would have given away his grandmother to have a bar mitzvah!

"Barry," Stan says, "how're you *doing*?" He is holding a bottle of ginger ale, ready to pour.

"You know—" I point a thumb down. God, I *am* weary.

"You ought to come by someday and look at my shop. Maybe you'll get an idea or two." He pours himself a glass of ginger ale. "You've got to think of angles. This week we're doing the second pair of glasses made from the same prescription half price. You'd be surprised how many prescription sunglasses we turned out this week alone!"

"Nah. I'm too busy."

Stan's mouth slides into a bemused smile as he sips his ginger ale.

"Really, Stan, I'm on to something important now."

I can always count on slow, deliberate Stan. Still, I hesitate to describe my work on the rainbow. Like everybody else, he'll think of fairy tales, pots of gold. They don't know that Spinoza and the great philosophers of the seventeenth century wrote treatises on the rainbow. My favorite question was whether or not rainbows appeared before the deluge. Or was Noah the first human being (he with his reputation for drunkenness, tottering at the edge of the ark), the very first to behold a rainbow thrown across the sky? Go trust a lush. I know that nocturnal vertebrates see chiefly blue; birds see red, but are subsensitive to green, blue, and violet. What about insects? Primitive forms of life? Did the rainbow exist if they couldn't see it? Did giraffes know where orange ended and yellow began? Does Stan know where Glassman ends and Marilyn and Donahue begin?

"It's a little work on refraction. I'm analyzing the degree of intensity in the colors of the rainbow in polluted areas. Have you ever seen a rainbow over New Jersey, near the refineries? You can't breathe for the stench, but what a sight! Only in polluted Athens high over the Acropolis do you get a comparable phenomenon. By calculating the intensity of certain colors, you can determine the composition of the pollution in the air. I think there's a connection between the angle of refraction and retention of contact lenses by people who wear them in polluted cities."

"You are marvelous, Barry baby. Marvelous."

"Well—" It is possible Stan is a little polluted.

"Marilyn still helps you?"

I shrug. Rashkin and Gluck are listening; I am interesting everybody too much, I think.

"What does *that* mean?" Stan asks.

"I don't know," I say truthfully. I have said enough and push back from the table to rise.

"Wait," Stan interjects. "Why don't you and Marilyn come out to Detroit to the Optometrical Society meetings in January? Gluck and Donahue are making plans to go. It might do you good to see what the pros are up to."

I move in on him as someone passes, too close and too sudden. "Are you saying I'm still an amateur?"

"God, no, Barry," he says, backing off. "One of these days, Barry boy, you're going to make it big—bigger than any of us dream. You've got ideas cooking all the time. I think you're another Huygens—a professor—"

"*But*—!"

"But you could be making money, too. Listen, this party must have cost you a pretty penny."

"I only have one kid—"

"Wrong, Barry. Your mind should be making big bucks for you. Look at Donahue and me—neither of us ever wrote a sentence for *Optica Acta* or any of the other journals you write for, but we're easily worth three or four times what we were ten years ago. In Bob's case," he twists his mouth to one side, "a pile!"

Stan is not through murdering me with his Dun and Bradstreet report on Donahue. "Tell you what, Glassman. I'll set up an appointment for you. The R and D people at Bausch & Lomb ought to have a drink with you. You'd get a royalty on anything they patent. Why not? You're the inventor. I happen to know one of the research V.P.'s at Bausch & Lomb. I'll speak to him. Count on me."

The ballroom is beginning to thump, guests clanking a fork or knife edge against a glass of water, others pounding the table with their hands. It is time for the toast to Michael.

"You're a prince," I say to Stan. We embrace. "I'll call you in January."

"Right."

"Stan, I'm glad you could come."

Do I mean it, this excessive thanks and gratefulness? I believe I do. I down a glass of Scotch before I go, vowing to work on Marilyn's betrayal by renting a place of my own where I can read and fit events into my system. And I vow to throw myself into my optical calculations as soon as the bar mitzvah is over, this very night! I swear it.

We have agreed that Rabbi Mayberg toast Michael. But he has taken me aside and declined—on the verge of a throat infection, he says, pressing a finger to his neck. So I go to the front of the ballroom, slipping in and out among the tables, avoiding Dolores and Marilyn, and grabbing a microphone that stands at the front on a low stage. I search about, hunting for the object of my toast; finally, on the right, I see a couple in the rear bay window, one a female with long wavy hair, the other a male, sacked out across the bay, his dark head in the female's lap. She is twisting his tie between her fingers. When the room quiets down and I begin to talk, they both stand up. She is at least a head taller, and I know they are Deirdre Hoddeson and Michael, their heads bent toward each other and calmly conspiring, like husband and wife. So I make my toast, raising my glass of champagne to the right rear of the ballroom:

"Michael, we have come to share with you our possessions, especially those of love and spirit. This bar mitzvah marks our good fortune in having this spiritual experience together. We adore you, Michael. If we could, we would banish all discord from your life.

"Michael, three practical things: Ask questions. Think about truth. Grow."

Throwing my head back, I drink the champagne in a gulp.

The ballroom heaves with a new round of thumping and ringing of glassware.

Do any of them understand that my heart is breaking?

CHAPTER 4

Such are the post–bar mitzvah perplexities that beset me, still holed up in my basement after the shop closes, subsisting on tuna fish, pumpernickel, and coffee. Paint from the friable ceiling dissolves into my cup like powdered sugar. Despite her obsessive cleanliness and the sweet smell of coconut oil on her flesh, Marilyn has stopped wavering. One philosophical evening too much and she has abandoned me for good. Glassman, I say to myself, your loveliest innocence is behind you. Let her go. There is a new life in you. The old life with Marilyn is over. Search into every leftover memory for truth. Make a few lists. Hark back to the Waterlooplein ghetto and the early days of Spinoza. Hey, Baruch, don't surrender. Separate the real from the rotten, the essential from the ostensible.

Follow that little enlightened soul around Amsterdam as if your own mother, brother, and sister had grown ill. Luck was just as scarce in the seventeenth century as it is for you, a storm blown in from the sea, an infant (God forbid!) dead, a house swept off its pilings as if it had never stood. Boats hooted along the Amstel around a separated Christian community, and the Jews stitched themselves into their own inquisitorial dressing gown on the Waterlooplein (Bayside's Temple *B'nai Chesed*), concealing their mortality from each other, as a father conceals it from a son, as you would conceal it from Michael.

In the street, the stench of the canals left a bitter taste on Baruch Spinoza's tongue. Walking to the synagogue tired him. The fleas were everywhere. He coughed and coughed, thinking a cloud of fleas had brushed past his lips, invading his mouth with a ghostly flutter. The neighborhood of Vlooienburg—Fleaborough!—took its name from the infestation of fleas in the huge refuse dumps near the Burgwal, where he had been born. (Who could forget the corner lots in the Bronx that filled with chicken carcasses, green ends of salami, stale and mildewed bread, shipwrecked couches, and abandoned, rusted iceboxes. We played there, climbed over the litter like ambitious little rats, coughing, screaming with nine-year-old joy, yet mindful that our mothers forbade us to be there. "You'll get the plague! You'll never go to college! Play on the sidewalk!") Fears from infancy were of catastrophic events (garbage, no college), sea and river rising above the levees, and always the men struggling to hold back the sea (hold back the sweltering Bronx apartments). A ring-dike enclosing a ring-canal was built around marshy ground, a row of windmills draining water out of the polders into the canal and out to sea. But for Baruch Spinoza, the struggle against nature resided not only in the Vlooienburg market and on the dikes and canals, but indoors, where disease and death created, deep within the boy, a private and privileged sanctuary, his household defeated regularly by the stillness of fever followed by the lassitude and certainty of death. Home was an unfriendly, unfathomable place (who could fathom Mother's gropings for a universal truth?), filled with the dread of knowing what we must never know, that death is our fate. And who can say what to make of it? He and his father Michael regularly made the ten-mile walk to the Portuguese-Israelitic cemetery south of Amsterdam in Ouderkerk aan Amstel, laying in their dead—the infant brother and sister, Ishac and Mirjam, three of father's wives, Rachel, Hannah Debra (Baruch's own mother), and Ester—on the banks of the Amstel, down from the bent and aged oak trees standing in a cluster. The leaders of the community were buried in high ground. Their stone monuments, graced by Hebrew and Portuguese inscriptions, showed sensuous sculptures of angels in high relief (my mother tormenting me with cremation, no monument, no inscription, not even a footstone), their Moorish faces and swirling gowns a chiseled legacy of more passionate days in Portugal. But on the gravestones of the Spinozas, good plain Portuguese lettering: *Espinosa*, a few dates, nothing else.

What can a sickly, faint-hearted boy do as he survives? When no one at home was dying, his father was occupied with his business. Business and the business of dying; there wasn't time to soothe an anxious child. Only the synagogue school drew Baruch's mind to other matters. (After my father's death, I too fell in with the mighty distractions of study. It tempted me. It ran me in circles. Was I equal to it?) What pleasure to be enclosed by lessons instead of death! To read, to argue (to hear Professor Winning, trained at Columbia), to hear Rabbi Morteira, trained in Venice among the Medicis, and to carry home those flashes of logic to the Houtgracht (to Kossuth Street) under a piece of bright sky still breaking in the late afternoon, the tall poplars (the bus stops) marking the succession of avenues that crossed the darkening canals.

Glassman! Take warning! Spinoza is dead at forty-four of phthisis, lens powder suffocating his lungs. Get out of that basement. Already you have pains in your chest, doubtless too from the lenses you have ground, and an inclination to awaken in the middle of the night in a fit of coughing.

It is true. My coughing is bitter company in the dead of night. Sometimes, upstairs, I hear Michael tiptoeing to the head of the basement steps. He opens the door a crack. "Are you all right, Dad?" he calls down. I suddenly smell the leftover kitchen odors of dinner.

"Yeah. Just my cold. I'll take an antibiotic this week and get rid of this harness on my chest," I say, heaving noiselessly up and down, up and down in an effort to suppress the cough. "Michael, sweetheart, go back to bed."

Michael, embarrassed by my interventions with the rabbi, is Marilyn's loyalist, a recruit in her army. His concern discharged, and to remind me of his irreversible partisanship, he slams the door.

But love has already comforted me, and my cough subsides. This is my Michael, fathering his own exiled father, his own balding and outspoken Baruch. Then upstairs the refrigerator door opens and shuts, and downstairs in my beloved little laboratory, a few yards from my journal-lined bunk, the oil burner whines on. Craving a little music, I pick up a program of hit songs from the sixties on my pocket transistor. Ah! Lie back. Listen. Take a few minutes for yourself. Ignore the postulates still at the gates.

Michael believes Marilyn has given me notice at the shop and mumbles something about Bob Donahue putting her to work. "I know," I say, "I know." But later as I disinfect my stinking little toilet in the back of the store (I admit that Marilyn used to do this), I imagine her and Donahue fucking in his new 31st floor apartment, near the Fifty-seventh Street Vision Centre, her fear of heights giving way to a passion for dizzying orgasms, the higher the better. Over the stained and splintering toilet seat and into the blackened bowl, I shake the mint green cleanser. The pipes clank with the announcement: *this is it*. I have left her. Can I manage in this world without her?

Marilyn married me because I freed her of her phobias, not only of neighborhood dogs and cats, but of heights and swimming. First I gave her articles to read from the *Harvard Medical School Health Letter* and the earliest issues of *Prevention*. Together we went over Proposition XII of the *Ethics* on absolute unity. Then I took her to the top of the Empire State Building, and with the wind flattening her hair against her face, and with a short rope tying our hands together (she thought of herself as a mountain climber), I led her to the railing to confront the city below. She looked, squeezed her eyes shut, but looked again, tugging me closer to the rail by the rope that bound us.

In the calm, murky waters off City Island, I taught her to do the dead man's float, and in my best hypnotic chant repeated, "You're a salmon, a tuna, you're as adorable as a red snapper. You won't go down. Keep your back arched and your arms out and your face submerged. I won't leave you. Now float. You belong here. The water loves you. You're doing it. I'm next to you, but I'm not holding you up." I said, "Not swimming is a superficial problem. You were born to swim." She spluttered, she splashed, she stiffened, and she floated away, delirious with accomplishment. In exchange, she dusted my books, kept my laboratory tidy, and welcomed my hand between her thighs. She kept the air conditioning on low in summer (I hate the penetrating chill of air conditioners going full blast) and the heat at 73 degrees in winter, and for years put up with my weak lungs, low sperm count, and second-rate optometry business, as well as my arguments with her father, who thrashed out at me in God's name with neither a systematic nor a Jewish alternative. (Only Mayberg argues with intelligence.)

But she finally grew weary. Her father died. Her mother died. Self-improvement was at a standstill; she broke into a sweat along the service roads, still unable to risk the three moving lanes of the Long Island Expressway. "You've pressed me into a textbook," she said again and again. "I'm stranded on the service roads. I need confidence. I need a few good jokes." It didn't take much for Donahue to pry her loose from my textbook.

The texts in the Amsterdam municipal archives conflict: here we are told that Michael Spinoza was a well-to-do trader, living on the Houtgracht in the Burgwal near Swannenburg in a tall, shuttered gentleman's house, that he was one of the *parnassim* of the synagogue, a member of the board of governors who made decisions for the community; yet here we see that Michael Spinoza buried his dead in Ouderkerk aan Amstel in the lowest ground, soft muddy terrain (oh, the feet remember my father's summer grave and the hard, sun-baked earth of Farmingdale, Long Island).

Which is the truth?

Are we *born* phobic, or are phobias thrust upon us?

Are we *born* philosophers, or do we only die philosophers? At night, the father and his mysteriously penetrating child appeared in their candlelight as if they had been in mourning for decades.

At ten, Baruch was sent by his father to collect money owed him by an old Jewish woman.

"Rebecca Fernandez, alias Abarbanel, I have come to collect what is due my father, Michael Spinoza."

The woman reached under the lace collar of her bosom and withdrew a small leather pouch. She removed the thick red Persian carpet that covered the table and began to count out the ducats on the exposed wooden surface. The boy stood and watched.

In Dutch she said, "Your father is an upright man. I sing his praises as one who never departs from the laws of Moses. He is a pillar of God."

The boy noticed that, even as she spoke these pieties, her eyes narrowed, and her hands moved distractingly across the table, so crisply in fact that had his eyes not been riveted to the sudden activity of her bony, spotted fingers, he would have missed her deception. She pushed the coins toward him in a heap. But Baruch's small fingers counted it out coin by coin. "Rebecca Fernandez, alias Abarbanel! You owe me two more ducats, the two you have let fall into the slit in your table. And he pitted himself against her in such a way that she could not free herself from behind the table. His slender index finger slid up and down along the slit. He collected his coins, then turned over his outstretched palm. Waited.

"Devilish child," she said, speaking now in Portuguese, her mother tongue and the language in which Baruch had been raised. Her dishonesty required the familiar.

Baruch stood his ground, pinning her behind the table as he leaned against it. Presently she fished under the table, extracted two coins from a drawer there and dropped them into his hand. He left without looking back.

I tell this anecdote (a) because it is one of the few that survive about Spinoza's childhood and (b) because as these former Marranos were unlearning one set of pious rituals—the bended knee, confession, a belief in saints and a priestly class—to take on another—the Sabbath, prayer in the synagogue, dietary laws—the boy Baruch stood somewhere outside of ritual, comprehending the irony of false piety. What pricked the heart of the child (his name—Espinosa—meant *thorn*)? Why did he not withdraw in fear, accept the money minus the two ducats, and run home fast to taste his soured childhood for years to come?

But childhood is slow to sour. I remember unaccountably blissful childhood walks home, mindless of everything but the riotous twelve-year-old self, kicking a stone or a bottle cap up Gun Hill Road as if I were at bat with two out and a pennant at stake for the Giants, unconsciously going over isosceles triangles and the Euclidean perfection I had witnessed that day in geometry.

Spinoza's walks were grimmer. Shadows hurried over the canals like skaters. The icy air chapped his face and made his eyes run. The fog hurt his lungs when he breathed. There was little joy in what he had discovered. It seemed to him rather as it had to me—we had glimpsed a law of the universe: that there are no signs of piety other than the leather glove fit of a geometric proof, premise A leading to premise B leading to conclusion C— providing you were smart enough! He quickened his steps. The ice on the canal was pious. A horse and cart jingled their devotions as they passed. The sound cheered him. There were always seductions, temptations toward the religious life. Chanting, music, camaraderie of the community. What about the truly religious, the dear teachers of the Talmud Torah—Mordochai de

Castro and Joseph de Faro? And the three highest teachers of the yeshiva: *Hahamim* (wise men) Isaac Aboab, Menasse ben Israel, and Saul Morteira, whose classes in Talmud and Gemarah he would one day enter on his way to the rabbinate. What of their piety?

The fact is he never entered those classes. There came an early end to professional religion (optometry displaces philosophy). Into his father's imported fruit business he went at age seventeen. Where was piety then?

Rabbi Mayberg, still clinging to revealed faith, but learning out of necessity in a suburban Temple to talk the language of rational insight—professors, scientists, mathematicians, humanists, and doctors all figured among his congregants: Dr. Arnold Steinman (economist), Dr. Carolyn Schwartz (rheumatologist), Professor Gene Peres-Pritzker (physicist)—even Dr. Barry Glassman, who for one year came nightly to say the kaddish for his dead, unaffiliated mother—they found a family there among the mourners, cheered by the workaday communal prayers that locked out private grief. And the rabbi, white-skinned, with elastic bands shortening his blue shirtsleeves, became his arch opponent and arch friend, eloquent in his admirable spirit, leisurely in his articulated faith. Mother! Don't die. *Magnified and sanctified be his great Name. Blessed, praised and glorified, exalted, extolled, and honored*, etc., etc., etc., reciting it every night, then driving home to face Marilyn's nagging, like pulling down the shades on a big light. But the truth is the child has allowed the mother to die! Nightly buttering up of God lest the child be the next victim. Hey, God, you're a superstar. Listen to your praises—you run the marathon every day—you get into Johns Hopkins—so leave me alone! Glassman, again you've got it wrong. A reminder of the speck we are against the infinite. Shall I chant the *yisgadal v'yiskadash* for Marilyn? Life hanging by a threnody. Can't Marilyn make it on her own? She swims laps. She feeds sugar cubes to horses.

I want to get Baruch Spinoza on the phone, but of course Mordecai Mayberg is on the other end. I try to think of him as one of the *hahamim* in the ranks of Aboab and Morteira and the great Menasse ben Israel, who crossed the channel in a small boat to see Cromwell about letting the Jews back into England. Menasse eyeballing it with Cromwell! But what is Cromwell to me? White-nosed Rabbi Maybe and doe-eyed Baruch Spinoza—that is the pair I crave.

Although I have telephoned for help, I am dominating the wire:

"_____."

"Glassman here, Mordecai. How are you?"

"_____."

"Listen, I could be worse. Michael is heartsick. I am walking out on Marilyn, and I am feeling like the scale of a snake, a drop of sleet, the dot from an *i*, but I am hanging in. And from this ridiculous standpoint, Rabbi Mayberg, this specklike existence, I have to accept that these calamities are happening to me. Good and evil have no meaning in relation to the universe as a whole. They have no meaning for God. What do *you* say—God tolerates evil? Wrong! Evil and ugliness and chaos—a child embarrassed and exhausted by a father who would repeatedly rub his nose in the truth, a wife fed up to her antlers, who gallops immediately into the arms of another—. But confessional is not a Jew's style. Jews need their sins. The universe with its myopic father-abusers, its menaced animals and despised vegetables (Big Boy tomatoes that somebody raised in a Long Island garden rot on the delivery truck, and the bloodied corpses of little pet dogs lie on the Long Island Expressway) is no other than the blessed, praised and glorified, exalted, extolled and honored God! Amen. What do you say, Rabbi Mordecai Mayberg, to *that*?"

"_____."

"Listen, Rabbi, I can quote right back to you:

> 'God nothing does nor suffers to be done
> But you would do yourself if you could see
> The end of all events the same as He.'

When the Messiah comes? Hah! I'll open a new shop. Lenses for the millennium!"

"_____."

"Speak up, Mayberg. You're not getting through."

"_____."

"Listen to a good friend? I called *you*, Mayberg. We've always counted on each other. I want you to give me a little advice. I have a lead, don't I? I know that love must be given to all, not only to the useful and the admirable."

"_____."

"I said *useful*. Yes, my mother was damned youthful and admirable, and

I loved her, and even so she intimidated me. The sight of her flirtatious good looks was unmotherly. She would have had me lift her up in one hand to show God how lucky she was to have such a son, a hand-ball player, a state scholarship winner, a Spinozist. She expected me to put myself through medical school after my father died. Win a scholarship to Harvard! she said, to Johns Hopkins! Her disappointment in me grew and grew. By the time she died, I was far on the other side of the eye chart and heard her calling across the *E*, 'Eternity is . . . a . . . long . . . time. Baruch, say . . . the . . . kad . . . dish.' "

"_____."

"Every night Marilyn and Michael sleep upstairs, in their own beds. That is, Michael is in his, and Marilyn, the pink satin night-gowned usurper—overlook the intimacy, rabbi—is in mine."

"_____."

"Only when I have to; otherwise I don't hear the sound of my voice. I shut the door to the basement until morning, imprisoning myself in my own house! I eat by myself. Believe me a sardine is enough for me now. A can of tuna is a banquet. But I bought a cookbook. The pictures looked so appetizing."

"_____."

"Don't. I'll call *you*, rabbi. I'm okay, I tell you, a little boneless and skinless but confident. You can count on it."

CHAPTER 5

We have separated without a moment to lose.

Do I feel persecuted? In truth, God loves and hates no one.

Still, a little of God's loving me back could go a long way right now.

God the Father? Spinoza's God is not exactly a teddy bear, not even a Big Daddy, authoritarian and judgmental, and my own father dead so many years I can no longer shut my eyes and summon his presence for guidance. I used to summon him, when the lights blew out and the kitchen became an arena, and my mother, "*Liebe* Leah," would expect me to rescue her from an exposed socket, its wire guts hanging out, and she with her wrinkled pillow cases and slips all dampened into little balls for ironing, running about in her nightdress with a flashlight to see what to do before the bundles dried. Not that my father knew anything about electricity; but she respected him. What he said went, even about fuses. What I said vanished into the air. It was then my father's silvery angel would appear to me: as late as my early twenties, still grieving for my lost father, I found consolation in the dead parent as go-between, the fairy godfather of good intentions between man and God. "Daddy, go beg God to make the lights go on," or, "Dad, please ask God for another miracle. Let the heat in Mama's iron last two more hours, until she finishes pressing all those damp little balls and calms down." (As the tiny cruse of oil for the menorah lasted eight days, so now give me another Chanukah!)

I no longer lie sleepless at night as I did after my father died, imagining him an angel hiding behind the glass plate of a ceiling light fixture and taking up a new place in the family of God. I used to tell him how betrayed I felt, left here on a cold and degrading earth while he went on to a garden of Eden like Fort Lauderdale or Nice! I thought in those dark hours about God. But to have God in thought and to imagine him are two completely different things. The former is possible, necessary, the second impossible. But I didn't know that then. I did the best I could—felt sorry for God in his long white beard, above which radiated my father's aquamarine eyes. Spinoza set me straight. "To your question whether I have as clear an idea of God as I have of a triangle, I shall answer No. For we cannot imagine God, but we can, indeed, conceive Him."

Still, even a triangle that loved me would be an asset right now—those three wonderful arms hugging me.

Why did I ever marry? When I met Marilyn, we were two against the world. Dead fathers and shrewdly surviving, insecure, vulgar, evasive, widowed mothers remained at a great distance from us. Nothing, no one, came close enough to cause turbulence. We were a twin-engined jet, cruising alone in the sky. We had all the luck in the world.

Why did Spinoza never marry?

Let us imagine his clear low voice explaining it: "A good thing that prevents us from enjoying a greater good is in truth an evil." In our youth the love of a faithful woman is the highest good. It takes about twenty years to replace that passion with a deeper need for understanding and a spirit of reconciliation that brings happiness. A marriage that hurls us back and forth between satisfaction and irritation is unmasked at midlife by the discovery of a higher good; marriage is the mediocre art of delays, a disregardful male ballet dancer with a bulge between his legs raising an ambitious female partner in an uncompletable dance. For he is never finished, that old flasher (oh no!) whose opened trouser reveals, finally, a noodle and a tangle of wool in the groin.

I can account for many reasons behind Spinoza's bachelorhood. It has been said that Spinoza's brilliant mind marked him. His fellow students began to whisper. Nothing they said could approach the clarity of Baruch's commentaries. Often they lurked in the shadows as he was leaving. Where did his ideas come from? (Stung, I once overheard Winning ask that about

Levi. Where does he *get* those proofs? For Levi's mind, like Spinoza's, had resources that mystified and angered classmates, turned us to bickering among ourselves and to realizing that our commonplace, orthodox ideas were nothing next to these profound unorthodoxies.) Worse, although the rabbis were also confounded by their troublesome student, the unexceptional group felt they had lost all hope of admiration from their teachers. "We can never be luminous while Bento is in our midst. His ideas amaze our teachers. He blinds them. Let us trick him into making heretical answers to our questions about the universe."

Ditto for Lorenzo Levi. And so I badgered him as he left the classroom.

"Lorenzo, Lorenzo. Do you believe in a hereafter? Hey, man, do you believe in a personal God? Can you believe the Pentateuch was directly revealed by God to Moses?"

He answered as Spinoza would, his face a slice of darkness above the peach silk shirt. "The only source for understanding Scripture is Scripture itself. God has no personality. He cannot be pictured through personal configurations. He does not favor one group over another. 'He who loves God cannot endeavor that God should love him in return.' The point of this axiom is not that I *ought* not want God to love me; I *cannot* want him to love me. God desires nothing, lacks nothing, has no purposes. 'One may not say that God demands anything of anyone and just as little that something is displeasing or pleasing to Him. All these are human attributes that have no place with God.' There is no hereafter, except what is eternal in God or Nature!"

So, Spinoza's classmates, not believing their luck, ran in a pack to report to the rabbis these heresies. No hereafter! No personality! One winter night, outside a theater, two of his classmates stepped out of the shadows, one seizing him while the other plunged a knife into his shoulder. He might have been dying, and no one to come to his rescue. He felt lonely and luckless. But rather than flee to the synagogue to ask God's forgiveness and help, he pressed his cape to the wound, feeling in its depths the oozing of his fate. God does not control my fate, he thought, God *is* my fate, and I will love my fate because it is all I have.

It is thought that the thickness of his cape in fact saved his life. In time he got over the attempt, though the home smells of cabbage, added to those of illness and death, lingered on his fingers and in his garments. But he was accustomed to not depending on friends and acquaintances, and their absence now only deepened his conviction that the life he would choose to lead would be solitary. A woman seemed an unnecessary distraction.

Spinoza never expected God to throw an arm around him: why should I?

I very quietly dispose of the question, was Spinoza gay? Always in the circle of students, who later in his life gathered for lessons in the new philosophy, were devoted young men, undersexed and overvexed. What rubbish to think any man—trader, exporter, painter, governor, philosopher—who chooses not to marry is gay. All too well we know cases of married men who lie in the marriage bed without desire. If Spinoza lusted after any woman, it was an infinitesimal desire as against his passion for understanding.

Did Spinoza visit brothels? "The love of a harlot, that is to say, the lust of sexual intercourse, which arises from mere external form, and absolutely all love that recognizes any other cause than the freedom of the mind, easily passes into hatred, unless, which is worse, it becomes a species of delirium, and thereby discord is cherished rather than concord."

And with regard to marriage: "It is plain that it is in accordance with reason, if the desire of connection is engendered not merely by external form [for five years, Marilyn, I couldn't get enough of your neat round Bronx ass], but by a love of begetting children [for seven years we fucked like jackals], and wisely educating them [Michael, it's yours! Keep my beloved *Encyclopædia Britannica*, 11th edition]; and if, in addition, the love both of the husband and wife has for its cause not external form merely, but chiefly liberty of mind."

And now, like Spinoza after the assault on his life, I guard against dejection. "There is a false appearance of piety and religion in dejection; and although dejection is the opposite of pride, the humble dejected man is very near akin to the proud." When I move out of here, I'll take up my existence in an inexpensive flat, get used to a new shower head and glarey lights blinking on and off from the street somewhere in Woodside or Brooklyn. Marilyn, you did me dirt. When I leave, I have to cast aside dejection and stop jabbering like a bar mitzvah boy who doesn't understand a word he recites. I've got to walk out a man, wiser, without hugs or good-byes. (She'll probably go and sit in a movie until I have cleared out.) Possibly I exaggerate. Possibly I am overlooking the truth of why Spinoza did not marry. He affirmed the dangers of a preoccupation with death: "The free man thinks of nothing less than of death." To Spinoza, the domestic life was a serpentine pavilion in which every move was a misstep leading to desire, childbearing, the coil of death. To avoid death, one had to abjure a wife and that serpent of all serpents, sexual intercourse. Enter marriage at one's peril! Childbirth just around the corner, the fattest, most venomous snake of all. Three of his father's wives buried, and two infants—wriggling little vipers, crying loudly at first, gradually unable to take milk without diarrhea, unable to breathe in and out, their congested breathing audible and grown so shallow that the older child strains in the night to hear the feeblest rattle of life before the trek to Ouderkerk aan Amstel and the tiresome routine of prayer, eulogy, interment, and handfuls of dirt thrown on the tiny boxes. To abjure marriage was to abjure death.

On the other hand, in spite of my affectionate emulation of Spinoza, I was eager to marry, scarcely aware that asepsis in childbirth had eliminated fear. But how quickly one forgets: the truth is that Marilyn and I spent years doctoring against infertility. Ought I to have read a warning in our inability to conceive? God's design and all that rot! (God *is* the design: God is night following day, spring winter, death old age.) The fire went out of our loins. Night after night like dogs, horses, jackals. Seven exhausting years of fucking. Flu or frostbite, we fucked on schedule. How we craved a holiday from fucking—to climb into bed at night and simply close one's eyes and sleep. Where was determinism when I needed it most? Where was necessity? My poor blind sperm shouting to her deaf little eggs over and over and over, in the very word Moses used as God appeared before him on the mount: *Hineni! Over here!* until in the middle of a cold January Marilyn failed to menstruate, and we dreamed her bloodlessness into warm September. I wanted to stretch an iron band across her uterus to keep those uterine walls from bloodying down. Like Joshua at Jericho, I fought the battle. I called her eleven times a day.

"Well?"

"Nothing!"

A week late! We were biting our nails. Three weeks. I took a week off from work (I did contact lenses then for Mayrowitz). Four weeks. I did not allow her out of my sight.

Soon Doctor Zola puffed out his chest. "Mrs. Glassman, we're six weeks pregnant!"

Then the evidence became empirical: urinating twenty times a day;

tiredness the scale of a whale; nausea; nipples blue as the Greek flag; it was a flawless pregnancy, continuing after that colossal travail as the most natural, the least strenuous condition. Her waistline thickened, her stomach stretched into a pale shine, and the rest is Glassman history.

I have been in the basement for two months, and though I dwell here in the present tense on the eternal verities, my cough is worsening. I have looked for an apartment, but rents are sky-high. Woodside is uneven and Brooklyn is unending. I am still looking. The truth is I long for the safety of a farmhouse and my own piece of land. I once read about Thoreau "inscribing" himself at Walden, as I did in my small Bayside garden. But this is not the time for autographs! A life dominated by a single passion is a narrow life, incompatible with the earth's kind of catholic wisdom. Yet here I am, shut damply into the world of my sorrow, satisfied in some ways as I have never been satisfied before to go on suffering. For to maintain one's suffering at an even keel is to forgo pain, since pain involves transition from a more perfect state to a less perfect state. An unvarying sorrow is painless.

Thus I abuse Spinoza's careful teachings on the passions. This morning before I am fully awake, Marilyn is knocking at the walls with her rings (aha! still wearing the diamond wedding band) and descending into the basement.

"Look," she says. "Barry, we are not here to injure each other. Michael says he will sleep in the living room. You can have his room. He sent me down to tell you to come upstairs."

"Come back later," I say, burying my head under the pillow.

"Yes or no? He's got to make his bus."

She is standing somewhere over me. A scant ray of sun falling from the basement windows temporarily blinds me. Her shadow looms in a blur of wheeling spots, and as she moves I get a whiff of the coconut foam she uses in the shower. Images of papaya and mango force an eyelid open to appraise her reality. The damp, the surrounding gloom of the basement demean my eyeball. "Jesus!" I mutter, squeezing both eyes shut. "Leave me alone."

She begins to shout. "Where is your brilliant philosophy now? Can't you see that you're getting sick?" She is stationary for a moment without speaking, forcing a squint from me again to check on her whereabouts. The silence is long enough for a daydream—Marilyn and I just getting off the plane in Puerto Rico; three Latin guitarists playing "A Lovely Bunch of Co-

conuts"; each guitarist in a trench coat—but Marilyn doesn't budge. She is still there, pressing the fingers of both hands together, the old phobic tension whitening her knuckles, her morning face unmade, her forehead hairy before the comb. But a softness is in her eyes, which I could have mistaken for love had I not judged it pity first. How Spinoza counsels against pity! Although it presents an appearance of piety, it arises from impotence of mind. In place of pity, the free woman or man acts to bring the pitied into a state of reason.

Is Marilyn here in the basement to improve my reason?

"Why are you here?" I ask her.

"I told you."

"I mean why are you *still* here. Waiting around like this. Doing nothing. You said what you came to say."

"Michael wants to know."

"Tell him to speak to me himself. He's my *kid*!"

Marilyn sighs heavily.

"When are you going to tell Michael the truth?" I demand.

It is *this* I cannot bear, the iciness, her glassy disregard, the chilled accidental intimacies, the ineffectuality of our being here under the same roof at all hours of the morning, the continuing evasions before Michael. She is very close to me. Without planning to, I grab her around the waist and pull her down on top of me. "Tell me why you are here, damn it. Go on, say it, Marilyn, say it." I am gripping her, my mouth warm on her cheek, tasting the salt behind her heavy brown memorable hair.

She struggles against me, though to her credit she won't scream. But her eyes are shrieking out of their darkness, and the tension of her body—back arched under her bra, nipples firm, waist sly with repulsion—afflicts me worse than a scream. When Michael pauses at the top of the steps to say his bus is here, I let her go. My penis, engorged and haughty, will not subside. She does not run away, does not call me maniac or rapist or fly to our dear Michael, but stands in the growing half-light smoothing her dark hair, finding a shoe that has fallen onto the concrete basement floor, straightening her blouse over her erupted nipples, tucking it into her skirt, slithering just enough for my semen to come jerking out in a spray. In a freezing voice she says, "Barry, if you don't get out, Michael and I will."

When we hear the door slam as Michael leaves, she clatters up the steps unevenly, one shoe on her foot, the other in her fist, and disappears.

CHAPTER 6

I haven't yet visited Uncle Nathan, who is a fifteen-minute car ride from my new apartment, though the Russian woman who shops and cooks for him three mornings a week advises—her voice low on the telephone when I call—that what this man needs are visitors, and she reminds me in her thick immigrant accent, that as we get older, "no more modder, no more fader, he have no children, he have pleasure from relatives."

Anya becomes something of a nuisance. I have to spend five minutes listening to her predictable monologue before she'll hand the phone to Nathan, who assures me that when she heard I was "Doctor" Glassman, that I had left my wife, that I was roughly her age, she became very interested in practicing her English with me. Although Nathan has never been married for long, he has had several wives, tenacious widows from Florida to Ohio, one of them a deceptively grandmotherly real estate broker in Trenton who laid claim to his house. But he was too canny for her, ignoring telephone calls from the casinos in Atlantic City and changing his number regularly. The day before their divorce, he wrote a check for $15,000 to the Cremation Society and then declared himself bankrupt. Now Anya is after him—a sex maniac off the Volga, he says to me. Look out!

"What does she look like?" I ask Nathan.

"A cross between Eleanor Roosevelt and Nikita Khrushchev—but she's some cook!"

"How are you feeling, Uncle Nathan?"

"Like Anya looks pretty good to me. So do you know how I'm feeling?"

"You haven't changed."

"Listen, who's complaining? Three times a week Anya and I have a little fun together. And once a month Enid Moscow shows up to take me to see the mummies."

"Are you sticking to your diet?"

"A mummy eats more salt than I do."

"You sound terrific, Nathan."

"Because I'm making my plans for the cremation. Listen, Barry, I've got to see you to talk about it. You're my closest relative."

"Now *you* listen. Let me set you straight. I don't relish cremations. The hardest thing I ever did in my life was take care of my mother's. Why don't I drive you out to Long Island one Sunday, and you'll see how nice it is. The family owns a double plot in Farmingdale. You can lie next to my father—he's all alone. You two played on the same violin—"

"Your mother said burial was unhygienic, and she's right. My mind's made up."

"You'll have to get someone else."

"Barry, honey, we'll talk. I have nothing against your father—"

"The earth is the great embracer. Nature accepts everything, and then goes on as if nothing happened. Indifference to death is best."

"It's no use, Barry. I'm a modern spirit. I want to be cremated."

"Nathan, when I come over we'll discuss it. But I assure you, I'd rather you live to be a hundred and twenty."

"I'll try."

I hear him fumblingly hand the phone to Anya. "So when you are coming?" she asks.

"Soon, Anya, soon."

"Is not good for you to be in house alone. Come. We watch TV together. Channel 11 have cute movies."

"I'll come."

During the next weeks, I can feel greatness fall away from me. When we were kids, my sister Frannie fell off the fire escape and split a front tooth. "There goes my Hollywood contract," she said, squinting at her gaping smile in the mirror, and though we both moaned over the broken tooth of fate, we deceived ourselves into believing that accident determines our course as we drift this way and that through the universe. Stardom, greatness, genius—we locate our glory relative to what drops from the sky. The more that befalls us, the less confident we are about our course.

But that is an innocent view.

In fact, the more that befalls us, the more certain we can be that the universe and our thoughtless mistakes in it are orderly. Generations of thoroughbreds, bees cross-pollinating—faint whiffs of sexual activity—go on and on. Men and women sniff about, discovering as we grow wiser that wisdom is partial and that our blundering and our mating are governed by laws that we will never fully know. To know them all is to be God.

Spinoza's lesson to me, then, is that I attain dignity not because I, Barry Glassman, have applied my individual system to the loss of my wife, who took her favors to that trench-coated *zhlub* Donahue—lately into culture: a membership at the Museum of Modern Art, a Sunday chamber music series at Queens College. My dignity comes with or without benefit of string quartets, through a continuing faith in reason, those delicate checks and balances that help me tuck my hacked-up self back into the universe where I safely belong, snug with the laws of Nature and the limits of a humanistic universe.

Spinoza presented his thinking by means of a Euclidean system of logical propositions and corollaries. The abstractness of it calms me as I sit at night in my Brooklyn room overlooking the bridle path in Prospect Park and read the *Ethics*. Spinoza, modest master of human freedoms, you alone are seeing me through my travail, you and the band of great men and women who were your disciples.

After your departure from Amsterdam, after your fruitful years in Rijnsburg, drafting your great metaphysics, you holed up in a room like this. When I left the house in Bayside, Michael had vanished for the day, gone off with Deirdre to a mall to avoid—over bowling and pizza—the pain of my departure. Marilyn, contrary to my expectations, was not at the RKO Fresh Meadows but sitting by as I walked back and forth in my stocking feet, noiselessly packing clothing in a suitcase and my books in cartons. A radiant sun slanted in from the Bay. She pretended to be engrossed by the issue of *Newsday* spread brightly before her at the kitchen table. I labored at reticence, but every now and then gave in to an involuntary groan. When the telephone rang, I heard her finally agree to her friend Toby's invitation to come for coffee.

"Toby thinks I'm masochistic for sticking around," she said, somewhat amused, tying the belt of her coat and swinging her shoulder bag over one tweed shoulder, but when I didn't share her amusement, her eyes harpooned me as though it were my fault that Toby had called her away and forced her to miss all the fun. Almost at the door, she ran back into the living room for a record album. She was in training for the late Beethoven quartets, she said, tucking the record under one arm, apparently still hot for a lover who could teach her a thing or two. When the phone rang again, I hurriedly put on my shoes and loaded several cartons out to the car in the driveway, leaving one box behind in my haste to beat it out of there before she hung up. She had tried to make light of the decision to part; but Spinoza would let me have none of it: choice often occurs against a background of death.

Spinoza, next to your house now stands the Spinoza Cafe, a drab storefront bar with trickles of rust running down the sign. Ten years ago it was dark and disorderly within. Through the windows long-haired men could be seen sitting on boxes and drinking beer, totally at variance with the wisdom and modesty I had come to associate with the name "Espinosa." While waiting for one o'clock and the hour of our appointment with the caretaker of your house, Marilyn and I wandered in for a glass of Dutch ale. The interior smelled of beer and decay. Men sat in groups, an occasional woman among them, talking in Dutch, looking like derelicts; I know now that their untidy appearance said nothing about industry, education, virtue. Nonetheless it shocked me that this seeming dissipation coexisted on the other side of a masonry wall with the Spinoza House and the regular monthly meetings of the Spinoza Society in the book-filled room downstairs. I know now the untidy cafe next door breathed with a liveliness fresh from the street life of the Hague. At the time, of course, Marilyn couldn't see what all the fuss was about. Why did a cafe have to be infused with philosophy? she asked. Three hundred years have passed, she said. Life is intrinsically unphilosophical, was her point. But her comments only frustrated me the more. The life of the cafe went incuriously, unconcernedly on, deaf to the formidable and regular proceedings of the thinkers in your house next door.

Here, then, in a run-down part of town, at 72–74 Paviljoensgracht, stands Spinoza's final home. Can ordinary people with work to do and grandchildren (glossy enlargements of blonde Dutch babies hang on the walls) live where Spinoza lived? The ailing philosopher boarded in the up-stairs attic room overlooking the Paviljoensgracht, a room with pitched attic ceilings and wide enough to span the front of the house.

Here is where Spinoza dies in February 1677. The doctor climbs up to this wintry room, without fireplace or fire, glass dust obscuring the air, and, still standing on the table, Spinoza's regular diet—warm beer and bread.

I remember feeling entirely transplanted to that room in the Hague, and I remember feeling baffled by it. How could so humdrum and chill a room contain the existence of so great a man? In that walled space with its rectangle of window, wearing his customary heavy brown woolen clothing, he ground lenses to maintain a livelihood, paying the housepainter van der Spyck for his board. In that room with its sharply slanting gables, next to the cold attic (when the van der Spyck servants hung wet nightgowns there to dry, ice crystals stiffened them into corpses with pleading arms), he worked, he slept, he lived out intense days amid a bone-chilling frugality. The single-minded writing of Baruch Spinoza left no moment to pine for the comforts others would secure for themselves during their passage through the prosperous world of Holland in the 1670s. Time passed without heat or love, except for the friction of one idea against another.

What does a man need? In Brooklyn I have a radiator, a hot-plate on which I brew coffee or boil an egg, a refrigerator, a rug on the floor—more than Spinoza had in the Paviljoensgracht. In Brooklyn I have a high-riser, a sofa that sleeps two, though I have not yet opened it. Who would share it with me? Marilyn is gone (Spinoza, like you I want to be a man without a past); I feel neither bachelor nor widower. Although she never mothered me, I know alternately that Marilyn has freed me and orphaned me. Exactly at this moment, I lie on my back across the shut studio bed, body limp, in T-shirt and briefs, a cigar clamped between my teeth, my belly more noticeable than my sex, remembering erections worthy of a Grand Prix for speed and danger; on the one hand I am an aging schoolboy, too young and inexperienced to be at this cruel frontier, and on the other I am panic-stricken that no generation is left between me and death. I am as free to die as to live; and no widow to mourn my passing.

But Michael? *If she won't tell him, I will.*

Barry, forget Michael for now. The faded blue couch is lumpy and the room unfamiliar and freezing cold in the night when Mrs. Messenger, the landlady who occupies the downstairs apartment with a blind son, turns the heat down and throws open her windows. One blanket is not enough. I get up and pull on my pants and a sweatshirt. I stand and smoke a cigar for a while, gazing out the window into the ordinary Brooklyn street. I catch my reflection against the night, a thin face rising to a high moonlike forehead, my reddish hair so undetectable in the glass that I must raise my hand to feel that it is still there. When the smoke irritates my throat, I snuff out the cigar, return to the couch, and cover myself up to my eyes, continually protecting one frigid ear.

I will bring Michael here. If I have to kidnap him, I will have him witness his old man in this room, not to exercise his pity (a sign of impotence) but to fill in the core of his life's history. Witnesses still troop to Paviljoensgracht, up the two steep flights of stairs, through the laundry-hung attic, to stand in the room of Spinoza's last years. Can a man expect less of his son?

In the early morning, a Sunday, I am standing at the high-riser, a cloud of dust released into the air as I trundle out the lower half, verifying that, if indeed my plan of action calls for a woman in this room, I can swing it. The early-morning room reeks of stale cigar smoke. I do not know which would be worse for my cough, a damp and penetrating Brooklyn breeze or a sudden burst of dust. I crank open the window, an old-fashioned casement affair that leaks the cold. After a good deal of effort, it admits a modest blast of air, equivalent to what can pass through two small square panes. Still, through the windows lies a pastoral scene I have no right to possess—the park is enchanting! A light mist truncates a line of little rainbows in the street lamps, which are still lit this early in the day, the display of color a flash more iridescent wherever the globes have been vandalized. The bridle path is deserted. Brooklyn's horses are sleeping. The horizon draws my eye to the distance, and in the general quiet and calm, a trembling seizes my body and hammers soundlessly under my skin, my heart too big for my chest, my blood too headlong. I cross my arms to hold back my energy, as though the dizzying miniature rainbows have emerged from within me, and I will go on making them. Will this be my permanent condition, a lonely, powerful cast-off in a furnished room? The thought of another woman terrifies me, but it is present nonetheless. I'm no big shot hermit, I tell myself. I'd go nuts if I had to live like Spinoza. At the same time, it would do me good for a while. If you want to take stock, I think soberly, it's best to take it unattached. A leaden sun is slowly rising, and then, to the right, I see faint across the Brooklyn sky a rainbow, its colors barely distinct as it vanishes and reappears in the mist. I blink my eyes; and see it still. The wonder of that imperfect arc survives my misery, bolsters my weakening resolve to plan for the future. Coat on and hatted, muffler wrapped twice around my throat, wearing an old white raincoat to my ankles, I speedily head down the flight of stairs and out into the blurred morning street to the park. The old Brooklyn houses are gray and solemn as wolves in the first light of day.

The edge of the bridle path. A man walking a small white dog on a leash. He is in a security guard's uniform. Nods. I appreciate his friendliness and reward him by pointing up above his head. "Did you notice the rainbow?"

Yanks the dog around, turns, and looks too high overhead.

"No. Further away," I say, coming up behind, extending my arm just over his shoulder.

He jolts back, fending off my uninvited intimacy; but elevates his head nonetheless to take in the sight. We are both walking up the bridle path, and the rainbow is following us.

Then he is left cursing under his breath, for I am running toward the rainbow. As I glance back over my shoulder, he decides to run the other way, his little white dog flying in the air on its tiny legs. The tough guy's afraid of me, I think with a chuckle. From that safer distance, he pauses for a minute, noticing my long white raincoat, holding his dog on a short leash. "Hey, are you a Hare Krishna or something?" he yells ridiculously into the mist.

I have cut across to a field, ragged with dried weeds and bordered by tall, bare poplar trees. By the time I catch my breath, the sky is vaporous, and I am enveloped by silence and loss. The minutest details of my failed formulations sweep through my mind. As I stand under the vanished rainbow, waiting for the clouds to pass and the colors to reappear, I think of other universes where to *see* a rainbow is enough, where the mind is an ally of the senses and liberated from analyzing *why* the rainbow appears, *how* the light refracts, *how* the colors bend into their cradling arc. But I am driven to make calculations. After scanning the horizon for twenty more minutes, stamping my shoes up and down to keep warm, all the while reviewing in my mind the calculus of my work and the impasse I have encountered, I make my way slowly and with dignity back to my new place of residence, trailing my raincoat up the weedy path. It is a stately old house. The porch light is still on. I go quietly up the stairs and unlock the door.

I shall get help, then. Who can say what greatness might not emerge from this humble chamber?

By the time I am again in my room, I smell my landlady's coffee. Outside, the mist has cleared; I hear movements downstairs, blunt noises. Perhaps it is Mrs. Messenger's blind son who makes the morning coffee. I can hear the heat flushing through the radiators, a sound I haven't heard since Frannie and I were schoolchildren in the Bronx, pulling warmed socks onto frozen feet in the early winter morning, my mother having risen at 6 A.M. to read her lessons and warm our socks against the bathroom pipes. Sunday morning begins. Upstairs, too, coffee perks; and an egg boils. I am starved for a piece of toast. I fling open the doors to all three cabinets in the efficiency corner of my room; I bang pots and pans, lift linens, poke through the broom closet, but a simple convenience like a toaster is nowhere to be found. A slice of toasted bread is a significant absence in my life, and I have to pause, physically halt all motion, and counsel myself not to permit so trivial an obsession to throw this day into disarray.

How would great men and women cope with the overwhelming passion for a piece of toast? I swallow egg, nibble slice of spongey, untoasted wheat bread, and gulp coffee, ready with books, pen, and paper to begin the work of the day.

Men and Women Influenced by Spinoza (and One of Them Coping Without a Slice of Toast):

(1) Samuel Taylor Coleridge, a druggy little smile on his face. Envisaged writing a poem "of Spinoza"; referred to Spinoza cryptically in the presence of an agent of the British government as *Spy Nozy*. Henry Crabb Robinson, eighteenth-century conversationalist and diarist, originator of fabulous breakfast parties, says that he "saw STC kiss Spinoza's face on the title page of the *Ethics* and say, 'This book is a gospel to me.'"

(2) Goethe, who rediscovers Spinoza, says (I copy it faithfully): "This man, who had wrought so powerfully on me, and who was destined to affect

so deeply my entire mode of thinking, was Spinoza. After looking around the world in vain for the means of developing my strange nature I met with the *Ethics* of that philosopher. . . . I found in it a sedative for my passions, and it seemed to unveil a clear, broad view over the material and moral world. But what especially riveted me to him was the boundless disinterestedness which shone forth in every sentence. That wonderful sentiment, 'He who truly loves God must not require God to love him in return. . . .' "

(3) George Eliot's earliest and perhaps most formidable intellectual project was the translation of Spinoza's *Ethics*. Never published, her manuscript is in the Beineke Library at Yale. (Had she published her *Ethics* in 1856 as she had planned, her biographers fear that she might never have turned to fiction.)

(4) Aha! An exquisite working model of universal laws. Does the idea of God, then, fully occupy Einstein's mind? The late Banesh Hoffman, biographer of Einstein, also ascribes to him a pragmatically stubborn faith in God: "As was his custom when facing deep problems of science, he tried to regard things from the point of view of God. [How the very idea turns me inside out!] Was it likely that God would have created a probabilistic universe? Einstein felt that the answer had to be no. . . . Einstein summed up his intuitive feeling about the quantum theory in the picturesque phrase '*Gott würfelt nicht.*' . . . It can be ploddingly translated 'God does not play dice.' " Now they are leaping beyond the quantum leaps, hinting that Einstein was on the right track after all.

For the rest, I go out armed with my book on Einstein to a phone booth on St. John's Place and get Rabbi Mayberg on the phone to clarify for him Einstein's (and Glassman's) status as a Jew:

"Rabbi, I am quoting from Banesh Hoffman's biography. 'It would be wrong to think of Einstein as a ritualistic Jew.' "

"_____."

"Rabbi, just take it easy. Don't interrupt. I want you to hear *all* of this. When asked via transatlantic cable if he believed in God, Einstein had cabled in reply: 'I believe in Spinoza's God, who reveals himself in the orderly harmony of what exists, not in a God who concerns himself with the fates and actions of human beings.' "

"_____."

"Mayberg, what I have been trying to tell you is that I too believe in Spinoza's God. Einstein said it: Spinoza is 'one of the deepest and purest souls our Jewish people has produced.'"

"———."

"No, I'm in Brooklyn. I can see Prospect Park from this phone booth. A pretty Asian girl in jodhpurs and a cap is riding a horse. It's not a bad spot to be in. So, Mordecai, I don't want to bug you, but one final question. Answer yes or no: Would you have called Einstein a marginal Jew?"

CHAPTER 7

Bernard Messenger has an impressive head of brilliantined black hair and a gaunt, handsome face, disfigured only by the eyes themselves, opaque and sightless, the surrounding lids and skin bluish, as if they had been bruised.

For eight weeks, passing November and December implacably in a preferred solitude, I have bundled against the damp chill of my room. I spent New Year's Eve, after a solemn drink with Feliz in the back of the shop, in an all-night movie theater on Kings Highway. As the couples slowly left, a few solitary figures remained, slumped in the dark, and I slept through the arrival of the new year among the losers in the well-heated, snug movie house, the Dolby sound bellowing in my dreams, my bones warmer than they'd been in weeks. Though I am attempting to complain to Mrs. Messenger that there isn't enough heat, my attempt is aborted by her blind son, who appears at the door similarly bundled against the resident chill. His mother, who usually receives me, is in bed with palpitations. He lets me in, and I arrive like a blast of cold weather, for he draws his sweater closer and belts it.

He greets me effusively, and I realize how hopeless it is to stand and complain about the chill to Bernard. Oh, the dangers of pity I know well, but in the presence of a handsome, gaunt blind man, I have few reserves of logic. Open on a green silk footstool is a book in Braille. When I ask Bernard what he is reading, he replies, with some embarrassment, "The *Pensées* of Blaise Pascal."

A pause.

"Does that interest you, Mr. Glassman?" Intently.

"Not only does it interest me, it takes my breath away."

Whereupon his delight is audible, deep satisfying sounds emanating like woodwinds. Immediately he seats himself in the easy chair before his book. The arms of the chair are worn, the soiled, matted stuffing showing through the shredded green silk. He reads with both hands, the fingers moving inward from the edges of the page. "The heart has its reasons, which reason does not know." He tips his head up, his blind eyes groping somewhere to the right of me. "I spent the morning on that sentence. Time is one of my luxuries. There's a connection, you know, between time and eternity. Have you ever thought of dying—?"

The question appears to be thrown to some catcher behind me. Instinctively I turn to be certain no one is there, glad not to be observed during this foolish interval.

"You don't need to answer. My questions often are greedy, I know. The heart has its reasons," he says.

From inside, his mother's raspy voice calls out, "Bernard, is that Norman?"

He turns in the direction of her voice. From the dining room, she suddenly appears, pink underpants over her loose, fleshy belly, a towel barely covering her naked breasts.

"No. It's the renter, Mr. Glassman," the blind son is saying, but it is too late. Her face is astonished. It seems to know everything. Silently, it registers that I am not Norman. She confronts me wordlessly, accusingly, as though her shame is my fault. "No need to come in, Mother. It's just a friendly visit." He gropes again in my direction. "Am I right? It's just a friendly visit?"

"Oh, yes," I say, as the woman pulls the towel sharply across her pendulous breasts and vanishes. My voice is disheartened. I went to high school with a five-foot-two sex maniac we called Stormin' Norman. "I merely wanted to say if you ever need some help—you seem to be quite independent—" a pause, the blind man's face is affable, "should your mother ever need anything while I'm upstairs, any kind of emergency—"

"Thank you." He extends his hand and holds it out perilously free until I walk over, take it in my own, and shake it up and down for a long moment; then I leave.

The image of Bernard's undressed mother asking if I were Norman, smoldering as she discovers her error, and Bernard's unexpected question about death stay with me all day. A certain uncomfortable appetite for life was present in that room, running by its own laws in the face of sorrow and loss. In the shop, at about noon (9 A.M. California time), my sister Frannie calls from San Diego. I am glad to hear from her, but having to talk to her distresses me, for when I hear Frannie's voice, nostalgia for family and the shock of Bernard's ménage trespass on my nerves. I have indeed been underground. She hasn't heard from us in months, she couldn't fly in for the bar mitzvah because of Alan's car accident (he is just now out of his neck brace), she never had a thank-you from Michael for the check, was advised by Michael where to call. (At first, "*Hi*, Aunt Frannie." Then a cool "Daddy doesn't live here any more. Try the shop.")

"What's going on, Barr—?"

"It's a long story, Frannie. But I'll be all right."

"Have you and Marilyn split?"

"Maybe."

"*Gottenyu*," she says, injuring me beyond her realizing with that old Yiddish endearment our mother used to use. "Mama used to say you two were her AT&T stock."

"Frannie, that was only because *your* husbands *cost* her money."

Her voice softens. "What *happened*?" she whispers.

"It's too long to go into."

"Is Michael in the house with Marilyn?"

"He is."

"By his own choice?"

"By his own choice."

"I can't believe it. He adores you!" she mutters bitterly.

"There's school and Deirdre and the orthodontist—"

"And you?"

"I have a decent place in Brooklyn, near the park, and I'm in the shop in twenty minutes, twenty-five tops."

"Are you depressed? Barr, I speak from experience!"

"Someone asked me just this morning if I ever felt like dying."

"Barr—tell me the truth. No philosophical funny business. Are you eating? Are you able to get a night's sleep?"

"Yeah, yeah. The worst is that Michael wants nothing to do with me. That keeps me up. The rest I'll get over. People do."

"The rest?"

"Oh, let's not go into a *megillah* on long distance. How're the girls? Is Karen getting along with Alan?"

"Karen starts Santa Cruz in the fall. She avoids Alan. It broke her heart to send him a seventy-five cent get-well card while he was in traction. Frankly, I'll be glad when she leaves."

"Don't be so glad!"

"Listen, Barr—, I'm going to fly out to see you. You sound awful. Why did someone ask if you felt like dying? Who on earth asked you that? A doctor? Are you getting help? Barry, you're not sui*cid*al, are you?"

"No. I still get my reading done. Unhappiness is a moral state. I'm looking into it."

"What kind of *question* was that?"

"I have a blind neighbor, Bernard Messenger. He asked me."

"A blind messenger! How apocalyptic."

I have to laugh. "Actually, it was not a bad question. It amplified a certain moaning in me that I can now get rid of. I really don't plan to die."

"*Gottenyu*," she says again. "I'll let you know what flight. Can you put me up?"

"Sure, but it's one room."

"It'll be like old times on Kossuth Street."

When I hang up, I notice that Feliz has been listening. In an hour she calls back. Friday at 7 P.M., La Guardia, TWA flight 546. I reassure her that I go to work every day like clockwork. She tells me that what you do in a storm is lie low.

"Go get some lunch," I tell Feliz. But he is reluctant to go, as if he understands that while he is gone I may decide to fire him. A cigar clamped between his teeth, he paces the length of the counter and in a pretense of housekeeping collects scraps of paper, clearing the dusty counter with one stiff hand edge as he aligns displays with the other. Then his muttering begins, a coil of words sliding frantically between his teeth: "No time to breathe. Jesus God, not even time for a hot dog. Two sets of contacts all week and both is due today. You never think of me, Barry. No one thinks of me," bending his face, hiding from me the swelling ego that menaces in the hastening redness of his neck. He drags his shoes from bench to buffer, a lightweight in the world of runners, a heavyweight in my shop. I no longer know what is under his mask. He is as inscrutable as one of his Portuguese proverbs.

Four days until Frannie arrives. Two of those days float by. I stay late in the shop, doing inventory on contact lenses and accessories, placing an ad in the *Times* for a new optician/benchman, then abruptly changing my mind because I feel overwhelmed by Feliz's predicament. I concede that were my life more even, Feliz would be a less emotional assistant. I resolve to be more self-possessed, keep my personal life to myself, and retain Feliz. He cries tears of thanks, which I despise, for they reduce both of us to actors. I can tell the blame is all in me, however. To Feliz, the boss is part of a whimsical universe, whose decisions confirm how accidental our fate is.

The third night, having grown increasingly restless and sulky, irritated in fact by the unpredictable nature of Frannie's impending visit to me, I set out to find Uncle Nathan and take him out for a meal. At the last minute I decide to invite Bernard Messenger along for an outing. He is surprised, believes he has misunderstood, stands in the doorway, eyes staring beyond me into the night, hair black and polished, calling excitedly in to his mother that he has an invitation to dinner, will she be all right, have her palpitations subsided? Yes, yes, it is an ordinary event, he is to go out with the renter.

I phone ahead to alert Nathan of our coming. The blind man, bundled into winter coat and muffler, is seated next to me on the front seat of my car. In his hand he carries his mobility stick, and although it is night he is wearing dark glasses. There can be no question: he is unmistakably blind. In an animated voice he asks where we are headed. This is clearly a festive occasion. I drive out along the park, and when we come to the first large intersection, I am mumbling about still being a stranger in Brooklyn.

"Are we now at Flatbush Avenue?" he asks.

I peer at the street sign, nod, and remembering, quickly say aloud, "Yes."

"All right. Take a left here. Go about half a mile, until you come to a sprawling vegetable and fruit market on your right, Bay Produce, I believe. A Shell station will be on your left. Turn there." Bay Produce, an all-night market, looms on my right, a blaze of spotlights illuminating stands of eggplants, bananas, green peppers. And the orange glow of a Shell station clicks in on my left. I make my turn. Meanwhile he has been chatting about a documentary on the Afghan resistance that he "saw" on TV last night, how tyrannized the life of the people, how austere. Then he says, "All right. We're on Avenue 'U.' Take Avenue 'U' until McKinney's Funeral Parlor, well-lit, a blue sign. It's five or six minutes on the right, a low brick building with potted pines out in front. A little shabby."

Traffic is slow. The corners of the windshield are dusting with snow flurries. The lights are against us. But within minutes, a small blue neon sign designating McKinney's Funeral Parlor is visible in the night, spotlights, potted pines, and all.

"Hey!" I say. "You're cheating."

He is roaring with laughter.

"Did you lose your sight recently?"

"I was eight," he says.

"Eight!"

"The neighborhood changes very little, especially at the major intersections where the larger businesses are. My mother is the eyes and ears of the world. And until my father died last May, I used to go everywhere with him. We sold ladies' blouses, and Brooklyn was our territory. He noted all the changes on our routes. He took me through Brooklyn the way Virgil took Dante through hell. When you live with a blind person—if it's somebody you love and regard—you learn to talk about everything. My parents were talking machines. I sometimes think my father talked himself to death. They glossed everything they did. My mother still does."

As I listen to Bernard, I feel a twinge of envy for a father who could so befriend a son, work side by side in search of the great American dream, the one describing and adoring, the other brilliant and blind and ambitious. And in the strictest privacy of my soul, I debate whether the blindness of a child(!) is worth it, a question that embarrasses me. I loved my father, but my love did not extend to the mutual dependency of two men wrenching a single living from the world. And against my son's stupendous absence I am fighting ferociously, for now in our love's dilemma I realize that our error— mine and Marilyn's—was that we didn't know how to love each other as much as we knew how to love Michael. To conceive only one child; to submit to Nature in the guise of bum sperm; to be mocked by kids procreating everywhere like flounders; teenage pregnancies; young wastrels loping up and down Eighth Avenue, carrying their "stuff" in paper bags, their huge radios in their free hands, and snuggled into their scrotums thousands of monster sperm, while their eyes lust after bigger radios and designer eyeglasses. To read about sperm banks and college students who produce eugenic sperm at will and sell it for profit, populating Boston, Atlanta, Salt Lake City with unknown counterparts of themselves. And now to imagine Marilyn impregnated (at last!) by Bob Donahue (Agnes took their four children to Hartford). How willingly she would spread her thighs, pump passionately against his velvet hardness, pray to her dead mother and father for one more child before her clock runs out, *longing* for a child from Donahue and holding him and holding him and holding him as he comes deep, deep within her.

And I weep to think that according to my best reading of the *Ethics*, she is virtuous!

To myself I repeat that the desire of connection must be engendered "not merely by external form, but by a love of begetting children and wisely educating them." Of course Spinoza is speaking of marriage, but come on, Glassman! we all know this is the last of the twentieth century. And for Michael a half-brother or sister—could I deny him this? He would no longer feel the freak, an unmatched pea in the universe. And yes, she would educate her child; Marilyn would scrub floors, would immolate herself with kerosene, would walk to Jerusalem if she had to.

And so, driving through Brooklyn's nighttime maze of avenues, guided by a blind man who becomes less and less blind as the journey continues, my faithless wife less and less faithless, I see; I understand. In my groin I know her yearning and her need. Do I feel fingers poking at my thigh?

"Excuse me. You didn't answer. I said, aren't we close to your uncle's address?"

I squeeze my legs together and swerve them sharply away. The touch radiates through my groin and penis in waves of indignation. "Yes, yes," I say. "This is his block." I feel transparent, as if this blind man, who cannot see *me*, can see my confusion. But of course he has no idea that he has touched so close to my life. He was merely probing an unfatherly silence.

I offer to take Bernard in, but he declines, preferring to wait in the car until we can head for the restaurant, one of Uncle Nathan's choosing.

Uncle Nathan lives alone in the downstairs apartment of an ancient two-family house, which he owns. Anya keeps the kitchen going, though the living room is a clutter of dead plants and plastic flowers wired into dry dirt. The carpeting is badly spotted. I have not been here in a year or two, but I look instinctively for the remembered photograph of Nathan standing with Leah, my mother, as children, arm in arm, in long bathing suits, in front of a sand castle they have built beside the ocean in Asbury Park. There it is, still in its gray cardboard frame, on a mahogany end table with a wrought iron railing now fallen into rust. A pipe with ancient spittle dried on its stem leans next to it. I look into those faces in search of resemblances, and instantly I see Michael, more in the young Nathan than in Leah. I have a moment of alarm picturing Michael in sixty years, barrel-chested and crippled. But genes play sinister tricks. Michael himself could surely be mistaken for a son of Donahue's, his tendency to dimples, for example, and light eyes. I help Uncle Nathan with his jacket, but the trick string of genetics has me in knots as I wheel him out to the car, explaining to Bernard that my uncle is an invalid, and make the transfer from chair to back car seat. Uncle Nathan, a strong man with broad shoulders and a broad chest, is a great weight to move, and I doubt that my undergrown Michael will ever reach such an imposing physical presence. Uncle Nathan cracks jokes as he reaches in front to shake the hand of the blind dinner guest. He settles in. Wheelchair safely folded and stowed in the trunk, I am ready, sweat trickling down my back from the exertion, my cargo of the infirm securely aboard. A more jovial group would be hard to imagine, so lighthearted is this outing, this unplanned, uncomplaining freight of the impaired.

The activity is a tonic; their need of me annihilates pity. The technique is to take each one in turn. Bernard waits at the curb, probing with his long, metallic stick, dislodging a puff of snow as he smooths his careful black hair. I resettle Nathan, wheeling him near. Then we three enter together, the blind man, stick first, moving tentatively on the now slippery sidewalk, while I push Nathan just behind.

We are in a Hungarian restaurant, bustling and noisy, tiled walls and old-fashioned oval mirrors glistening like cream. Nathan immediately stretches his head from his wheelchair to search the room, apparently for an empty table, one that can accommodate his chair without interfering with the flow of the waitresses, who are speaking Russian and Hungarian as they rush by. In a minute his hand sweeps into the air.

"There she is," he says, immediately wheeling himself along, a waitress with dishes of food steaming on her forearm saying "Hello Nathan!" as he passes; he has taken off in the direction of my cousin Enid Moscow, who sits alone at a table near the swinging door to the kitchen. Bernard is at attention, a bird motionless on a branch, readying himself for changed logistics. I move to his elbow and together we follow Nathan to Enid's table.

Let me summarize my reactions to this trickery conceived by my Uncle Nathan:

(1) Only a very few men attain to a virtuous life through reason alone. Scriptures, revelation, allegories, and parables—all genres of masquerade and trickery—meet the needs of finite thinking beings.

(2) The daily reality of religion in the life of the people was not overlooked by Baruch Spinoza, who had the common sense to "evaluate Holy Writ or revelation very highly from the standpoint of its utility and necessity." Nathan approaches his death as a fellow of passion and holiness, for whom utility and necessity may mean, "Don't be chicken-livered, get her to the restaurant even if you have to lie through your teeth."

(3) Nathan in his seventy-sixth year esteems himself a sage and prophet. It is the testimony of the prophets "which has brought so much consolation precisely to those who are not strong of mind, which has been of no little utility to the state, and which we can believe without harm or danger."

(4) Is Nathan pious or blasphemous? Judge a man only by his works and not by his opinions or protestations. Enid Moscow is blushing in embarrassment. She is as much a victim as I. Nathan, on the other hand, meows happily in his wheelchair, a big movie-star pussycat enjoying his canary. I *could* begin to feel happy myself, seeing the girlish, artless response of Enid Moscow, seated next to me, her rumpled tweed sleeve brushing my arm, her eyes bright green through her badly tinted contact lenses.

I could; and I do.

(5) I do not desire Enid Moscow because she is good; she is good because I desire her. I sit next to her, and we say ordinary words about whether to have the veal paprikash or the stuffed cabbage. I know the veal will be very good because I very much desire it.

CHAPTER 8

Net gains after the Hungarian outing:

Nathan has had a glorious time, reveling in our company, his memory running back and forth over the events of his life like a typewriter ribbon. I discover that at fifteen he left the home my mother had provided for him because "*Liebe* Leah" in one of her phases had become a Christian Scientist and would not allow him to use gentian violet on a badly scraped knee. It festered, and he was dragged, screaming in pain, by the observant mother of his friend Hesh to Montefiore Hospital to have it lanced. Fearing for his life with a woman who disdained gentian violet, Argyrol, ear drops, and other miracles of modern medicine, he took the money he had earned as a tailor's helper and sneaked away one night, boarding a train for Lexington, Kentucky. Gone for two years, he returned with his intuition intact ("always trust a hunch you get before dinner") and enough cash to buy a Ford truck and deliver for a dry-cleaning establishment. By eighteen he was in his own business. By twenty he had his own apartment and a route in fashionable Prospect Park West, providing pick-up service for the old guard there and in Brooklyn Heights around Remsen Street, contracting finally to do the pressing himself. As I leave him in his cluttered, dusty living room with its tasseled lampshades and cloisonné lilies, its smells of urine and lavender air freshener, he swears it was his intuition that drove him to call Cousin Enid to spend a night with family.

Enid has been consoled by my presence. Since the deaths of her parents and the tragic disappearance of her brother, whom she adored, she is the only survivor of a once close and happy clan. I sense her fondness for me, a heedless kind of affection that one family member expresses for another. By the time we are having the apricot *politsinta*, I have told her about my work on the rainbow. Her interest delights my soul, though it is Bernard who immediately grasps my professional intent, who ignores the peripheral comment about the size and shape of the raindrops and cuts down to the essentials that would relieve people in polluted areas of eye infections and poor retention of lenses. Although she is quietly relaxing in her chair, attention is Enid's most natural condition, I can see that; at one point she slips off her suit jacket, fishes out a piece of paper and a pen from her large leather bag, and to my excitement draws a diagram of how the refracted ray is reflected twice and sometimes three times within a polluted drop of water. She draws meticulously, marking with artfully curved arrows each point of contact, carefully blackening in the head of each arrow. Then, for the benefit of Bernard, she explains aloud exactly what she has drawn, shakes her bristly brown hair off her forehead, and looks at me hopefully. I now remember her as the family brain: Bronx High School of Science, a Ph.D. somewhere in Pennsylvania. She becomes voluble, tells me of her interest in Egyptology and how she plays tennis near the museum every Sunday morning at eight with one of the curators. I tell her about the rainbow I witnessed the other morning over Prospect Park, and how it pulsed into and out of view, finally vanishing in the early morning light. Bernard suggests I go down to the Promenade in Brooklyn Heights. He speaks with the confidence of a zoologist who has spent a lifetime locating the natural habitat of a particular species of grasshopper. Seated between us, she is snapping with pleasure, overflowing the constraints of her slightly obsessive mannerisms. She straightens his plate, hands him her fork when his is misplaced, stretches a napkin over his tie. We gossip like old friends, staying so long that only a few diners remain. Many of the lights are out, and our shadows dance murkily on the tiled walls. She delights in taking charge, requests the bill of the waitress, makes the necessary calculations, and insists on splitting the cost with me. As she rummages for her wallet, the exertion produces a light sweat on her upper lip. Although Bernard and Nathan decline, she and I share a final glass of port the management brings as a gift. A vague stirring in my groin surprises me as brilliant Cousin Enid submits to an unexpected request by Bernard.

The present in which Bernard lives is a region of speculative blackness. He lives there theoretically and energetically, with an intellect so triumphant as to obscure his tragic affliction. He sits on the other side of Cousin Enid as Russia itself sits on the other side of Europe, and I realize with envy that he has pulled her into his orbit, having more to say to her than I do. His conversation sparkles with anecdote and imagination; when he illuminates his ideas, a shock of daylight falls accurately onto the midnight. I have to remember he is a salesman. For all his intellect he relies on wit and gab. And though he is also a believer in the heart, his lucidity cuts sharper than an edge of glass. He elicits from her much that is autobiographical: she is a physicist for the Grumman company; was married to a European physicist at NYU for nine years until their marriage collapsed (Lutz Moscow by name, a specialist in semiconductors); no children; no regrets; suffers from lower back pain (and from excessive tearing, I observe, as she continually dabs at her eyes with a tissue, Bernard, of course, seeing none of this). I fear that Bernard will approach her at the end of the dinner, ask for her number, and promise to phone. But so far there is no "May I see you again?" *See* her again! Instead, he says, "Forgive me, I must ask a favor of you."

She is expectant.

"May I touch your face? I want to remember you."

Enid falters, then presses his arm, her lips fluttering, and raises his hand to her cheek. She compulsively tucks a strand of stubborn hair behind her ear. Then her hand falls away. The blind man is on his own.

His long fingers move the sheath of her hair back from her brow; he traces each brow, slowly and reverently the curve of the nose, and with the tip of a finger the clean circle of each nostril. He raises the other hand, and as he had done while reading from Pascal's *Pensées*, works both hands in from the edges, across the flushed hollow of cheeks, and back again to the small ears, running an index finger into the well of each ear, reading expertly this kind of Braille, rapidly now, gently, sliding across and downward, downward toward the prominent chin, dropping one hand, and completing the search with the other, for a lip, two lips, parting them, lightly tapping the small front teeth with a fingernail, slipping down into the cleft of chin, the underpath to the neck, the chest—and his hand stops, drops to find the other on the table, and clasps it.

In the long silence, no one speaks. I have explored Enid's face as I have never seen Marilyn's. Enid's shoulders have risen and narrowed; in the end she is perspiring and vulnerable.

Once again Bernard becomes the blind man, retreats into the obsessive darkness, tentative and insecure, stick sweeping the way in front of him, dark glasses alerting the world to his condition. Just behind, I push Nathan in his wheelchair. On our way out, I say to Enid, "May I see you again? My sister Frannie is coming for a visit. Why don't we do this again with her?" Bernard has paused, eyelids dropped, and I recognize the ardor of his listening, his slender figure and gaunt alertness, even a certain condescension, a slight hiss of attention escaping between his lips. On the way home, having safely installed Nathan in his house, just the two of us are on the front seat of the car; I dial some popular music on the radio. We listen in silence, backtracking over his former directions. As I escort him into his apartment, he pauses to thank me. It was a wonderful evening, he says, and he encourages me to strike up a relationship with my cousin. "Avoid living alone," he says, "at any cost."

Carefully, I refrain from suggesting that he do the same and place my slack hand in his.

CHAPTER 9

It is Frannie's idea that Michael spend Saturday with us in Brooklyn, and as Frannie's kid brother, I have over the years learned to respect her waves of domination as a swimmer respects what is permanent about the sea. Michael can bring a sleeping bag and stay overnight, she says. You can drop him off when you drive me to the airport on Sunday.

But Michael does not agree. Not so fast, he tells her. She is speaking to him from an open phone booth at La Guardia; soon she pulls the door shut. I can see only that she is plowing through this conversation, yanking the red beret off her strawberry blonde hair and talking very fast, waving one set of red fingernails. When she comes out, she says, "He'll come. But he won't stay over. Send him back by subway, the little shit."

I am uneasy. Frannie's older daughter, Karen, bores her, and Larisa (the younger is named for Zhivago's beloved) moved into Bialystok's terrazzo house in L.A., upsetting the divorce settlement by choosing at the last minute to live with her suave father. Will my volatile sister now succeed in turning Michael against me? How I regret Frannie's windswept arrival, mixing precipitously into my life with her short temper and long fingernails. Off the plane not ten minutes, bags still unclaimed, and already she is calling my darling Michael a "little shit."

Frannie drags me back into the exhaust fumes of history, hopelessly dissipating the ether of my philosophic life, my lifeline to Spinoza. Glassman, take hold. Eschew melodrama. You can handle old Frannie. She's all you've got left of Mama and Daddy—see, there's Mama's enterprising smile on her slim wide mouth and Daddy's slightly lurching, energetic walk. Spinoza says there is a bond between reasonable human beings. Pick up her bags and be reasonable. Mama was a reasonable woman, training us to be readers and thinkers, to memorize long lists of things—the rivers of Europe, the kings and queens of England, the archangels. She quizzed us at dinner—Frannie, Daddy, and me—considered testing us her duty because she was the only one who had time to read the *Times* from beginning to end. Frannie was sharp at government, knew which deals were being swung in the Senate, followed Taft-Hartley, and so mastered the rhetoric of politics that she finally thought life a bore with a husband, however elegant, who could not rise to the demands she kept negotiating. I specialized in medical science, the latest in rice treatments for hypertension, new techniques in high-speed hernia operations. I dreamed of Nobel prize winners, their hobbies, their lovely European wives. Dad followed the human interest stories, mostly the aftermath of the war news: on pastel-colored maps thumb-tacked up in the entrance hall, he tracked Nazis on the lam in Paraguay. He marked the jungles of the Solomon Islands where Japanese turned up years later, appearing in Wirephotos with their hands up, not knowing the war was over. What *we* didn't know was that my father's life was almost over. Mama had her specialties, too: hydroponics, Eastern religions, life after death.

I lift Frannie's bag off the carousel and, bearing up, set off at her side, out of the terminal and across the lighted evening to the short-term parking, listening to how I should stop handling my kid with kid gloves. "He'll walk all over you," she says.

I really do not want to hear that refrain ever again. Haven't I just heard the same from Feliz: "Give them eyeglasses, not ethics." It sets me coughing, and the airport wind passing through my open coat doesn't help. Inside the car, I wipe my tearing eyes and button up. I cannot talk for fear the exertion will bring on another fit of coughing. When we reach my room in Brooklyn, Frannie has nothing to say about my novel circumstances, but goes straight to the phone (which I have hurried to install before her arrival, fearing a replay of one woebegone night, between husbands, when I sat with her in a cheap phoneless motel room outside of San Diego as she ranted at *me* instead of at Bialystok; Frannie—mime, Scrabble champion of Evander

Childs High School, graduate of EST and primal scream—my sister is no slouch at ranting). Dinner time in California, and she catches both Karen and Larisa at their respective tables. She has eaten on the plane. For myself, I open a can of tomato soup, heat it, throw in a clot of leftover rice from the Chinese take-out place, and read the paper while Fran talks a full twenty minutes with each girl. To her credit, she is even-voiced, a bit glacial with Karen, but sunny and solicitous with the absent Larisa, who apparently has just split with her weight-lifting boyfriend. "He *was* wonderful, honey," she tells her daughter, passing an emery board across her nails, "but now you have every right to despise him for what he did. Send back everything, and tell him to drop dead if you feel like it. But the 14k gold dumbbell charm is yours—birthday gifts *never* get returned," she instructs.

Eventually we confront each other in the living room. In her robe, perched on the high-riser, her face scrubbed, she is the old teen-aged Frannie again; I am in the only easy chair in the room, near the casement window. "Well, you're thinner," she decides, reaching across to grab both my hands in hers. "You're not eating."

"I eat plenty."

"You're going through hell," she says. "Nobody knows that better than I."

"I miss Marilyn! I'd be a liar if I said I didn't. But she doesn't want to be married to me anymore."

"Who could believe it!"

"She's forgotten everything—what a basket case she was."

"I remember. You coaxed her. You treated her like a kitten."

"Don't lay it on, Frannie. I know you were crazy about Marilyn," I add bitterly.

"All those years. She worked so hard at overcoming—"

"You mean *I* worked so hard. Tell me something. Was she a nut case when I married her or not? Tell me the truth. Who else would have married her?"

"You forget how stunning she was— All the guys were in awe of her. So she had a *meshugaas* or two. Who doesn't?"

"She was never satisfied."

"My God, Barry, you gave her confidence."

"Did *she* know that?"

"And you made her young!"

"But did she *know* that?"

"Well the two of you had a common goal. And you reached it."

"*I* reached it. She reached for the first pair of pants that was hot for her."
Frannie says nothing.

"And it happens to be my old buddy Donahue. Frannie, I thought I
was having a heart attack. He comes into my shop—" But why go on? "I
was working on the self-confidence of a whore all those years and never
knew it."

"Barry! I don't want you to regret this conversation, you hear me? You
may be a wonderboy, Barry, but you know what?"

"What."

"I couldn't live with you for a week. Not for a weekend. You're a hermit.
If a person doesn't speak to you, you have nothing to say."

"But I always loved her."

"You should have told her."

"I always needed her."

"Words." Frannie's polished fingernails are pulling imaginary words out
from between her lips. "You have to speak."

"Marilyn knows I didn't ignore her."

"It's not the same as talking. So you were a sexy hermit. You could have
been Jesus Christ. But if you don't play the game—"

"If I didn't play the game, how come I lost?"

"Don't be a wise guy. You lose when you don't win."

"I thought you came out here to help me."

"Don't worry. I'm on *your* side. Though your philosophy—"

"I could never interest her in the very philosophy that changed her life.
She became a swimmer, a designer, a League of Women Voter— She
became a materialist, always in a hurry. Philosophy takes time."

"You want the truth?"

"No!"

"Where are your brains? I thought you were a philosopher!"

"Frannie, maybe I'll take a hotel room for tonight—"

"You could stand a little materialism."

"Listen, even you and I have different values. Marilyn wants gold jewelry.
I heard you telling your kid to rip off her boyfriend. Keep the gold charm,
you said. Not everyone's made out of money! Especially not a kid."

"The kids in L.A. have 14 karat chains on their pacifiers. Barry, that's what I mean. You misjudge. You're not practical. You have a wife who—"

"*Had*—"

"But you were so in love," Fran says. "I was so jealous, because all the guys I hung around with couldn't come up to my kid brother. You were such a mensch. I adored you. Who knew you could *be* incestuous? In those days, *thinking* about incest was incest." She laughs. "Marilyn and I are like sisters. I tell her my problems. I tell her everything. Did you know she sent me two hundred and fifty bucks for the Santa Barbara institute after Bialy and I split? But that's not all."

Any Spinozist knows that it's never *all*.

"Actually, she called to tell me you had moved out. And I spoke to Michael. It wasn't a fun call. They both say it's your fault, Barry."

"Aaaah. I don't want to hear this."

"Well, what *do* you want to hear? Rock 'n' roll? They're angry!"

"You asked Michael?"

"Of course."

"Leave Michael out of this."

"Kids *know* things. They're like dogs. They sense bad news."

"I don't want Michael to know that he knows."

"Consciousness raising develops the will—even in an angry kid."

"Well, the good news is that I'm getting a lot of work done— I think I'm ready to start writing." The possibility that Michael believes it is my fault floods my twenty-twenty vision.

I wait for her to ask me what I am writing about, but she is adrift. Frannie, I want to say, blinking back tears, it is about optics and the rainbow, heady stuff, Mama would be proud of me.

"I hope I can sleep tonight," she says. "I've become an insomniac. If you hear me stumbling around, don't blame your ritzy accommodations. It has nothing to do with you." She stands up and walks behind me, hugging my shoulders, pressing her lips to the top of my head. "You're a good guy, Barry," she whispers into my hair, "always were. Just like Daddy. Not a mean bone in your body."

I would feel comforted by this affectionate display did I not detect in it an overture. The truth is old Frannie is just warming up.

"You ought to see Larisa. She wears antique clothing—fur sleeves, lace boots. She looks exactly the way I looked at that age, you know, outlandish, *thin*, only she's a California blonde, a golden girl. A woman of a thousand voices, she does Meryl Streep, she does Bill Cosby, she does a microwave oven—" Here Frannie sucks in her cheeks, creates a loud whooshing sound, then beeps twice narrowly through pursed lips. We laugh. "Remember the way I did the neighbors on Kossuth Street?" And here she goes right into her old act—it must be twenty-five years—fourth floor rear, skinny nervous Mrs. Schwartzman's lisp—"I thent my Thtanley to thchool with a thore throat today" and sixth floor front, Frenchy LeBrun, rolling her heavy buttocks in front of the he-man Yugoslavian super: "Ze drain in ze kitchen, *n'est-ce pas?* Come up before *lez enfants* are coming 'ome from ze 'igh school." It is wonderful to hear the old routines.

We both nurse a little sherry along, warmed by nostalgia. "Life was so uncomplicated then," she says.

"Only simple problems," I say, "like starvation. We owed four different grocers for cream cheese. And death at an early age. He was forty-three."

Her eyes leak over to mine, "You and I and the ambulance squad from Montefiore and Mama away at one of her meetings. Was it Christian Science then or Rosicrucians? If I was nineteen, then you were seventeen. Like Karen and Larisa. And he was dead before the soup finished dribbling out of his mouth."

Silence. A long silence.

"That's why I think Alan and I are wasting our time. For God's sake, life is short, and Alan is such a slob. Barry, my ex-husband is showing an interest in me again. He took me to Palm Springs for a $100 a plate dinner. I sat next to the whole Chicago Black Hawk team. We had a long talk, Bialystok and I."

"He never *sounds* romantic."

"I always call him that because his first name—"

"Raoul—" I become a lion. "R-r-r-ow-oool."

"Imagine being married to a man whose name you can't pronounce! *Alan* is so easy— It's been a year and a half with Alan, three months of which he's been totaled—his fault, you know, his goddamned fault. The boob falls asleep on the freeway delivering pool supplies. He works like a dray horse."

"I thought the problem with Bialystok was the opposite. All talk and no money. At least Alan makes a living."

"I come all this way thinking I'm going to help *you*—" She pauses. "Barry, will you put me up for a week? I feel so decisive just now. I believe I can get hold of myself here. If Alan calls, discourage him. Tell him I went up to Boston to look at schools for Karen. Tell him I'm learning to cook vegetarian. Tell him anything!"

My heart takes a dive. The room is too small, Fran is too headstrong, I am too troubled. Events are taking over. But then I remember that ethical practice replaces history. Spinoza had no historicity. Reason and ethics were his universe.

"We'll talk it over tomorrow night. I've got to go pick up Michael early in the morning, so I'm going to hit the sack."

"He's old enough to come out by subway."

"From Queens? He's a kid from the sticks."

She smiles at me. "He's your one and only now, isn't he?"

I pull apart the high-riser and roll one clattering frame and its blue mattress to the other side of the room. The last thing I hear is Fran getting up to pull on another sweater.

In the morning, as I am ready to leave for Michael, she hollers out to me that she has changed her mind. Mrs. Messenger's frigid apartment is no place for my California sister. "I'm taking a motel room for tonight at the airport, and then I'm going back. This place is an icebox."

In the bulk of his navy and red ski parka, Michael looks taller and broader. Carrying nothing, no pack on his back, standing alone at the curb on Fifty-first Avenue with bare hands hanging at his side, bareheaded, he looks utterly frozen, which worries me, and older, which startles me. He trots around to the other side of the car and gets in. Leaning across, I throw an arm around his shoulder and hug him. I do not release him immediately.

Michael tolerates my hold. Glassman, you are already ahead, I think happily. "Dad." He begins promisingly. "Your directional is pointing the wrong way."

I flick the directional the other way. As I smile my thanks, I notice that a light fuzz is nestling in the dimple of his chin. I'll have to teach him to shave, I think. But where? when?

"Isn't Aunt Frannie here?"

"She's waiting for us in Brooklyn."

"She wasn't very nice to me on the telephone last night. I don't like being yelled at. She's a neurotic bitch."

"Well, we're brother and sister."

"*You're* not neurotic. You just don't give up when you get an idea in your head. You obsess."

"Is that a new word you've learned?"

"There's a club in school for kids whose parents are divorcing. They tell us not to obsess about it."

"You can obsess about not obsessing."

"Dad!"

"Good advice, actually."

"Not really."

"Then why go?"

He shrugs. "Do you know why you do everything you do?"

"Of course," I say immediately.

Michael snickers.

The Brooklyn Queens Expressway is slower than the LIE: merging into one lane, honking, standing, inching forward. I keep the radio on. For a few minutes we are gabbing like old times, disagreeing about the third quarter of the Super Bowl last weekend. Then silence. Michael is staring at the New York skyline on the other shore of the river.

"We're almost there," I say, leaving the BQE.

Silence.

"This used to be an elegant part of Brooklyn."

By now Michael is into a serious sulk, still peering out the window. Shabbier houses come into view. Within a few blocks the neighborhood is run-down genteel.

"Do you live in a dump?" he finally asks.

"It's no mansion, but it's not exactly a dump."

"How many beds?"

"I have a high-riser—that's a couch that forms two—"

"*God*, I *know* what a high-riser is!"

"*Okay*. We never had one—"

"*God*, you don't give me credit for very much—"

"Well, how should I know what you know——"

"I'm holding my own. I got a 96 in a chem test. I'm even playing tennis. My coach says I have a serve like a sonofabitch."

I pull up at the curb in front of the Messenger house. "Michael," I say, blocking his gesture to open the door. "You are my favorite person in this whole world." I press the toe of my shoe against his sneaker, holding him. "Wait——"

He wiggles his foot, but it is merely a test. He does not try to escape. By now the door on Michael's side is hanging open. The kid is abject. "Oh, fuck it all," he says through his teeth, "I know all about it," and, freeing his foot, he slides out. Dutifully, he pushes the button down to lock the door and slams it. Inside the hall, an opera is thundering from the Messenger apartment. I push Michael on up ahead of me. Halfway up, Michael grabs my arm. "Dad, I have to tell *you* something."

I stop on the step below him and lean close to his face. Though the music is very loud, I am sure I hear his heartbeat.

He is shouting. "I want you to think about coming back home. Mom is making a big mistake with this guy Donahue. I can't stand Donahue. He pushes Mom around. He laughs at us, maybe because we're Jewish, I'm not sure. And he's pro-Arab! Besides, he keeps buying us clothes and stuff, as if that would make a difference."

"Does he spend a lot of time at the house?"

Michael's face reddens. "If you think I'm going to tell you whether he stays overnight or not, you're crazy. All I want you to know is that I hate his guts. But listen, if you don't come home, we'll be all right. We don't need anybody's help, Mom and me. You just go on reading your books——"

"I'd do anything for you, Mike——"

"Except come home, right?"

I run my hands through his hair. "Who knows?"

"And another thing that's come up. I believe in Israel, but I'm not sure I believe in God any more. Deirdre and I have been reading the Old Testament. It's so melodramatic the way He gets written up. I can't buy all that fire and thunder. To me God is a different idea."

"Michael, you have to decide important questions from strength. You're in a weak period just now." Abruptly the music is gone, and I realize that we are screaming. "This is no time for monumental decisions," I whisper, hoping that Frannie has not heard, detecting for the first time that I am pleading.

I feel like the abominable Jew. God, replacing Placido Domingo's voice, is filling the stairwell, the banister, Michael's dark mop of hair, and I am very vulnerable. "Please. I'll think about what you've asked me," I say, "and you think about nothing. Okay? Nothing at all. Anyway, I doubt that Bob Donahue is an anti-Semite. I've known him all my life, the bastard."

"You think I don't know an anti-Semite when I see one?" Michael says.

He is one miserable being and I am another. Together we climb the rest of the way up to face Frannie, who, still in her bathrobe at the kitchen table, is also huddled inside an old overcoat of mine; she is having a cup of coffee and doing yesterday's crossword puzzle in the *Times*. I haven't quite rallied after Michael's last-minute confession on the staircase. He, however, is all over the apartment, flinging open cabinets, looking out the window, cranking the casement handles, plopping on the high-riser (dust escapes; I ask him not to do that). He allows his aunt to kiss him, but it is an effort for me to follow the dialogue between aunt and nephew. All I can think about is Donahue springing anti-Israel, anti-Semitic innuendos against my kid—I should kill him for that! All those unrequited bar mitzvahs, watching his Jewish chums making successes out of themselves at thirteen, pocketing their checks in the pockets of new clothes. (Our bar mitzvah suits probably drove him nuts. I see him and his three macho brothers, four moon-faced toughs in hand-me-down uniforms from Catholic school, patched navy elbows and high-water plaid pants two inches above the ankle.) He doesn't even know how fucking anti-Semitic he is, the bastard! It takes sensitive, baby-faced Michael to fucking know it, to really know it, as only a Jew knows it. And Marilyn? How can she be so insensitive to what's going on, she, the "normative" Jew, the defender of the faith?

They need me; I believe it, as I believe in Substance and in light bending and in eye banks. Even Marilyn deserves better, though she was always impetuous. A July night; the bus stopped on the Grand Concourse and Fordham Road; she foretold our marriage, heavy dark hair swinging, an arm thrown around the belt of my pants, fingers hooked in my belt loops as we boarded; we tossed our quarters together into the hopper, symbolizing the joint casting of our lots, she, looking out for bats all the way up the Concourse as a small piece in the newspapers had warned of an invasion of bats from Sullivan County. I was a blind risk, but she took it, bit the bullet, as they say now, said I was not like the other guys, knew instantly she could trust me with her life—*so what if you are a universalist; in my heart I believe, come fire, earthquake, or wild dogs, that you will rush in and save me first.* (Within two years I had cured Marilyn of an irrational fear of German shepherds by instilling in her a belief in the oneness of all the beings in the universe.) Fortunately, I was never put to the test.

Until now.

Michael needs me, but rushing to his side now would itself be an evil thing. "A good thing that prevents us from enjoying a greater good is in truth an evil." The thought of neglecting him, however, constricts my chest. I don't cough, but I can't breathe. Oh, how tired I am of these physical crises. In a few seconds, I am aware of a paralysis in the room. Everyone goes into slow motion, Michael loping toward me, Frannie gliding to the sink and toward me. Water. Drink it. Someone is pounding my back. I am hanging from the side of a boat, from the wing of a jet, but I don't let on; I am arguing with the rabbi that Substance is God is the *Ain Soph* until I am breathless.

And then it passes. I breathe. Michael's hand strokes my back. Frannie begins to scold. "You're neglecting yourself. *Gottenyu*, Barry, go see a doctor."

And from Michael, wagging his beautiful head, "You mean you still haven't *gone?*"

I have been doctoring the soul: it is like doctoring the penis; the dread of depression and insomnia is like the dread of impotence and an enlarged prostate; if we live long enough, we all get it. To borrow Michael's word, you can obsess on either one. I vow to submit this week to a physical exam; but I do not vow to perform a rescue operation for Michael. There is no such institution as day-care for souls, no one else into whose professional arms one can turn over one's infant soul on the way to work. Did I need my soul in the store? Would I miss it? How childlike was my soul? I suppose without it my business acumen would improve, at least according to Feliz's theory that too much heart renders me a pushover as a businessman. (Feliz wants assets, a good credit rating, Italian shoes. Is it a wonder I am still in a muddle over Feliz?)

But is a passion for truth *truth*?

"Michael," I say again, "I promise to go to the doctor. And you must promise me something: not to expect me—or anyone—to make your life perfect."

Frannie says, "I'll tell Karen and Larisa to give you a call, Mike."

"No *thanks*," Michael says.

"Your mother can take care of herself, Michael. We girls don't fall apart without a man in the house."

"Leave my mother out of this! She's none of your fucking business. She's *my* fucking business."

"Your business right now, Michael, is to get good marks in school, learn to be tolerant of your dad, and play a game—soccer, tiddlywinks, anything—to get rid of all the free-floating anger inside of you."

Michael is breathing like a volcano. Frannie is at the edge of her seat, my big coat a boxer's robe hanging unevenly about her. I hastily suggest that Michael and I pick up some lunch and bring it back to the room. And at the same time I tell Fran I have a couple of errands to run. Then I call Feliz to make sure the relief optometrist the agency was to send has arrived.

"Is a woman!" Feliz says with glee. "All bones, but very shrewd. You'll see what we are doing here together. Barry, you can stay home every Saturday!" He is exhilarated. "She is 100 percent."

"Is she a kid?" I ask, fearful that I may have given a youngster too much responsibility.

"Who can tell? Under her lab coat she wears a T-shirt."

"Feliz, *look* at her!"

A pause. "Not a kid. Thirty-three, thirty-four?"

"Good. Put her on," I say.

Her name is Linda Kemp. She is polite, all business. I remind her about the duplicate file we keep for soft contact lens prescriptions. She says she and Feliz have already had a brisk morning. I thank her.

Michael is coming out of the toilet. "What a dump," he says miserably, pointing to his splashed pants and wet sneakers.

"Grown-ups know how to turn things on gently," Frannie says.

I think Michael is getting ready to sock her.

"C'mon," I say to Michael, covering her mean little laugh, and we are on our way, walking to Flatbush Avenue for deli sandwiches. Michael starts out hunched, with both hands in his pockets; I am glad to be outdoors. On the block away from the park, a row of recent apartment buildings changes the skyline of the neighborhood. The smell of lint and soap cleanses the sidewalk in the bright Saturday air, the hum of washers and driers propels us along, as we walk by the vented basement windows of these new brick buildings. Both the stately Brooklyn homes and the new apartment buildings are unfamiliar to Michael, for he grew up in a tract house in Bayside, a high ranch, the entire living quarters on one floor, a flight above a rec room at basement level. From the living room there is a view of the Expressway. The sanctuary downstairs with no view whatever is what I miss most, my lab, my library—though at this moment I cannot recollect the hours, the years I spent there (I try to compose myself), except those last days, hiding like a wounded bear as mate and cub carried on above without me.

I suppress all desire to put demands on Michael during this walk. And the truth is I am glad he does not put demands on me. Instead, the mild January Saturday does its work. We walk unhurriedly, happy to be breathing in and out; soon we are both swinging our arms, relieved to be out of range of Frannie's one-woman firing squad. I go over the kinds of sandwiches it is possible to get at the deli. A sign of his new adolescence is that Michael enjoys talking about food. He licks his lips. We'll each have a pastrami on rye and split a turkey and roast beef combo, mustard, Sprite, heavy on the pickle. Pretty soon I know that fathers desire happiness with their sons and sons desire equality with their fathers. If men are governed by reason, they will seek nothing for themselves that they do not desire for their sons. Although I had planned to reintroduce Frannie and Michael to Nathan and Enid, I understand what an error such an outing would be at this time. Add to the giant *E*: *E*at. *E*rror. *E*quality. And *E*nid Moscow. We pick up Frannie and eat our sandwiches in the park. It is a balmy afternoon. Frannie has fished a paperback out of her bag and in the sixty-degree sun is serenely reading *Smart Cookies Don't Crumble: A Modern Woman's Guide to Living and Loving Her Own Life*. At the foot of a boulder adjacent to a baseball field, Michael and I discover a half-dead pigskin, which we knock around in a game of touch football. I feel like one of the surviving Kennedys on the family compound in Hyannis.

CHAPTER 10

Stan Gunn has it from Donahue that Marilyn and I have split. He is wide-eyed in my defense. How I love that guy. "All the more reason for you to fly out to the congress with us Sunday morning," he says. "I can find someone to relieve you Monday and Tuesday."

I consider leaving Linda Kemp and Feliz in the store for the two days of the Detroit meetings. Optometrist Kemp has turned out to be a thirty-eight-year-old, frizzy-blonde super saleswoman in high-fashion eyeglasses, a lot of rouge, a sequined T-shirt under her white lab coat, and light gray eyes; competent and tough. She sold more sets of expensive frames on that one Saturday than I sell in a month. "Have nothing more to do with the agency. They're on the take," she said confidentially. "I don't owe them a thing! Call me at home any time you need help." In a projected career change, she is going to NYU law school at night and can use the extra cash.

But still I hesitate to go. Conventions are not my cup of tea. I dislike the stepped-up pseudo-professionalism that requires hanging around smoky bars in glitzy hotel lobbies and joking with people you don't give a crap about. I dislike the boring commercialism of the exhibits, the spherical key chain ornaments that tilt to show how a contact lens fits over an eye. Rarely anything theoretical, except an occasional film about laser surgery, or Bausch & Lomb, of course, who have mounted wonderful historical exhibits on Christian Huygens, Carl Friedrich Gauss, Newton. I remember a lovely exhibit about James Bradley, eighteenth-century professor of astronomy at Oxford, who discovered that an apparent motion of the stars, which he described as *aberration*, was owing to the motion of the earth in its orbit. This is not to be confused with *parallax*, which causes stars to appear displaced, relative to the backdrop of the more distant stars, when they are viewed from different points in the earth's orbit. (Recently I have suffered from a parallax of the passions, the more distant satisfactions of a happy childhood taking on a sharper melancholy now than when viewed from the happier years of my marriage.) I remember the diorama of Bradley sailing splendidly on the Thames as he chanced to observe changes in the apparent direction of the wind, which in turn led his imagination to his theories of aberration. Nowadays, I cannot summon the energy to attend, for I dislike being an optometrist for a solid seventy-two hours, as if nothing outside of that were useful or desirable to me. My weakness as a businessman gives rise to pain. I fear that rather than cheering me up, a trip to Detroit may bring on an overnight slide into dejection and false feelings of envy, induced by unexpected moments of comparison to men I haven't seen in five or ten years. Not going to Detroit is my way of adjusting my external life so as not to perforate the delicate web of my internal life.

I manage to ask Gunn whether Donahue and Marilyn plan to go (I picture them in earphones, sleeping across each other's arm rests on the flight out), but my question embarrasses him. He has no idea and is genuinely bewildered at our split. But he reiterates his promise to mention my research to Bausch & Lomb.

"Even one or the other," I say jokingly.

That Saturday night in January, just before closing time, with his coat collar turned up, Feliz hands me an envelope. He is ready to make a quick getaway, but I sense something stupendous is in the air and I restrain him. He resists; then, overcome by loyalty, he stands by. I hear a nervous little tune vibrating across his lips, as he shifts his trim weight from one foot to the other.

"Is all in the letter," he says unhappily, filling the intolerable silence. "I am wrong to stay on with you! In my country, is not like here. A man have to earn a good living, take care of wife and family." His voice is trembling with irritation that his plan to present the letter and vanish has backfired. "Is all in the letter," he repeats, slapping with his bare fingers the envelope I am holding. Yet there is some majesty in the way his eyes fasten to mine, proud, ambitious, perhaps resolute. "Santina comes from good family. Her father is a banker in Milan and her mother is doctor. I am a good match for her. But here I am bored. Jesus knows, you keep my chances at a minimum. I am wrong to stay on with you." He makes a sweeping gesture at the shop, the splintering counter, the optical machinery huddling on the side behind the glass partition, the fading posters of bespectacled models, some of them in outdated hairdos, and the frames suspended in rows across thin cords under bluish neon lights. "I want to help you. We make everything more modern, more high-tech. You need a good partner, Barry—" He looks away, his chest heaving with the unexpected liberty he has taken.

I tear open the envelope.

Dear Barry [I read],

What I must say to you now is painful; I feel you are like a brother to me, a brother that I love. But I am not making a career for myself in your shop. Your soft way of doing business is not my way of doing business. In short, I must believe we are imcompatible. I have thought to become a partner for you, I am good with the Hispanic community who need eyeglasses, but I see no sign of that, in spite of I work hard and care personally for you. Therefore, I resign, with best wishes for your health and happiness and one week's notice,

Feliz Algarve

I feel as if I have been hurried out on the ice without my skates tied. Feliz is clever, and he is ambitious, and I am about to break my neck. I should have seen this coming, but the slippery affairs of my store have not been uppermost in my mind. Which is why Feliz is leaving, I remind myself. He plans to marry his dark-eyed Santina and raise a family. Who can blame him? Santina, an affectionate, chic Florentine designer (the last time I saw her, in her clingy blue sailor dress, she looked a little pregnant), might also be behind this, I think understandingly. In fact, I understand the entire situation. I may be a B+ philosopher, but I am A+ at understanding! Then why does my shirt dampen as the sweat soaks down my back? Feliz, *don't go*, I want to scream. Although Frannie and Michael left on excellent terms with each other, after their departure I sank into a nervous depression. On Sunday Frannie called just before her flight to apologize for clouding our meeting with her aimless problems. "I understand," I told her, A+ etched again into my forehead like a third eye, though that Sunday I could not get out of bed, didn't shave, didn't bathe, kept repeating my position regarding the blazing indigo, making no headway whatever with the inert gas that causes it and how large the particles are. When Michael called to say the ten dollar bill Frannie had slipped him must have fallen out of his pocket in the car, I told him not to worry, I understood everything. Everything.

"But the ten dollars," he said. "Did you find it?"

"Not to worry. If it's there, it is necessary that we find it, Mike."

"Dad, please. Take a look on the back seat under the belts."

And now Feliz. Striving for happiness and perfectibility. Feliz has a right to the usual rewards of life esteemed by men—fame, riches, pleasures of sense—as long as these are not the end of life but the means to happiness and perfectibility. To Santina. To a nursery of dark-eyed babies.

"Feliz," I bawl, "what are you going to do?"

At this question, he puts his arms out and embraces me.

"Do you have something else?"

"Possible," he says, buttoning his coat to the neck and heading for the door.

A thought seizes me. I run toward him and grip his arm. "Vision Centres, is that it? Did that snake Donahue get to you?"

Feliz does not answer. I drop my hands, and we glare at each other.

"Will you come to my wedding?" Feliz mumbles.

But I do not blame Feliz for his ambition. The intellect and the will are one and the same.

I lock up; and sit half the night reading part four of the *Ethics*. "He who wishes to avenge injuries by hating in return does indeed live miserably." (The true liberty of man requires fortitude. Generosity. Strength of mind. So what if Michael hasn't called all week?) "Everyone who is guided by reason desires for others the good that he seeks for himself."

By the time I fall asleep, I see Bob Donahue as no more than a toothache in my life, an untied shoelace, a stuck turnstile temporarily barring my ride to truth.

The newscaster on the car radio Monday morning must have announced it, but it is not until Feliz arrives—late and brashly unapologetic during this final week of his employ—that I learn about the tragedy. Feliz pauses long enough in the telling to marvel that I am so out of touch as not to have listened to a single news report, neither Sunday nor Monday morning. (It would have been worse to tell him that I had WINS on all the way across the Brooklyn Bridge, fighting traffic crosstown, parking, but that I heard only the sound of my own physiology plumbing in my pipes.) "Everybody who is half-alive in New York listens to the news," he shrieks at me, incredulous. "If I thought for a minute you didn't know, I would have call you yesterday. Nobody call you?"

As if the plane crash were not bad enough, I am grieving for my lost connectedness to life, the once blissful maelstrom of the neighborhood, the smug circle of a wife's best friends, who are unfailingly on the other end of the phone with their self-centered, nasal stories. During the entire weekend my phone never rang.

The first impact of the report shows how upside down my world is: Donahue, I think next, crossed up by his own admission of lust. So that's why he came to the shop—to prepare me for seeing them together in Detroit—and instantly the cannonball strikes my intestines and explodes: Marilyn! Is she? Did she? I'm afraid to hear. What if. Michael's mother. My good old Marilyn. Dying with the whoring new. What if. "The joy that arises from our imagining that what we hate has been destroyed or has been injured is not unaccompanied with some sorrow." I'm too weak to know. Michael's mother, my good old Marilyn, so *soon*?

I rush to the telephone. Michael is in school. But he's not in school if. If—, he would have called. Someone would have called. I dial my old number. No answer. The absence of an answer becomes the cause of hope. I dial the Vision Centre near Bloomingdale's. I ask for Mr. Donahue. I ask for Mrs. Glassman.

"Well, who do you want?" says the operator.

"Are they both in today?"

"Every day. Mrs. Glassman is right here."

It is Marilyn all right. They went to hear Donahue's kid give a saxophone recital in Hartford yesterday. But she gives me the news. The plane carrying Stan and Cathy Gunn, Albie and Cynthia Rashkin, Herm Gluck (Theresa Gluck's stepfather had had a heart attack and she had canceled at the last

minute), and thirty-eight other optometrists from the New York metropolitan area, many wives, and a handful of children exploded over Dunkirk,
New York, southwest of Buffalo, on the shores of Lake Erie, crashing into
a roller rink. No survivors. Thank God it was a Sunday morning; the rink's
first session began at noon.

I sink against the wall. To Feliz's credit, he hovers over me as he has hovered in crises past. I beg for more details, but he has already added everything he knows: clear weather, no fog, not a DC10 but a 727 with an excellent safety record, no message from the pilot, no warnings from air safety
control, Marilyn safe. Witnesses said the plane was an erratic ball of fire as it
descended. Feliz becomes dramatic for the second time. One girl on her way
to skating said it looked like a burning gymnast doing somersaults—Feliz
extends his arms—its wings outstretched like fiery arms. They are hunting
for the cockpit voice recorder and the flight data recorder (the black box),
but the intensity of the fire makes recovery doubtful and their usefulness uncertain. I run out to buy a *Times*. "Authorities have come up with no apparent reason for the crash."

Morons, I think to myself, stupids! Though the reason is unknown, it exists. We perceive a thing best through only one mode of perception: not
through hearsay (human failure, some say), nor through mere experience
(that most disabled planes burn), nor through inference (the plane is larger
than it first appears as it begins to descend, finally setting ablaze an extensive
area beyond the rink), but from a grasp of its essence or through knowledge
of its proximate cause.

Proximate cause. A federal committee has been formed to look into the
cause of the crash. The American Optometrical Congress in Detroit holds
a memorial service at its annual dinner Sunday evening and votes (three to
two) to cancel the rest of the meetings, while the *Times* carries an interview
with a disgruntled Seattle optometrist named Raisonner, who says Israeli
terrorists must have boarded in New York, there must have been a bomb in
the baggage compartment: "Are we going to let Mayrowitz and the Eastern
Establishment get away with this? Are we going to cancel our annual meetings because of the Zionists?"

On Tuesday, Bausch & Lomb runs a corporate half-page ad in the *Times*,
under a photograph of the wreckage in Dunkirk, bordered in black, an-

nouncing a $20,000 prize *In memoriam* for the best essay on an optical sub-
ject submitted to a panel of judges before October 31. By Monday noon Nathan has called to find out what I know about the crash.

But Anya gets on first.

"We see on televizhya so many doctors is dead. I worry. He turn white
like sheet from bed. I say drink tea, but no tea, he want to make call to governor. Nathan telephone first to your boy, then he say thanks to your God
you are not going on airplane."

"Please. Put him on."

"When are you coming?"

"I will come, Anya. Let me have Nathan. Now," I add.

Nathan's voice is solemn. "Barry? You came close."

"Not at all. I never planned to go."

"You'd be finished—kaput. I went to the museum on Sunday, so I didn't
hear until this morning. Enid called in a panic."

"Enid Mintz?"

"Moscow. She thought you might have been on board."

"Pretty nice of her," I murmur.

"And your bar mitzvah was non-communicado, said he was late for
school."

"And Marilyn?"

"Who speaks to Marilyn? I have nothing against her, but these days—
So, Barry, enough of tragedy and close calls. How's your brilliant friend?"

I have no idea who Nathan means.

"The handsome one."

On the third try: "The one we had dinner with, the blind man."

"Oh! Bernard Messenger. I hardly see him."

"Well, you're even. He hardly sees you," Nathan says, laughing at his
joke.

"Yeah. Well, keep laughing, Uncle Nathan."

"Actually, my feet are swollen today. And S.O.B."

"S.O.B.?"

"Shortness of Breath. Goodbye, Barra-le. For a few breathless minutes,
my dear nephew, I thought I had survived you!"

"Keep your feet elevated, Nathan, and you may yet survive me. Tell Anya
I said to raise your legs."

"So long, Barry. I prayed to your mother, and you are alive!"

I wait until 4:30 to call Michael and reassure him. He remembers Gluck and Rashkin from his bar mitzvah. A host of others swarm into mind: John Sweeney, a sweetheart of a guy from Canarsie; happy-go-lucky, tennis-playing Dominick Cutrone from Massapequa; and, oh yes, Leo Van Helden, who practically lived with us in Elmhurst when Michael was a baby. I peruse the list of victims. Dominick Cutrone's name is not listed. John Sweeney *is* there, and Leo, Leslie, and Douglas Van Helden. God. He was a family of three. My heart plunges in fresh grief. I never even knew he was married!

Human beings have only a partial knowledge of the events of the world, I tell Michael, but a reason for the crash *will* emerge.

He asks me how many of the forty-one I knew. "About thirty."

Then he says, "Donahue is not on the list."

His remark is all bone and blade. "But if Donahue had gone, Michael, Mommy would probably have gone, too."

"Not necessarily." Michael is hissing into the receiver. "Not necessarily."

"I know you are a high-minded boy," I say.

No response.

"These feelings will pass. They are understandable." I can't believe I am still feeding him understanding!

"I've got chem to do."

"Do me a favor?"

"What?"

"If you hear of any funeral plans from your mother or Donahue—especially for Gunn or Rashkin or Gluck—call me at the store. I want to try to make as many as I can, especially Stan Gunn. Michael, write it down, Stan Gunn."

"The remains have not been identified yet," Michael says. "Donahue thinks they may never be."

"Oh."

"I've got chem to do. Please let me hang up."

"I'll put the ten dollars in the mail for you, Mike."

Although I have never found the ten dollars in the back of the car, I can think of no other cheer to offer, money, like any evil, being entirely relative and at this precise moment relatively useful and good.

At a memorial service arranged by the local optometrical society, I learn that Stan and Cathy Gunn's wake will take place on Friday and the funeral on Saturday. (Their remains are among only a dozen bodies to have been positively identified.)

Two plump teen-aged daughters, dazed and tearless, are being shepherded by an uncle, Stan's brother, eerily just as blonde and soft-faced as Stan, who does not unlock his arms from the girls'; and Stan's mother, an Irish octogenarian in a pink ski jacket, keeps shrieking from her wheelchair, "Oh, mother of God, I should be dead by now. I should be dead by now, dear mother of God." In the pew next to her, both of Cathy's parents, a tiny, neatly dressed couple in their seventies, with wet staring eyes, face stiffly ahead, as if only total immobility could fend off the other woman's pitiable outcries.

The vast gray and gilt interior of Our Lady of Perpetual Help is filling with mourners, colleagues whom I recognize, friends, relatives, teen-aged friends of the girls, with awkward smiles on their faces, nodding across the rows as another uncertain teenager arrives. Organ music begins, faintly, and I realize it is a meditative rendering of "Oh, Danny Boy," infusing a gentle Irish undertow into the waves of people finding places. Two rows in front and immediately to my left, Marilyn and Donahue are taking seats. From the moment they sit down, my agitation is uncontrollable. It is as if until now I have been painting a storm inside of a studio, and at last I drag paints and easel out of doors to paint the raging wind, the gray, soaked earth, rain drenching me in the downpour, hurtling against the canvas, deadening all of nature's colors into a single, brooding slanted gray blur. It is the real thing, and it concerns only me. The organ's gradual efflorescence subsides. The priest's eye is alert. "God of all consolations . . . I bless you Stanley and Cathleen . . . as Christ was raised that you might live a new life. I ask you all to join in prayer for Stanley and Cathleen Gunn, who begin a new life." The priest begins his chant. I cannot take my eyes from the rows to the left of me. They sit side by side, scarcely touching, Marilyn in the white suit she wore to Michael's bar mitzvah and sporting a new frosty hairdo, blown and trendy; Donahue in his trench coat. They do nothing at all; and they do it brazenly! I realize I am quivering: my knees shaking inside cold pants, my eyes stripping her to the flesh, my imagination lashing him onto a cross, like the gray and gilded wooden Christ crucified above the altar, dominating the church. I drive nails into the palms of his hands; and then punch him in the groin. I take her on the bench, ripping her skirt, sliding off the panty hose that she hates, her bikini underpants. I slap her behind, then slap her face when she falls asleep. "Those who have fallen asleep in Christ have perished," the priest is saying. "May those who have been denied the fulness of days receive the fulness of eternity. What you have hidden from the learned and clever, you have revealed to the merest children." As the priest intones the mass, I am suddenly filled with remorse at how little Stan and Cathy Gunn are on my mind. It is as if an angel has been released from my heart and a stampeding horse invaded it. I seek to calm myself with revelations from the Scholium at the end of the second part of the *Ethics*: how to deal with the things of fortune, or those that are not in our power, "that is to say, which do not follow from our own nature." Nothing in my nature could have elicited this betrayal, this offense to my eyes. Spinoza's doctrine teaches us "with equal mind to wait for and bear each form of fortune, because we know that all things follow from the eternal decree of God. . . ."

"We bring God's gifts to the altar . . . the bread and the wine. This is the cup of my blood. In mercy, in love, unite all your children."

" . . . according to that same necessity by which it follows from the essence of a triangle that its three angles are equal to two right angles."

Spinoza's damned triangles—if I could be free of them! The congregation is kneeling, suffering its rites together. In the crowded church I have my own triangle: I form a straight line with Marilyn (two upright Jews) and an oblique one to Donahue (kneeling Roman Catholic). Then from a side door two altar boys appear in white robes, one a red-haired child, the other an olive-skinned Indian boy, dark face against white robes. The Indian clasps the cruet before him and backs adroitly away, both boys trailing behind the priest in his glistening white silk chasuble, who now ceremoniously shakes his censer to left and right over the twin coffins—each embellished by a long spray of white carnations with a single red rose at the center. The boys' faces are angelic. Had I ever seen cherubim, I would say these boys were part of the cherubic host. Their faces, the flowers, the music—I am missing my own militant archangel, Michael, who in his way is bribing me home. *He*, of course, is the bribe, in the flesh, reading the Old Testament with haughty Deirdre Hoddeson, growing up under my nose and shaving that sweet baby flesh at my side in our own medicine-chest mirror, weights, smelly Reeboks, and all. And what am ambush! What an effort for me to resist. Why *do* I resist my own child? Death and grief everywhere. I could be a corpse in a week, in an hour. I recall another episode of bribery: Amsterdam 1656. Already the loneliness is mournful, for bribery rises out of the brevity of our days.

In June (the year Spinoza was twenty-four), a committee of *parnassim* made their way to Baruch Spinoza's house and invited him for a walk. The weather: cool for June. A salt breeze coasting along the canals, splashing the surface of the water. A yellow fog lingering modestly under the bridges. Baruch's reputation as a freethinker and free speaker had spread ominously throughout the Amsterdam community, not only because his discourse was so surprising and not only because of Uriel D'Acosta (whose excommunication had culminated in a scandalous suicide sixteen years earlier), but because Rabbi Morteira had become vexed and disappointed—vengeful perhaps—at the continuing heresies of his adored and brilliant student.

Spinoza agreed to meet the *parnassim*. His father had died, and his business partnership with his brother Gabriel depended on flourishing relationships with the Jews of Amsterdam, most of whom engaged in a network of import-export businesses dependent on one another's connections. But the *parnassim* did not have business on their minds. In June of 1656 they stood at the corner of the Herengracht, forming a little circle around Baruch, and offered him a bribe. Baruch, all we want is lip service to prayer and ritual. Keep your ideas quiet. Study. Read Descartes from dawn to dusk if you like, but take 1,000 florins a year as a subsidy and heed our advice. Maintain a place in the community. Do not injure your teachers, who have such a high regard for you. Your dead father was one of us: he sat among the *parnassim*, his arrival in Amsterdam arranged by none other than Morteira himself. Can you willfully cut such a bond? Who are you to disregard a people, a chosen people at that?

Be a man of reason. Bento, accept the 1,000-florin annuity. Life is compromise, not paradise.

But Bento interrupts them and leaves before they have finished.

"May paradise be open to your servants," the priest is saying, his eyes appealing to the blank and stony daughters. "Make suffering not easy, but meaningful."

I leave the church service before it is over, refusing to be bribed by anyone, not even by Michael, excusing myself into the aisle and out into the sleet that is falling. For moments during the mass, I had lost touch with humanity and with God: all my readings since college have failed me, the memory of my beloved Stan and Cathy has died a vile death. Whereas a common grief protected the others like a warm sun, I was cold and shivering in my philosophy—half-religious, half-profane. I start the car urgently, putting Michael out of mind. The windshield wipers jerk and squeal across the frozen glass: *scro-ink, scro-ink, scro-ink*. But the sleet in its halfway condition between rain and snow exists as neither and strikes the windshield as it must, a wet, partly frozen rain.

CHAPTER **11**

All my highest hopes are dashed. Philosophy drops a curtain of doubt around me, a darkness inhospitable to life. To Spinoza the infinite, which contains everything, is complete, not additive; Substance is always complete; it bears no past, present, or future; it is the eternal now. Yet I know no comfort. I think endlessly of the moment of death, and why I am alive, and why time goes on. I ask why I must square up to an irrational world and, since the funeral for the Gunns, why I have been cut off from the friends I love, from Michael, from my parents, from Frannie, from a wife—worse, from the *idea* of a wife. Disaster is relentlessly with me, consciousness of my own Jewish betrayal a joke told badly and repeated badly in my ear. Not since my father's death have I endured such a load of grief—a leaden philosophic dilemma within—the contradiction of being at once softened and hardened by death. I eat bags of Oreos and boxes of chocolates, which sit like lead in the bottom of my stomach.

But since Substance must exist, death subtracts nothing from the universe. Some powerful law of compensation exists and, though I cannot explain it, late night readings in the *Ethics* numb my sense of loss, and after many weeks, one day the numbness gives way to a mystical excitement like that first day long ago, eleven months after my father's death when I awoke knowing for the first time that he was appropriately in the ground, properly where he belonged, and I had a right to walk the planet, from one end to the other if I chose, without him. It was such a relief, such justice, I fairly danced into the subway and to school. I spoke to strangers, brought my mother three pink carnations in a cone of florist's paper, and washed the bathroom and kitchen floors for her with a scrub brush when I came home. She understood: it was not that my mourning had ended, rather that I had discovered the peace that always is present in the universe. She held me close and laughed out loud with me on the wet kitchen floor, directing me to a few grimy spots I had missed under the table. That spring I helped Mama with her hydroponics, but water was insufficient to me: I needed to grope with my fingers in the same dirt in which my father lay buried. I filled a cheesebox with soil and, like a nine-year-old on a school project, planted zinnias on the fire escape over Kossuth Street. When the zinnias came up at Crotona Park, where I sold Mister Softee ice cream that spring and summer, I ran home to see what had gone wrong in my windowbox; but there! nature's clock was working, feather green shoots in the little box of soil on the fire escape over Kossuth Street, bonding me to my father in his rightful grave in Farmingdale. *Natura naturata*. Inside of two weeks, a multiflowered end to grief in a bobbing line of zinnias.

The other day I weighed myself. The scale must have been a relic of the 1940s: honest weight, one cent. For a penny I stood in the tropical fish department of the five and dime where the scale still stands, a bit rusted from years of dampness, and discovered that I am eleven pounds over my usual weight: 160 instead of 149. Tiny golden-red fish do aerobics back and forth in their tanks, but I get no exercise, thighs flabby, pants pulling at the seams. When a painful blister bloats at the back of my heel, I discover that my shoes are tighter than they ought to be, my feet locked in like herrings in a box. And I have been wearing so many sweaters this winter that I am a stranger to my own body. Undressing for a shower is an embarrassing act.

Am I eating, Frannie wants to know! Yes, of course, and gaining substance every day. Where in the universe does it come from? I reject the suspicion that my life has peaked, risen out of one eternity, now sloping toward another. But my cough has a new character: it is no longer loose, postulating sickness amid health, but goes into dry, wrathful paroxysms. The timbre of my voice deepens; and is lost to laryngitis as night falls. During the days I cough with a bronchial whoop, but at night soundlessly, rackingly. Bad health slips into a routine. While others play their Jane Fonda exercise records, eat granola and millet, pull on sweat clothes, yellow sweatbands around their foreheads, and bound across the Brooklyn Bridge, I curl under the covers with Mounds bars to listen to my old tapes of Professor Winning at Baruch College lecturing on Spinoza's correspondence with Henry Oldenburg of the Royal Society. "No one can blame God because he has given him or her an infirm nature or an impotent mind. For it would be just as absurd for a circle to complain that God has not given it the properties of a sphere." Winning, damn it, I am still completing your course! I miss you, you Marxist bastard with the harsh, firm mind, you who taught our crowded Philo 205 class in jeans and a work shirt, with your back pressed against the blackboard and a philosopher's scowl on your good-looking mug, a container of tea in one hand, a piece of chalk in the other. How I scrutinized the Lipton tag for a sign of how to be an intellectual. Oh, how I expected an A from you, from *you* a perfect A: in the end—a B+; muddled, you said, on the final exam.

In the week before Feliz leaves, I go to see Dr. Scarf. The plane crash has lit a match under me. Life on this planet is to be taken seriously, since we do not know what the cause of death will be. I have a premonition that accident is not my destiny; there is nothing dramatic at the end of my undistinguished chain. A slow, tedious sonata playing out the proximate cause (prostate cancer, heart disease, kidney failure), hands playing with difficulty, then, lifted above the keyboard and suddenly dropped, crashing at the end into a muddled chord.

For the first time in my life I am overweight! Dr. Scarf, a big careful man of about sixty, has blunt features that sit comically low beneath a huge forehead. But he is not funny. He puts me on a diet—fresh fruits and vegetables, lots of fish. He reads the menu through bitten lips, and his chrome and vinyl waiting room, though located in a trendy condominium in Bayside, is a serious place, crowded with blue-collar people, fitting in a doctor's visit where there ought to be a beer after work or the seven o'clock news. I like waiting my turn there, a mortal among mortals. When I go to a doctor I do not want to feel elite; I am a specimen of averageness, middle height and build, big teeth, excellent vision, an upper respiratory weakness, and bad knees, though lately functioning. Dr. Scarf withholds comment, except to say he'll need a chest X ray.

"Have I got TB?"

"Doubt it," he says, calling his technician to take the film. The technician is hollering the instructions from out in the hall. "Okay, you can breathe." I wait around, looking at a magazine, breathing, but Dr. Scarf has an emergency and won't read the X ray until tomorrow.

As I make my way back to the store, the newscaster has one small item about the plane crash: that the members of a federal commission have been named. They include the CEO of Bausch & Lomb and Senator Jake Garn, Republican of Utah, who rode the last successful shuttle before the Challenger. The announcement ends by noting that the eyes of the metropolitan area are currently underserved owing to the deaths of forty-one optometrists and the shutting of many shops. Bob Donahue, cruising from one Vision Centre to the other in his cashmere sweater and trench coat, must be raking it in. And I hear that Theresa Gluck is having a hard time keeping her shop professionally supervised. Bony, sharp-eyed Linda Kemp ought to quit law school and open up a shop. Marilyn might go to optometry school. Who *knows* what Money-Bags Donahue will treat her to next! Even my shop shows a healthy spurt of profits, Feliz's cheek twitching bitterly over what the rush might have meant to him in dollars and cents had he not resigned (I vow not to take him back!). I shuffle from examining room to cash register many times a day, though several times an afternoon, knowing I am about to have dinner, I duck outside for a falafel or a hot dog, losing myself among the ethnic citizenry in their disorderly glide uptown.

Bernard Messenger surprises me as I climb up to my room that night. I have Dr. Scarf on my mind and a muffler twice around my neck. Just as I raise my foot for the last step, Messenger bursts through his apartment door downstairs.

"I was listening for you." He is facing the wall opposite his door. "I want to invite you to hear some music. Murray Perahia plays Schumann tomorrow night. Your cousin and I want to show you how relieved we are you are alive. She plans to call you later tonight. How about it?"

The invitation is treacherous. Were they planning this outing—one of a series well under way between them—and decided to ask me along? He says "your cousin," constricting Enid and me within our biological relationship. Or was this outing *conceived* as a threesome for this purpose, the only outing, no other goddamn thing between them? And what news will tomorrow bring from Dr. Scarf? Will I *know* by tomorrow? I feel trapped in ignorance, which I despise. I would clearly go if I were not intruding. On the other hand, I ought to prove intrusion to myself rationally. Whether intruding or not, then, I have to go, though ambivalence strips me of pleasure.

"For a couple of days, I didn't hear a thing upstairs. I thought the worst. Enid called your uncle."

"But your mother must have seen my car."

"Mother's in the hospital. Not serious," he says, sensing my surprise. "When her palpitations are very frequent she goes in for tests. The electrocardiograms are okay, and so far the enzyme tests are okay. No infarction. I thought we could have a night out before she gets home."

"If there's anything you need—" I say, coming down a few steps.

"Say yes. Come with us."

"Are you and Enid—" I have trouble putting the question.

"She'll talk to you," he says. "So?" He is highly animated, his hands rubbing each other, his eyelids blinking rapidly. Then he holds up one hand, as if to say he has heard my answer. His hand is a prophecy.

"I'll be glad to drive."

"Wonderful. Let me go in and call the Academy for tickets."

In the dark of my mind Bernard Messenger exists as an acolyte of Sabbetai Zevi, the false messiah, whose fame started in the Ottoman Empire, then swept across Europe to England. Jews everywhere rejoiced that redemption was near. Yeshiva boys in Amsterdam wore green silk ribbons to honor the approaching redemption. Students reported that streams had turned in their courses. Children ran through the streets telling of wondrous portents. The canals were first green as grass, then red as the sun. Comets, they said, fell like hail. Strange ships with Hebrew letters on their sails were sighted at dawn on the Amstel. I am not dreaming this. I am fiercely thinking it as I lie across my bed waiting for Enid Moscow's call. Sleep does not come. Messenger appears self-possessed and handsome, but blinded by ecstasy, floating, as blind people often seem to do, from village to village in the Europe of the seventeenth century. The Jews of the villages are on the lookout for him, especially the *tzadikim*, the righteous; to them he is all the more miraculous for being blind. They feed him chickens and wash his feet; give him woolen caps and gifts of silver. They consult him on questions of birth and death;

they ask him how to grow onions in stony ground; what to do when young women outnumber the marriageable men. What does a shooting star mean? how can a rainbow appear at night? is it a sign? a return to Eretz Israel? is it true that the wife of a *tzadik* reaches orgasm twice in one night?

Bernard Messenger adores the questions. He becomes messianic. That Spinoza could develop a rational system of thought while a short distance away the false messiahs preached their ignorant cant seems to me a miracle! Miracles, I remember, like the parting of the Red Sea, are events whose natural causes we do not yet know.

What has been happening between Messenger and Moscow? Has a miracle flowered between them? I am so consumed by the necessary changes in my life—Frannie's visit, Michael's contempt for Donahue, Feliz's resignation—and now the plane crash, all of which I try to understand as necessary as part of the savage completeness of the universe. I am so preoccupied with concerns of self that my earliest premonitions about Messenger and Moscow have gone unattended.

I expected more of Messenger! sneaking in on Enid when I wasn't looking. He comes on so helpless, so innocent and defenseless! A blind man, for God's sake! seducing my own cousin out from under my nose. He is no miracle. He occupies the same place in nature as any of us and must be held accountable to the same decency and morality.

I am the blind one! standing helpless, banging my white stick against the curb; but no one comes to my rescue. No "Can I help you? Take my arm. We'll cross together." And I am still on the wrong side of romance, opening my eyes for a moment to see the empty sidewalk before closing them, as alone as I was before. Oh, he's a shrewdie, all right. I expected more of him. And why not? Doesn't he *know* what suffering is? what it *means* to be different, to lack what everyone else has? Do I lack the capacity to be loved by a woman, to be her one and only? Does he lack the capacity to see? Seeing matters, not sight. And loving matters, not love. The mind's capacity to imagine is its freedom—and its link to error. Bernard Messenger has trained himself in human freedom. While I am in bondage.

When the phone rings, I become aggressive. We have both been duped, Enid as well as I.

"I hear you and Bernard are taking me to a concert tomorrow night."

"_____."

"Enid, I have to talk to you. About the essay I am writing. I would like to submit it to the memorial contest. I thought you might consider coauthoring—"

"_____."

"Yes, of course I have. In the *Journal of the American Optometrical Society*, in *Optica Acta*, a note in the *Spinoza Quarterly*. I publish regularly."

"_____."

"Correct. *Spinoza*. But that's not the point now. Think about it, and we'll be there at seven. See you at seven."

At 3 A.M. I awaken to a huge banging and bumping, as if one of the great pyramids has been hauled up to my door. Bernard Messenger is pummeling the wall with his fists, reaching my door, shouting my name. I shiver to the door. Sweat is glistening on the sides of his face. Could I drive him to the hospital. His mother has had a massive coronary. I get on some clothes, lead him down the stairs, and out into the car. He is a sight! A blue and white pajama top shows through his coat, his hair standing straight up on his head, his mouth grim, one lip crusted with food; he has no socks on, and his shoes are untied. Neither stick nor dark glasses declare that he is blind. He looks like a man escaped from a madhouse in the middle of the night.

But in the car, perfectly coherent, he is aware that he may look in disarray. I assure him it is understandable, but he presses me to adjust his collar. When we stop for a light, he says *please*, and I lean over and straighten his coat, concealing his pajamas underneath the collar, smoothing his lapels. He pulls a maroon wool muffler out of his pocket and stuffs it around his neck as if his immediate obligation is to a dignified appearance. I cross it carefully in front and tuck the ends in. We are both polite, his blindness mitigating the embarrassment of our touching. He mumbles something about a fastener on his coat that needs replacing, and he feels down the length of the coat until he reveals a torn flap on the inside edge. At his touch, it comes off in his hand.

Quite calmly, the flap of fabric pressed in his fingers, he says, "If my mother dies, I will not be able to manage alone."

"Have you given that any thought before now?"

"Months pass when I think of nothing else," he says. "But I have no solution. I'll probably go into a home for the blind. I've never had to be independent. My parents were too good to me."

"There may be other possibilities."

"We'll have to see," he says softly, as we arrive.

I offer either to wait for him in the waiting room or go up with him. A man is holding a very young baby on his chest in the corner of the empty waiting room. Both are asleep, their bodies breathing as one. Bernard suggests I wait. A nurse appears to lead him away. With my eyes lavishing protection on him, I follow them as he steps mincingly alongside of her into the elevator.

But the memory blasphemes. Who is lying ill on the seventh floor, a beautiful young woman in her thirties, the adored remembered mother of an eight-year-old boy, or an imagined old nag of a mother? Is that what it is like tonight to be Bernard Messenger?

CHAPTER 12

Enid Moscow is waiting. Before she notices my Plymouth pulling up outside her apartment building, I enjoy watching her glum, unbroken attitude of attention through the heavy mahogany-framed glass doors of the lobby. I do not willingly distract her, but when she catches sight of me, I wave. She steps out with an instantaneous shift of demeanor, head high, one of the gods emerging at Valhalla. I had offered to park the car and come up for her, but she brushed the offer away, denying me a magnified look at what I speculated to be her scientific daily life—an apartment full of plants, gadgets, computer terminal and printer, walls of books.

A car has its own intimacies, however, a woman slipping into the front seat beside me, bringing a fragrance, not of asepsis, but of flowers rushing in on the cold night air, orange blossom and lily of the valley; Gershwin is on the radio. She leans across and barely presses her lips to my cheek, but it is enough to remind me that regardless of how many people are killed in plane crashes or die of heart attacks or endure underground or have a thankless child, the flesh feels better when kissed. Cousinly, pre-concert affection, to be sure, friends herding together when another is in trouble. Consolation, nonetheless.

"She's still in the CCU," I say in response to her immediate question about Mrs. Messenger, "the last electrocardiogram shows heavy damage to the heart."

"Is Bernard holding up? I mean there's so much at stake now. What will he do—"

"He mentioned admitting himself. Let's be realistic. He's surprisingly helpless."

"Bernard in a home? Why that's inconceivable—" Enid says. She reaches over and snaps off the radio.

I, too, recoil at the thought: the man's colorful genius bleached by institutionalized sameness, another shuffling blind man in rooms full of blind men and women; his books, his opera, his peculiar savvy about the world— what happens to all of *that*? And I didn't even know the guy six months ago! Now there's all this human feeling to overcome, simply to get to a concert without being obstructed on the way by an immovable ton of guilt, like a jack-knifed tractor trailer or an airport limousine stalled on the Expressway. I can hardly bear it, Enid and I using our eyes with no more appreciation than a couple of fish peering around the bottom of the ocean. We are only doing what is necessary. Freedom of the eyes is not freedom not to see. An eye must see.

"He insisted we go without him," she says.

"And he's right, of course," I say. "The free man does not dwell on death."

"Death is not the worst thing in this world, Barry," she says. I know instinctively she is alluding to her lost brother Harris, who at age nineteen, in 1969, went for a walk between halves of a civil service exam and was never seen again. Was he the victim of a druggie? a street gang? Or did he simply split? get on an express bus somewhere, or a plane? My mother held that since Harris's body was never recovered, he simply fled the pressure and is somewhere in Europe or Canada or on an ashram in the Himalayas, cooking his grains and vegetables, doing card tricks and staying as skinny and deadpan as he likes. "Sometimes I think my brother mugged me and raped me and drowned me, and then poof! left me with no one to hate or put into the ground. I hope you don't mind my talking about him. I rarely do anymore. But you're family, and you remember him. You do remember him, don't you?"

"The only six-footer in the family and about 135 pounds! When he came to visit us my mother mashed potatoes into his eggs to fatten him up."

"What I wouldn't give to know he was dead!" The word is precise and bitter.

"Are there any new theories?"

"God knows I didn't mean to talk about Harris tonight. Every couple of years I get a call about some vagrant in the police lineup whose name is Harris or Harry or Harrison and is a long drink of water. The detective assigned to the case is, frankly, shit. All the good ones have long been reassigned. This one has his own personal theory that in the sixties *no one* between the ages of eighteen and thirty was normal and no one had to face exams. There were too many outs. Either Harris couldn't concentrate or couldn't face getting stuck in the system. Whether he was buzzed out or not, I may never know, and having a superstar sister wasn't exactly what the doctor ordered. So he took a dive. My own theory is that he never intended to drop out, just needed time to think. But either he damn well liked being free of us, or met a woman (we once had a call from some Southerner named Georgina who tried to extort money from us)—anyway, *something* happened."

"Listen, it could have been his metabolism. Maybe he banged his head."

"You're a believer in natural causes? Well, I'm sorry, Barry, I believe he was a pretty galling kid. Barry, a disappearance is nothing short of astounding. It so thoroughly galls you that you never eat or sleep again in the same way. You never know the limits of what was taken from you. All you know is that your eyes never close, you're on the prowl twenty-four hours a day. Sometimes I wish I were blind—like Bernard!—so I could get a little peace. I look into every face. Is that *his* nose? Did his face get fat? Once a police artist did a computer sketch of what he would look like now. The computer drew him mean, like a larcenist. I framed it, then buried it in a drawer, but I used to take it out around the holidays and pretend he was married to that creep Georgina and had a couple of kids and we were all together on Passover the way we used to be—Harris, my father singing the seder like Caruso, my mother serving the gefilte fish, me, maybe my kids."

It's the first mention of Enid's desire for children of her own, and for a few seconds I fall under the spell of imagining her with a family: toddlers in rumpled overalls in a school for the gifted.

"What a laugh!" Enid says. "The truth is, our family is wiped out. I was too young when I married Lutz; he was my teacher and I adored him—I couldn't live a normal life with my husband. Harris haunted me to distraction. Finally, Lutz began to get even—a great loss, I suppose, he was such a promising physicist—little things he wasn't even aware of, like letting his shirts pile up at the laundry, writing bad checks, not mailing my insurance claims—not to mention all the sexual stuff!"

What didn't I imagine? Wires hooked to her breasts, pipetting tubes in her vagina?

"I thought he'd get over it, but then he began to skip his lectures at NYU. His graduate students couldn't find him. One day a Filipino came to our house with a gun looking for him, and by the time we split up, Lutz was living alone in a furnished room in Tel Aviv. Every now and then he writes to me, elaborate pleading letters. 'Come and start over with me, the one lily of my life—' He writes like Thomas Mann, in exquisite detail. You know, he describes the arguments on Dizengoff Street, word for word he quotes the politics of electricians in a cafe. Or he entices me with golden views of Caesarea at dawn, and the advances at the Technion in laser work, or sends me publications, begs me to come over. 'Let's try,' he says. But though Tel Aviv attracts me, I don't want to be expatriated with anybody, not even him, not even in Israel. It undercuts you, especially in times of trouble. Where would I go? How do Jews in Israel separate?" She swallows audibly. "Did you know that Lutz was born in Treblinka? That's like being born in a sewer. And the women of the sewer kept him alive after his mother died. He swears Israel is the best home he's found. Ha! But I still belong here in Brooklyn!" she says. "If not for Harris, maybe we'd have had a home, but Harris tore Lutz apart. How could someone *want* to disappear? In *America*? It destroyed him, he could not understand it. If not for Harris, I'd probably be a parent, have grown kids, instead of—"

"Instead of being a strong, capable, appealing professional, contributing to—"

She is dismayed. "Don't be taken in by my apparent coherence. I never lost it professionally, but my private life was going berserk. Harris and Lutz drove me bonkers."

"You're unforgiving."

"Lately, I am."

"If your brother met with foul play—"

"Then I'm a rat, okay? Then I'll pay for my sins one day."

"I hate to hear that kind of talk."

"I hate to talk that kind of talk."

By the time we arrive, she has to work at pulling herself together. She takes a comb out of her bag and begins to pull it through her hair, hunting for a mirror on the underside of the sun visor.

"How's my hair?" she asks.

Hers is the kind of short bristly hair that combing has little effect on. It surprises me that she cares.

"You won't believe this," she adds, dreamily, "but Lutz was preoccupied with my hair. I wore it long for him—kind of bushy. One of his few memories of Treblinka is that the women's skulls were shaved."

"It's better," I say.

The concert is a delight, though tears stand in Enid's eyes during the *Kinderszenen*, "Traümerei" recalling her childhood, she says, "when my life was complete." I vow privately to sit her down and talk to her about the completeness of Substance, but this is not the time for it. On a more practical level, I believe a baby would cure Enid's disappointments, an unpromising idea in the face of my history of weak sperm. But the shyness of the music throws us quietly together. Perahia is tender and poetic; the simple music without artistic self-consciousness moves the audience. The *Waldszenen* selections are romantic, fragile but distinct.

After the concert, in the congested vestibule of the Academy, I dial Bernard's phone number. The phone rings and rings. Outside the crowd has thinned. Enid asks to come back with me to get the news; but at the Messenger door our knock still brings no answer.

"We can wait upstairs," I say. "Let me talk to you about my rainbow equations."

In one sweeping glance, she sizes up my room. "You've got a good work space and I bet good natural light." Dropping her pocketbook on the kitchen table, she sits down; I pull out my notebook of recent calculations. Her glasses, my pens, a pot of tea, a pocket calculator, bent heads—we sit together and pore over each calculation. I explain that I am interested in the perception of the rainbow more than in its production, which seems to have less application to optical problems. She says the psycho-mechanics of vision are still not fully understood. What goes on between the eye and the brain, she says, giving me the eye, is like what goes on between lovers.

I hurry to produce photos I have taken of the particular indigo that interests me. The luminosity of the color attracts her, though we cannot be certain it is not the result of the glossy print. She playfully agrees to ride out to New Jersey with me—on a misty summer day—and have a look. The interaction of light energy with matter within a raindrop is intimate and fascinating, and the connection to perception of color and retention of contact lenses strikes her as a useful application. Of course, I am speculating hopelessly whether she is merely polite or genuinely impressed with my work. Nonetheless, her mathematical agility awes me, as she pencils in adjustments to account for the range of drop size from 10 to 50 microns (the usual size of occurrences in clouds), substituting a more precise method to find the intensity (I) of light for points on the curve near the cusp (C). Nothing significant, she assures me, this "phrasing" has more range and is ultimately more elegant. Speed in math was macho when I was in junior high school, and we "mathletes" were the idol of a group of literary girls who read Amy Lowell and wrote poems about death. Enid's performance has a similar sensual exuberance, holding her gold Cross pencil like a cigarette, her intelligence in hot-blooded pursuit of my ideas, the smile of pleasure over a row of babyish teeth giving off a whiff of delectation. She assures me there are tables and charts showing how changes in the rainbow's intensity and shape correspond to changes in the size of the raindrops. Very large drops—as in a rain forest in the tropics—may lack the uniformity necessary to produce a rainbow. But uniform, oversized drops produce brilliant rainbows. That's documented. She is high-spirited and high-breasted. Every nuance of explanation is full of juice.

Or are my months of abstinence telling, months of cultivating a Spinozistically monklike restraint? What I'd like most is to give Enid a baby! Think what a child of Enid's and mine would possess! Science. Philosophy. Not to mention intuition—Enid is intuitive *and* practical. For example, she reminds me that rainbow theory needs to be harnessed, the way electricity has been. "Remember that electricity sat in the air for centuries," she grins, "pre-Franklin. And now, here's the rainbow—pre-Glassman."

Throughout our discussions, of course, we are listening for the return of Bernard Messenger. Several times she has wandered to the window, still talking cusps, to check out a rasping car motor or a car door slammed in the night. Having a woman of science at hand has drained me of all other interests, but a loud noise prompts me to have a look through the deep blue windows, each pane flushed with the reflections of lamplight; I see droplets of water collecting on the glass, not a rain, a light condensation of the kind I associate with country mornings and dewy vapors in the Catskills. I linger. Patches of chalky fog float past the window. "Enid," I say, "this is the kind of night when the moon creates a bow." She is at my side, lilies and orange blossom in the air, venturing a glance through the glass. My knees die under me. "Shall we go out and have a look at the sky?" Now I am grinning.

"Sure," she says. "Why not?"

I step cautiously to the closet, giving my knees a moment to come back to life. "Here, take a scarf," I pull one out of the closet, "it's damp and chilly out there."

She swings a blue and gold plaid thing my father used to wear (I have cherished it all these years) around her throat, throws on her coat, and is ready, her greenish eyes glinting, her smile young and without lipstick, framed by my father's ancestral scarf. The fingers of one hand hold deeply to my shoulder as we make our way down the badly lit stairway, and I move carefully so as not to dislodge her; it's been a long while since a woman has clung to me.

The entrance to the park is deserted, the day's litter—joint wrappers, newspapers, beer cans—kicked or blown to the edges, except for a suspicious looking pair of men in pea coats in the midst of a vicious argument. Clutching her handbag, Enid mutters that she ought to have left it in my room. The rainbow effect around the streetlamps is not at all marked tonight. She becomes edgy, eyes darting back to the two men, a city woman out in the night and worried about her valuables. Though the men head off out of the park and up St. John's Place, her mood has shifted. "We can get killed out here," says Enid.

The moon, full and gleaming, has a corona around it, pink, distant, round, and oozing a milky light. "Come on," she says, as I stand, nose toward the heavens, scanning the skies for traces of color. "Come over and protect me," I say, attempting to lighten the moment. Is she annoyed? She takes a few running steps toward me after all, tilting her chin up in the path of moonlight. I reach out to touch her face, her cold damp cheek, pass a finger over her lashes glistening with an amber light under the moon. But the novelty of desire renders me ambitious: I gravitate closer, pressing my lips to hers, my arms melting inside her coat, and pulling her warm breathing body against my chest.

A moment. Perhaps only seconds.

"What was *that* all about, Cousin Barry?" she asks quietly, drawing herself up.

We walk back to the house side by side, not touching. I have several precise ideas what her question might imply, but the kiss is fast becoming an effigy, vulgar and insignificant.

The rotating red eye of the police car confuses our ability to judge distance, diffused as light is by heavy mist in darkness. Without a word, we both run toward it, hearing now the police reports stuttering out of the car radio into the night. The car, nearer than it appears, is angled in the middle of the road, in front of the Messenger house. A police officer is at the rear door of the car assisting Bernard, who stands in the damp street, taking his bearings, a hulking figure in the winter darkness, touching the car with outstretched fingertips. For a moment the car radio falls into silence. The officer a second time extends his hand into the car, and a short elderly man in a gray fedora hobbles out, who in turn steadies his footing, then presents Bernard his arm. "Bernard! It's Barry and Enid," I shout. The sound of my voice dumbfounding him, he thrusts his face sharply forward. The older man, wheezing audibly, turns toward us.

"We're friends of the Messengers," I call to him. "What happened?"

"Norman," Bernard's voice is loud in the empty street, "these are my friends, the man from upstairs and his cousin Enid Moscow. No need for you to stay now. Maybe the officer can drop you at your house. Anyone out this late has trouble getting a cab."

Before I reach Bernard, the police officer has taken me aside. "You live upstairs?"

I nod.

"His mother died tonight. He's kind of shaken. Can you look in on him?"

"Oh, God," I say, glimpsing Bernard's raised head commanding the night. "Sure," I say, "We'll look after him. Who's the other man?"

"A friend of the family," the cop says. "Been mumbling about promising the mother that he wouldn't leave the son alone." The cop is moved. "Nothing sadder than being blind," the cop says. He is very moved. "Although I tell you, the blind guy is okay. Shaken, but both feet on the ground. You want my opinion, the old guy is in the way. He ought to be in his bed."

So this bewildered man is Stormin' Norman! About the right size, but his face has a collapsed look about it. Enid meanwhile has drifted to Bernard's side, and he is leaning against her, the streetlamps throwing a dark shadow across her figure. She is murmuring to him, but the static from the car radio has resumed, and I cannot hear her words.

The older man is talking through his coat collar, raised against the night air. "I got nothing to do. I can spend the night with Bernard," he says. "I was a close friend of Dora's. I made her a promise . . ." He is gasping. "It's a shock, of course," gasp, "but Bernard is a remarkable fellow."

"Look," I say, "I give you my assurance that I won't be far away. You ought to go home. You don't sound very good."

"Well, here's the thing. I sleep in a semi-sitting position, and I have medication to take that I don't carry with me. You're sure? I suppose I could get my pills and come back—"

"You have my promise."

Norman shakes my hand. Then he embraces Bernard for a long moment.

"So that's it," Bernard mumbles, a sob escaping his composure. "Thanks, Norman." His voice is hoarse.

"I'll call you in the morning—"

"She wouldn't want anything ornate," Bernard has a hand on the man's shoulder.

"But she's a big woman. She needs a handsome coffin."

The police officer throws an arm around Bernard. "I'm the cop who drove you. We all go through it, Mac. Goodberry's the name, 14th precinct, if you ever need anything." Then he slides in behind the wheel of his car, Norman's hatted figure low in the seat alongside, waves his hand once, and drives away.

Consideration for Bernard came first, of course. A man grieving for his mother renders himself tender and childlike. The queerness of the love between a boy and a woman shows up in all walks of life, but strikes the onlooker as defective—tragic—when the son is blind. What is the degree of dependence? How much guilt is there (on both sides)? How much pride (in playing out the cards that have been handed to you)? What the degree of assistance (overprotection, obsession)? What had lain in wait for these two, yoked together by circumstances that made of them creatures in an intense and suffocating household? How were they, finally, to be parted?

I am putting my day in order and preparing for bed; but I tiptoe about upstairs in my stocking feet, straining to identify the noises coming from below. Consideration for the bereaved, I explain to myself, *that* comes first. Listen, the arrangement appeared to be easy and natural, yet I ought not to have been so surprised. I was thrown, of course. Who wouldn't have been? Enid and Bernard and I, crowded together because death was no longer remote but an occupant, with us, in that room, Enid and I staring without comment at Mrs. Messenger's flowered apron and large white bra flung across the couch, her house shoes under the TV set, one turned on its side, a widely stretched instep gaping, its heel bent back, a woman heavy in her stride (would Enid's shoes look like that one day?), the other upright, though listing to the left on its worn heel. On the end table stood bottles of nail polish in several shades of red and a wad of cotton. Bernard must long since have lost track of what was where in the room, his phenomenal memory tested beyond limits during this interval of hospitals and absence.

Still disheveled, still in his pajama top, his shoelaces muddied from trailing on the ground, he made every effort to be gracious to us—fixed forever in his life as those who stood by when Mother died?—neither Enid nor I quite clear about the other's friendship, he alone knowing the extent of it, which put us in a decidedly inferior position. Exhausted, collapsed in his green satin easy chair with the shredding arms, a Braille book still open on the footstool before the chair, he suddenly asked, "Is the lamp on? We don't have to sit here in the dark."

But the lamp *was* on, apparently linked to a timer. "Yes," I told him. "The timer is working."

"What time is it?" he asked, then, touching his wristwatch before either of us could answer, said, "The lamp goes off in half an hour."

Enid asked very softly whether he would like a cup of coffee, tea, perhaps a bowl of soup. Tea, he said weakly. Tea would be nice. She went off, apparently knowing where, to fix the tea. Bernard asked me to locate a book of phone numbers near the telephone. "My mother has a sister in Toronto, and a married niece in Syracuse. I think we ought to call them now."

Although it was very late, he insisted on making the calls. I dialed the numbers; and he related the awful event to his relatives, each one apparently asking what would become of him. "That's still far ahead of me," he said to each. "Right now we have a funeral to arrange."

I offered to assist him, but he assured me that Norman, who was devoted to his mother (he never suggested in what way), expected to visit the chapel, choose the coffin, and so on. "But Norman is not a religious man. We'll need a rabbi. My mother wanted a Jewish ceremony, like my father's."

I promised to call Mordecai Mayberg in the morning. Reserve the chapel for day after tomorrow, Bernard said. By then the relatives could come.

Enid, adroitly and in subdued tones, guided Bernard into his bedroom. After a few moments she emerged, and, feeling the walls familiarly, he made his own way into the bathroom, speedily locking the door. Wondering what had passed between them in the other room, I had little to say to her as we waited politely. A good deal of complexity seemed intelligible just behind her eyes, though I couldn't be sure what it meant. Soon the toilet flushed, and Bernard emerged. I remember that I glanced to see whether his fly was zipped. Not only were his pants in order, but he had combed his hair and washed his face. He thanked us both, assuring us he would be all right. He had spent nights alone now and then and might as well get used to it. "I'll be right upstairs," I said, rising, but Enid had begun to clear the couch.

"I'm staying," she announced, removing the mother's apron, folding it and the bra and my father's scarf, oddly in place where she had dropped it on the couch among Mrs. Messenger's things, and piling the articles neatly on a chair. "Could you bring down a pillow and a blanket?" she asked, but Bernard disappeared into his mother's bedroom and emerged holding out a pillow, sheets, and a blanket, just as the lamp blinked silently off. Darkness descended on Enid and me like a membrane, of which he was unaware. "I'll take them," she was in the midst of saying.

"These are spares," he said, moving deftly through the darkness with the bedding, toward her voice, toward the couch where she was waiting. "Enid, this is wonderful of you."

And so in one night I have kissed her longingly and imagined her bedded down in a darkness confidently occupied by another man. However extreme the circumstances, they are both *there* at this moment, below me. I imagine her physicist's thighs spread unprofessionally on the couch, her abdomen breathing softly, much as I had witnessed the mother, fleshy, carelessly exposing herself, greedy in the way one eats when one is alone, asking if it were Norman. (Norman, with his missing medication and semi-sitting position!)

How weak do I feel, how misused? How destabilized? Let me attempt an answer.

(1) Reason is the greatest might among men. But it is very rare. I have just been in an accident, and my reason, like a license to drive, has been taken from me, since I have used it recklessly.

(2) A man's worst enemy is the man he most fears. I admire Bernard, but I fear him.

(3) Feliz has made me a laughingstock, helpless against his intuitions about my futile business sense. Would Feliz quit calling me a turkey if I rehired him? Forgetting about Enid and Bernard, I spend half an hour planning to see my lawyer about drawing up a partnership with Feliz. (Big deal! But it is the only way. After all, I might become ill, disabled, and what of the shop then?)

(4) Moreover, the results of my X ray are in nobody's brain. I cannot believe that my X ray, the most important thing in my life, lies at this very moment *un*disclosed in a drawer, or slumped *un*read in a folder on a shelf. In fact, I am enduring a life of other people's *un*s: *un*read X rays, *un*repressed lust, *un*discovered causes, *un*solicited partnership, *un*requited kissing, *un*exceptional, *un*eventful, *un*faithful, and—worst of all the *un*s—Michael, and the despair of having an *un*filial son.

Nathan wants a ride to Dora Messenger's funeral, but I refuse.

"Bernard is a great guy!" Nathan is very earnest, his affection for Bernard plain. "I want to tell him so while he's feeling lousy."

"You didn't even know her."

"You think I go to funerals only of people I know?"

"The weather says snow, Uncle Nathan. Stay in."

"Anya can get a cab. Half her relatives drive taxis."

"Absolutely not!"

But Nathan is already there when I arrive. Anya, I am surprised to see, is petite. She looks nothing like Eleanor Roosevelt or Gorbachev (was it Khrushchev?) but more like Sonja Henie in those ancient ice-skating movies. Hearing Anya's accent while looking at her tiny figure and neat waist renders her cultivated and European instead of Russian and comic. That womanizer Nathan! See how he lords it over the poor maligned woman, how seriously she takes everything he says, how attentive she is, her small mouth stricken into an O by his every request. I sit near them, while Enid, in a billowing down coat, occupies the second row, behind the two mourners, Bernard and the sister from Toronto. Norman, I notice, slides in next to Enid, pushing her coat aside. Eighteen or twenty people are in the chapel, no more. Bernard has called each one personally.

In the last month, too many funerals. Dying left and right. I don't quite know what to do. No word yet from Scarf, although I left a message with his answering service. I still cough and have a supply of honey drops with me for the service. As the mourners file in, a surge of feeling rises in me like electricity in a refrigerator.

Mayberg was reluctant to do this funeral. In contrast to Uncle Nathan's goodwill toward the unknowable dead, he conducts funerals only of people he has known personally, or whose close relatives he has known. It is his ethic. But he will do it for me, he said on the phone, though if it snows, a friend of his in Bensonhurst could officiate—and for a lot less. I told him we want *him*. "The son is an educated man," I said. (Flattery.) "And he's blind." (Compassion.)

"Blind?" Rabbi Mayberg said, predictably.

"The woman has one sister. That's all."

"Blind," Mayberg repeated. "A pity."

The funeral is unexceptional. Mayberg calls her *Dolores* Messenger and pronounces Ber*nard*'s name *Bern*ard. He calls her a woman of valor and dwells at some length—with fervor I think—on the mother's and father's creative devotion to the blind son. Bernard, who is dry-eyed throughout, has given him his material, and Mayberg delivers it straight. Nor does the aunt shed a tear. She is a strong, big-boned woman, dressed like an executive, in a suit and tie. Each pairs off with a niece and a nephew behind the coffin as it leaves the chapel.

Wellwood Cemetery at Exit 54 on the Long Island Expressway is far out in potato land. Enid, Norman, and the rabbi, who leaves his car in Brooklyn, travel the distance with me. Anya has taken Nathan home in her nephew's taxi, but not until she has pressed my hand in hers and told me what a giant I am in Nathan's life. She is a butterfly, with grave, experienced eyes; I have trouble letting her go. (Glassman, what do you want to get mixed up with a serious Russian for?)

The burial is quick. After the cemetery, Mayberg insists we stop into the coffee shop near where I live before he takes off for Bayside. I've lost track of Enid and Norman, who doubtless are riding home in the limousine with Bernard and his aunt.

"Thanks, rabbi, for helping."

He waves his hand as if to say it's nothing, don't mention it, but his shoulders are stooped in the old rabbinical posture of insecurity.

"How'd I do?" he asks.

"The truth?"

"Nothing but—"

"You were great."

He sighs, satisfied. "The last time I did a funeral like this, I called the deceased by the wrong name."

I bend my head into my coffee cup.

"No!" he says.

I nod.

"It's not Messenger?" he asks. "What is it, Monitor, Messerschmitt? What?"

"*Dora*," I say. "You called her *Dolores*."

"Oh, marginal," he says. "A small thing."

"Is that what you mean by *marginal*? Unimportant? Trivial?"

"What's the difference. It's a word! Words are less important than feelings."

"And reason is more important than both."

"The board of the congregation wants you to stop writing letters to them. They'd rather have your dues."

"Those letters were for *you*!"

"A rabbi gets a lot of mail. Anything for me should say *personal*. They didn't say *personal*. Barry, how many congregants do you think I have who write to me about the irreducibles of life? But the board would rather have your dues."

"Is that why you asked me out for coffee?" The *parnassim* are after me. "Listen, Mordecai. I've been through a lot. You heard about the plane crash. I lost forty-one colleagues."

He sucks in his breath. "A pity," he says. "And no cause."

"There *must* be a cause," I say.

"But unless someone finds it, there *is* no cause." He exaggerates his impatience with me.

"No, rabbi. Every moment we have to believe and remember that there's a cause we don't yet know. That is the secret of the universe, and you have to admit, it's very different from glibly thinking there's no cause. There's a *cause*!"

"Don't be belligerent."

"Who's belligerent? All I am is irritated as hell that Dolores Gutman and her Bayside *parnassim* sent you here to talk to me. You said *Dolores* instead of *Dora*."

"It's possible. The woman bothers me a great deal." (His wife's name, I realize, is Dvora, but he is my rabbi, after all, and I let that pass.)

"What if I don't pay?"

"Then you're out."

"And if I pay?"

"What are you getting at?"

Every word drags me closer. "Am I out anyway? Am I? In or out? Tell me, in or out?"

He is sipping a can of coke, a safe drink for a rabbi in an unkosher coffee shop. But the whole table smells of my steaming black coffee. "Is it just my money you're after?"

"Michael attends confirmation class. Teachers are expensive these days. This one is a drama student at Yale."

"What does a drama student know about religion?"

"How to bring it to life! He was a yeshiva boy in Jerusalem for six years. A Lubavitcher. He's married and has three babies. Now he wants to be an actor. He's delicious. The kids love him. I love him," Mayberg says. "Dvora and I only wish he were single and could marry our ballerina." His eyes sparkle. Mayberg's ardor rises like a bridegroom's when he talks about his daughter.

"So Michael is taking extreme religious unction from a drama student! What about theology?"

"Stop with the sacraments, Barry. You need emotion in religion. I'm going to tell you something. I was sympathetic when Steinman wanted to drop the sermons. You need to be astonished by feeling, by doing, not by sermons. When Michael acts out the story of the Warsaw Ghetto uprising, he has real tears in his eyes. He's living his own history! *That*'ll keep him Jewish. And singing! Reaffirming the faith of the martyrs on their way to the gas chambers: 'Ani Maamin.' And even a few Yiddish ones: 'Aufn Pripitchik' and 'Arum dem Feier.' You need to touch the heart, Barry, in addition to the head." He is thumping his skull so hard that his black silk yarmulke slips to his neck. He catches it and drops it back on his head. "Reason is limited. Ask any physicist about quantum theory. If you can't see that, you can't see reality. Reality goes beyond reason. The prophets were full of ecstasy." He fairly sings the word. "It was the heart that was the moral conscience of the Jews, not the brain, Barry, ecstasy! But how can I hold up my head as a rabbi if I don't give sermons?"

"I'll pay you what I owe you. I don't like to have doubts." Mayberg looks up sharply— "I mean debts." I believe I am too tired to continue. The heart has its reasons, Bernard Messenger had said. A universe of argument in a few grains of Pascal! "But rabbi" (I was incapable of quitting), "*ignorance* is the cause of injustice. Not sin. Not immorality. Plain *ignorance*. In the days of the prophets a person in debt was fuckin' sold for a pair of shoes, rabbi. It was only when men and women understood that they dwelled in the divine presence that the equation—person equals thing—didn't work."

"Okay, okay. Calm down. But how did they find that out? Barry, they found out because God revealed Himself to the Jews through what He did. 'And you shall say to your son, We were Pharaoh's slaves in Egypt; and the Lord brought us out of Egypt with a mighty hand.' That was the act by which God made Himself known to the Jews. That's why the Exodus is so important. Revelation came not through mind, not through a computer like the mind, but through deed and through ecstasy."

I take out my checkbook and start writing. "How much do I owe?"

"Oy, my dear Barry. In Hebraic thought, Nature is never divine. That is idolatry. That is pagan. The Hebrews destroyed the bond between God and Nature. There is only God—and we utter our reverence three times a day in prayers—God is the sovereign, God is transcendent, the King of the Universe. He does not pervade the universe" (a smell of coffee pervades the universe: Mayberg breathes a deep appreciative draft through his nostrils) "—nothing could be further from Judaism! God is a living, personal Will, a moral force. He is discontinuous with His universe, Barry." And he reaches across to the check I am writing and tears it in half. He may have gone on speaking, but I have stopped listening. I raise my eyebrows. "How should I know how much," he says. "I'm not the bookkeeper. Call the office. The bills are probably going to Marilyn."

I conclude with great control: "Reason is a part of divine necessity, rabbi, and we learn about God because we must. Necessity is the key! Events seem irrational only to our finite understanding. I pay what I owe because I choose, but I think what I think because I must."

A gang of high-schoolers has swooped in for afternoon snacks, circling every table with loud name-calling and settling into bored games of sleeve-pulling. Rae behind the counter takes our money mechanically, her attention vigilantly on the kids.

"If you could stand coming to services," Mayberg says, his hand squeezing my arm tightly, a little too tightly, slowing me down as I hurry along, "we'll talk." At this moment talk to him means holding a discussion in the social room of the Temple, where tea and nuts and raisins are set out, and Sabbath songs are declaimed, and the rabbi's face is robust, and what chance do I have of making myself rational, clear, unmistakably logical? The mouths of the congregation are open in song, or gossip, or news of the week's businessmen in Bayside, and my mouth would open too, lips dry as dirt, comforted not at all by that kind of peaceful consciousness of one's neighbors who meet in fellowship under the Chamber of Commerce or a watchful God. The rabbi enjoys me, owing, I believe, to the cruelty of Spinoza's position, the unrelenting distribution of God's intelligence that I know gives Mayberg his confidence, his place beneath azure skies that somewhere closet the benevolent, personal, and feisty God he is championing.

Mayberg's eyeglasses are still slipping down his nose. As I reach up, he is startled. I catch them—grab them off his face—but with a mighty hand, his blow landing squarely on my jaw, he has already felled me to the sidewalk, and there I am, spread-eagled, clutching his glasses instinctively to my chest. In my dizziness, I drop them to the ground.

"Mayberg, what the hell are you doing?" I say, rubbing my chin with both hands.

CHAPTER 13

He is peering down at me, recklessly, his fists still in the air.

"I only wanted to adjust the nose pads—"

"You're so belligerent. For the moment—"

"Rabbi! Who could believe you've got such an arm?"

"I'm sorry, Barry. I do everything with a full heart. I'm sorry. Here—" He pulls me to my feet, bending over to retrieve his glasses.

"You really don't trust me, do you, rabbi? Hnh, do you?" Snatching the glasses from him—the lenses are plastic and unbroken—I bend the earpieces and the nose pads between index finger and thumb. Then I shove them back on his face. He is blinking furiously.

"Let me drive you home," he says.

"Stay away from me!" I say, pulling myself out of his reach. "You come any closer, you're finished! You really think I'm a menace—"

"Nonsense. I've dealt with plenty of doubters in my day. But you're so fast, like a tiger. Come for a meal. Please. I'll get Dvora to invite Michael." He inches toward me. "Let me drive you home. How do you feel?"

I should have asked him how *should* a man feel who has just been knocked to the ground by his shithead of a rabbi while he is waiting for a report on his X rays, after his wife and child have left him, but the truth is I had forgotten about everything *but* truth until I got home and fell into bed.

I am given penicillin and put to bed for a month. Linda Kemp relieves me at the store, even comes one Sunday afternoon with a bunch of red tulips to visit me, full of solicitude, and on Saturdays I ask the agency to send an additional relief person to handle the rush. Feliz is wildly apologetic for causing me grief in recent weeks: a partnership in a busy shop, an impending marriage, an heir—Feliz is a happy man! I lie in bed under a mountain of blankets, an ice pack on my jaw, still seeing the sudden lurch of the rabbi brandishing his fists. I am seeing his fists, but am I seeing enough? As I relive the moment of hitting the sidewalk, in an instant of recognition, I see his terror slip away into bliss, the bliss of action. Mayberg has done me in, and he is glad! I press the pack to my throbbing jaw. As he struck his blow, he was unique, Mordecai Mayberg, preserver of the faith, acting under a terrific compulsion to preserve himself. Up flew his arms; out shot his fists; if it meant reducing Glassman to a speck, then speck I became.

It was only afterward, after he realized his craziness, his error, that fear stole back into his eyes. What had he done?

Ice numbs the gums, but ice brings no relief to this inner hurt by Mayberg of the murderous fists.

Dr. Scarf saw the pneumonia on my X rays. He advises a few weeks in Florida to recuperate after my lungs have cleared. (I told him I have been under a strain, though I went into no details about the breakup of my marriage or the assault by Mayberg.) Then I'm to repeat the X ray and do "whatever else is necessary." When I question him about "whatever else is necessary," he eventually gets to the point: difficult to read; other tests. Frankly, though concerned, I am neither surprised nor panicked. I know Dr. Scarf as a methodical physician who conveys to the patient what he learns, then wraps himself in data before he recommends. "You've been waltzing around with this pneumonia for a few months at least. It's shadowy. We may be looking at scar tissue," he says. When he takes down my Brooklyn address, he peers at me over rimless half-glasses: "Is that a permanent change?" ready to strike out my Bayside address with his pen.

"No," I say. Then, "Yes, yes."

I can now afford a better place to live, though making money on one's dead buddies is like picking your teeth after eating your pet dog. I discover in some confusion that the money is real, buys poached salmon with dill mayonnaise in the better take-out establishments, English wing-tip shoes, a good book whenever I want one, and a bottle of Perrier water handy if my digestion requires it. The apartment is noticeably warmer (since Dora Messenger's death, Bernard has banged the windows shut and moved the thermostat up), and as I lie under the mass of bed-coverings, my body no longer shivers, the fire in my leaden jaw subsides into cool slate, my toes are cramped but warm—still, the hurt continues. My own rabbi! Apostle of monotheistic rationalism. I reject any idea of a vacation at this time: Florida's grapefruit crops have frozen in March, and heavy rains have caused coastal flooding as far as Boca Raton. As for the Caribbean, I wouldn't know where to begin. I do not readily see myself in Club Med shorts under a palm tree sipping a piña colada, though Marilyn, passionate for a cruise, used to assure me that nothing would be easier. "All professional people take winter cruises." She pronounced it like a Socratic syllogism:

> All professional people take winter cruises.
> Glassman is a professional person.
> Therefore . . .

We never went. Score another grievance against the philosophic Glassman!

I am determined not to tell Michael of my illness; but Feliz spills it to him when the boy calls for my social security number one day. The man doesn't announce it outright; shrewd Michael must put two and two together. However, it is Marilyn who calls.

"Is it just pneumonia?" she asks.

"What do you mean *just*?" I say, fingering my lower front teeth with new confidence since they have begun to feel cold and tight. Apparently the rabbi has not leaked a word to anyone about our brawl in front of the coffee shop. "Both lungs. Plus a touch of pleurisy."

"Well, borrow our electric heater." (*Borrow*, she says!) "Frannie tells me your place is an icebox."

"It's warmer here now."

"You're still living like a monk, only now you're in an ice-cold cell. I'll call an agency and have a woman come in to cook for you, Barry."

The idea makes me laugh out loud. A messiah for every monk. An agency for every emergency. "Marilyn, you are an upwardly mobile Bronx wonder."

"Don't be mean, Barry. A person needs help, he shouldn't—"

"A person has a kid, the kid's mother could get him to *call* once in a while." I instantly regret what I've said, my greatest fear being a cynical, ungovernable self-pity.

"I'll tell him."

"No! Don't!" I say. "He's old enough to think of it himself. So what *is* it, Marilyn?"

"You saw Scarf?"

"Why?"

"Because Michael had an allergy shot and the nurse asked if we'd moved to Brooklyn."

"What'd he say?"

"You know Michael. He said he could be reached at either number." She laughs. "I'll send over some cooked food for you in a taxi, if you give me directions. The shop is pretty busy, but on the weekend—"

"Don't bother. I have friends. I'm on a diet," I say again, visualizing a yellow cab rolling up, loaded with Marilyn's specialties, sweet and sour cabbage, veal and tuna roast, curried zucchini soup, apricot cream cheese cake. My mouth is watering, my hands reach out, but the loaded taxi pulls away.

"Barry, I'd rather keep our relationship amicable. *I'm* willing—"

"Thanks for calling, Marilyn," I say, irreversibly starved, as I hang up.

But two days later a taxi arrives, the driver lugging plastic containers of soup, veal and tuna roast, halibut salad, anchovies and pimentos up to my door. I invite the driver to join me, but he demurs. His chin is dark with a kind of Arabic five o'clock shadow, and his English is shaky. I insist he take a sandwich, fix him veal on a roll. He stuffs it in his pocket and flies down the stairs. Despite feelings of mortification, I glut myself on the delicacies. Though my jaw still hurts, I eat it all, happy to be alone, dripping food stains on my bed amid a shuddering fear of bribery. The essential Barry Glassman endures. (Doesn't Marilyn *know* that?) Anything primitive in me is a manifestation of *my* reality. (Doesn't she know that aborigines can't be bribed?)

From Mayberg not another word! Too embarrassed to talk about it. Sworn Dvora to secrecy. One phone call to me the bloody night of the incident breathlessly advising me to see a doctor, he'll pay for any medical bills, and Dvora shouting in the background, "And you'll pay dental bills, too!"

"And dental bills!" the rabbi adds.

I am too obsessed with his powerful right arm to think it through. In a letter to "the very learned and prudent" Mr. William van Blyenburgh, Spinoza once wrote that some of the traits we admire in animals we detest in men. A dove's jealousy is sweet; but not a husband's. A bee's bellicosity is instinct at its sharpest; but not a rabbi's or a congregant's. What Mayberg slugged was the bee in me, the tumultuous whirring necessity to land; and sting. Or does my belligerence exist only as a phenomenon of *his* understanding and not in me at all? Who knows? He hung a right to the jaw worthy of Muhammad Ali (he should excuse the likeness of a rabbi to a Muslim).

Talk about a sting!

Thus the weeks pass. My friends do "look" in on me, though one of them is blind. He makes his way upstairs to sit at my bed and talk philosophy. With his mother's death, he is in search of a serene understanding, but he often arrives in a rage, for example over Leibniz's insulting imagination through which a table becomes a community of souls. Monads! He prefers nononsense, contemporary existentialist thought, plus a dash of Pascal, whose epigrammatic wit and acuity suit his style—"eloquence allows others to listen without pain"—though he admits that seeing a table as a collection of whirling neutrons is not much of an improvement over Leibniz. I can tell he has been involved with Enid—the exactness of his references, the clear hold he has on the principles of physics.

Enid has also been my visitor, arriving with Bernard, but also without; while in Bernard's presence she is as impersonal as an anesthesiologist, without Bernard, on a Friday night after work, say, arriving from Wok #1 with a quart of beef in black bean sauce and Captain Ho's chicken in a brown shopping bag already translucent with grease, she is familiar and helpful—wifely, in fact. Wifely.

I am much improved, so much so that we pull out the calculations and consider a few adjustments in the differentials between the angles of refraction. My woman of science begins the evening as sleek as her brain. In tight black pants and pearls, her face aglow from her walk through the neighborhood with dinner in hand, she nonetheless wears the same rumpled tweed jacket as a matter of course. It goes on and off with her coat, a single skin, except that when after an hour or so the night grows chillier, she pulls it apart from the coat, its sleeves emerging from the other set of sleeves, like an insect metamorphosing, and puts it on. By that time, she has slipped out her contact lenses and put on glasses. She looks scholarly. Without her lenses, her eyes go from green to gray. We never discuss *why* she comes alone some nights, and with Bernard on others. There are certain truths of perception; I have as self-evident that our happiness has increased during the course of my illness. She is caring for me; and she is good at it.

Neither of us has ever mentioned the kiss in the park the night of Mrs. Messenger's death, and when Enid lies across my bed, reading, lolling, running an emery board across her fingernails, looking at me earnestly, touching my forehead with her fingertips, the memory of that insignificant kiss comes up like the tiny shadow of an airplane on the landscape, far below the much larger plane in which you ride; for after several weeks it is Enid, a larger-than-life bouquet of orange blossom, who permits the blanket to slide down to my hip, stretching herself alongside of me, large as a lily is to a bee, her head propped on her hand; it is Enid who slips the palm of her warm hand under my neck to adjust the pillow. Far from a bouquet for the dead, her fragrance teases my penis under its tent, and as I buzz round her with my arm, she whispers, "I feel so at home here, in this house, upstairs and down. I've led such a solitary life since Lutz left—I can't begin to tell you how changed I am." With a forefinger grazing the tip of my nose, she says, "Soon you will be well, Cousin Barry."

"Most of me is *very* well," I reply. But I do not insist. Much as she stirs me, I *am* weakened: a mercurial desire to be taken care of, sometimes indistinguishable from a hazy well-being, is a sign of weakness. *Cousin* Barry. *Cousin* Enid. Marilyn was always most affectionate when she had the flu.

The social worker assigned to Bernard since Dora Messenger's death has not been satisfied with the trial period at home, despite household assistance supplied several times a week by the city's Department of Social Services. Apparently for all his bravura performance as companion and thinker, Bernard has trouble keeping himself tidy, so that he can locate his possessions. Whatever skill he had in remembering where he put things had come through his mother's relentless housekeeping. On his own, the disorder is colossal. He has to retrain himself completely: line up his shoes in pairs next to his bed at night, stand a used cup in the sink, square the coffee canister on the same edge of counter near the stove. In the habit of taking things with him, he uproots items freely, but now there is no one to re-root them (his mother's garden gone to weed), no one hovering over his movements, clinging to every key or sock or piece of underwear to set it where it can be found. A trainer comes from the Lighthouse to make physical changes in the apartment—textured labels, cords that can be tied and untied, a rope from door to porch, habitual placement of foods in the refrigerator, shelf by shelf; and on the plate, meat at 12:00, salad at 3:00, potatoes at 6:00.

When it is time for Enid to go, she calls a cab. I tell her I miss her already. You are my mommy and my daddy, my doctor and my nurse, I say with a grin.

One night when she left with Bernard, he leaving the door carelessly ajar behind him, I heard them laughing in the hall, he telling her how happy she made him. "You are my two brown eyes," I heard him say. "How can I ever get that across to you?" There had been a long pause, an elongated hum of voices, before I heard Enid's taxi door shut, the cab groaning away toward Flatbush Avenue.

Tonight, after Enid leaves, I am feeling exhilarated. Though still black and blue, the jaw itself is back to normal, the skin supple, the teeth tight without tension, the swelling and puffiness of the gums receded. I haven't coughed all day, and I want to exclaim to the universe that all things are interconnected. In fact, I call out God's name as I pull on jacket, muffler, and gloves against the night air. Now I must get a newspaper and study the freedom of a Brooklyn day, arson in Park Slope, abduction in Bed Stuy, a waitress bludgeoned to death under the Brooklyn Bridge, not to mention poison—in the chicken livers of the Board of Education as they meet on Livingston Street for lunch, hospitalizing the chancellor. I've heard it all on the radio; but I'm a reader, and I haven't seen a newspaper in a week. It is three blocks to the newspaper stand.

I am pretty steady on my feet. So all *right*, I remind myself, easy does it, Glassman. You're still a candidate for stroke or heart attack—or *worse*. Out on the porch a path of lamplight glistens from Bernard Messenger's living room, pearly in the evening air, set no doubt to the timer that goes on and off unseen and unheard, with nothing but a mechanical advantage in the blind man's life. I picture him sitting with his Braille book on his knees, his tapered fingers passing expertly over the dotted symbols in his new independence, which means the lamp is lit for *him*, not for any other living being. And late into the night, long after the light has slipped away, he reads, like a deer leaping silently away from the lit highway into the black cathedral of woods, and leaping still.

So I imagine Bernard Messenger. After I buy my paper at the newsstand, an all-nighter that caters to residents of the new apartment houses, I go into the coffee shop next door, still buoyed by having risen out of my sick bed to take up with the world. It is where Mayberg and I had our last discussion, the scene of his hauling off and punching me in the jaw. For a while, I was a regular there. I'd think of it as the Spinoza Cafe; but, an ordinary rundown Brooklyn coffee shop, it goes by the name of the Prospect Coffee Shop. In a rational world, the idea of a Spinoza Cafe is one of the great absurdities. Here the interconnection of all things breaks down and stands apart from the vision of their unity in God. Yes, the smell of coffee is everywhere in this place, but what did Mayberg mean? God is no coffee smell. He is discontinuous with the world He has created. He saves. Mayberg's God is as tempting as a good cup of coffee. I sit. I rest. I drink a cup of strong coffee.

Charlie is asking me if I want another cup. "No," I say, and as I pay, Rae is advising me to take it easy, I don't look well. "We haven't seen you here lately."

"Pneumonia," I say, heading toward the door.

"Two years April, Charlie and I had to close up for a few days. Like sick parakeets, the two of us, we just laid there. A pneumonia like the doctors had never seen before. Aren't you married?"

"Separated," I say, hearing that word for the first time on my lips.

"Well, let's take a look at you every now and then. Don't be a stranger."

The word "separated" acquires absurd resonances as I make my careful way back to the house. *Separated*, a menacing word, designating a forlorn kind of chaos I now knew as mine. Not single, not divorced, but separated—from wife and son and also from the larger society that moves through space and time in the orderly scheme known as couples. What had been joined, temporarily put asunder. Suggesting of course wife and son as sundered as I.

While still in my sick bed this week, I called Michael one evening. I could tell he wasn't alone when I called. His answers to my questions took on an abortive quality, not that he's been much of a talker lately, but these were monosyllabic responses to questions about basketball, TV, Mr. McQuade's rigorous chemistry class, no answer at all when I asked if he was shaving once a week, would he like one of those Braun electric razors for his next birthday; no answer, so it must have been Deirdre standing by, and where is Marilyn, or Ed Hoddeson, for godsakes, and you could hear how sorry he was that he had picked up the phone. Who were you expecting? I finally ask, and he says wouldn't I like to know, and I say I've been sick, I have to go for more tests, though I had no intention of telling him, but he has it coming, and he says, it's no wonder, as if I had told him I needed to stop for a tank of gas, and then he says he's been reading Leviticus, chapter 19, about shaving:

" 'You shall not round off the side-growth of your head or destroy the side-growth of your beard. You shall not make gashes in your flesh for the dead, or incise any marks on yourselves [that means no tattoos, he says]—I am the Lord.' Take a look at it Dad or don't you have a Bible in that creepy room?"

I have a Bible, I say, in that creepy room, and after I hang up, I lie in bed reading Leviticus 19, including "You shall not insult the deaf, or place a stumbling block before the blind." Michael and Deirdre reading Leviticus, a creepy pastime when most American teenagers prefer to "pick the vineyard bare," and I fall asleep echoing the rabbi's reminder that I the Lord am your God who brought you out from the land of Egypt. Separated—but not from the rumblings of religious memory.

With the paper tucked under my arm, I determine to leave off thinking these thoughts. Though I was heady with the systematic success of my outing, the connection of these two coffee shop people seems so earnest, so necessary, that I ask myself why there are systems of thought when two human beings can blunder into perfection without one.

A light is still on in Bernard's living room. Odd, I think, knowing it is well past midnight; the porch light is out, and the yellow glow from the far window spreads unfamiliarly to the further end of the porch, illuminating the black, glossy leaves of shrubs blowing like faces in the night wind at the side of the house. As I open the door I hear voices, Bernard's and a woman's. Before I realize what I am doing, I knock, thinking to join Bernard and Enid before Enid's departure. She must have encountered him in the hall on her way out.

I knock loudly. Sudden silence. A long wait. The door opens. It is Enid, barefoot but fully dressed, black pants, sweater, rumpled tweed jacket. The pearls are missing. The pearls have been removed.

"Barry, what are *you* doing out at this hour? You're supposed to be sick—"

"I was feeling so *good* after you left. . ."

Bernard is on the couch, in trousers and a T-shirt, feet in socks, and his pleasure exposed by the absurd smile on his lips, the fingers of one hand smoothing his stomach, flattening the fly of his pants.

"Ber*nard*!" I say louder. "It's Barry."

"Jesus, Barry. Isn't it late for a visit, or am I wrong? Is everything all right? Are you feeling worse?" He stands up and manages to look composed.

"Well, I'm glad you're so energetic," Enid says to me, her breasts heaving.

"I didn't mean to intrude."

"No need for apologies. From anyone," Bernard says.

Enid has slid back to the couch, touching Bernard's thumb as she arrives, knowing the coded gestures of greeting and response. Bernard, with a hand more deliberate than accidental, reaches toward her, brushing her lightly on the hip as if to tell whether the hip is bare or clothed.

"I'll just go on back upstairs. Please. It was stupid of me—"

Enid laces her arm through Bernard's. "Not at all. Don't stand there. Sit down. I was just telling Bernard how brilliant your work is. It's not every day I'm invited to coauthor a promising article in optics."

"Enid's admiration for you is unbounded," Bernard says, annoying the hell out of me, in the superior way he has of getting off on his own interpretations of things.

"Enid has told me that herself," I say, "or is about to."

"Please," Bernard says. "Are you sitting down? Please sit down."

I lower myself into Bernard's worn green chair.

"He is sitting," Enid says quietly.

I've interrupted something, I say to myself, blaming myself. Blame looks backward at what has already happened, but, Spinoza says, if the action could not have been avoided, then blame must be considered irrational. The world goes round and round and never stops.

"But what are you so *surprised* about?" Enid asks, her innocence giving way to impatience. "You didn't barge in, Barry. You were perfectly civilized. You knocked."

"Of course," Bernard begins, "if I could see your expression. After all—"

"After all, *I* can see *yours*. Is that what you mean, Bernard?"

He throws his head back and laughs. "You got it! That's what I always mean."

"I confess I had a standard of human nature, and I measured your behaviors by it. I saw Bernard's as highly moral."

"I'm surprised at you, making the mistake ordinary people make," Bernard says. "You're a philosopher, and you still expect a blind man to be more moral than anybody else? Anti-Semites feel the same way about Jews. A Jew is supposed to remain in the ghetto. And you'd put a blind man into a ghetto and be outraged if he goes after the normal desires of life—companionship, trust, laughter— You take my point, Barry?"

Brilliant Cousin Enid clutches her arms to her waist. Her bristly hair, the hair Lutz Moscow made into a fetish, is flattened on one side, and she gives a nervous shake to her head. I am waiting to see if she can carry this one off.

Bernard is carefully stepping back from her side, feeling for the couch behind; sits down; takes his head into his hands. She begins to stroke his unkempt black hair, absently, as one would a child's.

"I'm not at all sure I know what the hell is happening," I say. "I mean, you were so affectionate tonight." Then I sink into silence, demanding all my answers speechlessly. Why did you come to my apartment alone? Why did you lie down next to me? Why did I assume you were cheering me on?

Bernard's face is impassive, the prominent eyes staring without vitality.

"Barry," Enid steps around to be nearer. "Remember what I told you? I love *being* here. We're family."

Not even an eye blinks.

"And scientists," she breathes.

"But isn't that *wonderful*?" Bernard asks. "To have a relative like Enid? A relative like Barry?"

I speak very low, though it cannot be low enough. Still, I must ask her:

"Enid, you're not seeing Bernard out of pity, are you?" I know that pity in a reasonable person is unprofitable. "You're actually too rational for that, aren't you?"

Enid answers violently: "It's not pity. *What do you take me for?*"

"You misled me. You're having a good time just for the hell of it." I feel the beginnings of truth weighing in my groin like a pair of canteloupes.

Bernard, raising a hand, is ready to deal with me. "On the contrary. I say you've misled yourself, Barry. Your systems have misled you. They're too vast. You don't see the next guy's necessities. You worry only about *your* necessities. The philosophic life is a self-centered life that deludes itself into thinking it is not."

Enid's small upper teeth are biting into her lower lip. The strand of pearls, unclasped, is stretched on the coffee table next to the white holder for her contact lenses and her glasses. She reaches for her glasses and puts them on.

Am *I* not leading a socially benevolent life? Am *I* not part of the eternal whole and therefore *in* God? Our most perfect freedom consists in loving God. The reward of insight is insight, and a blind and impotent soul finds its punishment in its blindness. Oh, Enid baby, I see you, corrupt as an eyelash that has fallen into its own eye. Glassman, where's your universal perspective? Donahue, Zevi, the holocaust—this, too, is a predetermined monstrosity, compressing all eternity.

Oh, where is joy in the apprehension of truth? I unzip my jacket. The heat has made my head swim.

"I would like to coauthor your article," Enid is saying. "So far your work is very promising."

Sure, baby, I say to myself. I assumed you would. No sweat.

All things in the universe have been made for one another and not to please or aid man. Any particular thing is only relative to and intelligible as it appears in the whole cosmos. Hence, an ingredient of Spinoza's happiness is social, that "others may understand the same that I do, that their understandings and desires may wholly agree with mine." Here, Messenger, you arrogant schmuck, here is the social heart of human ethics.

I get up and let myself out, Enid hovering in her bare feet near the door, Bernard on the couch, their faces approving my departure with relief, as if I were a menacing elephant suddenly called to obedience by a trainer. I drift upstairs and fall into my sick bed to resume my illness.

CHAPTER 14

I had not seen Enid for several months when she called last weekend and said the weather possessed exactly the right humidity for moonbows to appear in the night sky. And since she had just bought a new Honda, how about an excursion to the refineries of Secaucus—in the name of science?

I had no assurances that her interest in Bernard Messenger had subsided, but I was much recovered, and in her sleeveless cotton dress, her extremely bare arms were lovely in the late afternoon, her glee was impartial, and the stringent passions of winter seemed suspended; her pleasure in showing off her sleek, white, air-conditioned Honda wiped away the past. Enid knew that Bernard was in Toronto for a few days visiting his aunt. This visit was mine. She drove skillfully, and I contrasted her ease behind the wheel with Marilyn's turbulence, her rhythmic scooting in and out with Marilyn's jerking back in line and inability to change lanes.

We parked along a desolate stretch of the Jersey Turnpike, just now slipping on a gorgeous veil of merging reds and oranges in the early sunset. We each had a notebook in hand, heads craned to peer through the shut windows of the air-conditioned car. Inside, the car was cool all right, but the moon was impossible to find with our heads bent that way, and Enid's perfume kept threatening to steer the atmosphere away from the mental; after a few minutes, my neck ached; my spine felt like microscopic metal filings.

Outside, despite the ferocity of the stench, we did better, trooping around in that no man's land, covering our noses with our handkerchiefs, protecting each other politely from tangled vines and sudden pits in the ground. Behind fences, the huge gas tanks loomed like Mayan ruins, their iron staircases silhouetted against the fiery sky. And just above the tallest was a clear, porcelain, circular moon, radiant in the mist. As night came on, the reds of the sunset fell away; Enid raised a pair of binoculars to her eyes; the moon shone on her bare arms.

She had the patience of the experimental scientist—more patience than I. Mosquitoes began to bite—my neck, my ankles, my forehead, attacking the insides of my thumbs in minute decimal sections. I remembered how the thought of muggers in Prospect Park had enraged her the night Dora Messenger died; here, however, in this untrafficked meadow, she was fearless. The sky was her laboratory. The mosquitoes respected her; me they were eating alive.

When she spotted the indigo we were hoping for, she passed her binoculars to me and hugged me. I peered through intermittently, because my head and hands were one huge, tight, unrelievable welt. I could barely hold the lenses, my thumbs itched so.

And soon Enid was thrashing about with her own difficulties, dabbing at her eyes with her handkerchief, squinting, rolling the eyeballs up into the lids so that she could blot up excess tearing. Still, she hung in, waiting for my reaction.

"It's a moonbow, all right," I said.

"The indigo," she said. "Look at how it glows. It's such a deep primitive blue. Everything else—"

"Absolutely. Fades out in comparison."

But I couldn't stand the itching anymore. I remembered Spinoza growing up in Vlooienburg among the fleas. A loud hum wiggled in the core of my ear like a worm in an ear of corn. Swat! the lobe of my ear sang with the pain of my strike. Instantly the hum shifted to my left ear. Swat! Both ears stinging, ringing, buzzing, I wanted Enid to take the binoculars so I could scratch my neck, my thumbs, my feet, but she was flailing in her own distress.

"Hold this," she said, thrusting her pocketbook at me. I slung both the bag and the strap of the binoculars over my shoulder. "Ooh," she said, screwing up her eyes. She had her compact open in her hand and was carefully removing her contact lenses. "Ooh!" she said, reaching into her pocketbook, that now hung on my shoulder, to slip them into their containers. "Whatever is in this air is damn near blinding me!"

"C'mon," I said. And we ran headlong for the car, a cloud of mosquitoes rushing before my eyes. Poor Spinoza! I thought, feeling the inescapable scourge of his flea-infested childhood as if it were my own. The binoculars and Enid's bag banged against my hip. She was just in front of me, and to be honest, a bit of a plodding runner, the contour of her little ass working hard to get away. But I liked what I saw.

We fell into the car, gasping. Then we laughed until the tears came, fugitives from research—the New Jersey wilderness, the turnpike streaming menacingly toward the unknown south, the moonbow barely a halo of glowing glass, a soft violet blue light visible against the navy blue sky—fugitives from science. Gigantic mosquitoes blew against the car windows, their threadlike legs and thoraxes grotesquely nimble and airborne.

She turned on the ignition. We luxuriated in the peaceful, cool protective rush of new-car-smelling air. It was hygienic. It healed her eyes, my bites. By the time she sped off onto the turnpike toward Metuchen and doubled back for New York at the next exit, we were in an engrossing discussion of holistic optometry.

I explained. "Soft lenses, like yours, soak up the vapors. The indigo light is a barometer of what's polluting the atmosphere. Depending on how dirty your lenses are, you'll feel the fumes in the air scalding your eyes. The whites of your eyes were as pink as some azaleas I've grown, Enid. I saw them. If that had continued, you'd have been in big trouble."

"Mea culpa, Dr. Glassman," she said. "I slept in my lenses last night."

"What we need to consider are full spectrum lenses. They're hard lenses, made of a material that allows the screening out of light wavelengths that might be harmful to the eye. Holistic optometrists are already screening out ultraviolet light wavelengths. These guys are on the fringe of the profession. Gluck was a pioneer in all that holistic stuff." (The poor bastard's unattended shop on West Eighty-first Street appeared in the center of my retina, big as the Museum of Natural History.) "There's no reason why that material can't be treated to protect the eye from other pollutants."

"Ooh!" Enid said, her right eye still squinting painfully over the steering wheel into the night. "I thought a torch was on fire in the socket of my eye."

"What we need to do is write up the connection between the indigo light and the noxious irritants we felt here tonight. We've got to call Exxon and Getty, find out exactly which gases shimmer in the air over those tanks."

Enid said, "But Barry—sometimes when I have my lenses on I go bananas if I'm in a room with raw onions. If the lens absorbs the harmful wavelengths, won't the gases irritate the eye as long as they remain in the lenses?"

There were problems, of course; Spinoza said the practical and the theoretical are identical. Enid was raising a million questions, happily snaking in and out of lanes. When she stopped for a light, she scribbled a sudden thought into her notebook, then shot off again. She seemed girlish in the driver's seat of her neat little Honda, a schoolgirl virgin neither theoretical nor practical, just curious. But her questions dashed my nerve. I thought of Rashkin, Gunn, and the thirty-nine other victims of the crash. Still no cause! Lots of theories, but none of them provable in practice. I began to feel sad, part of a less and less competent world. Spinoza, my darling Spinoza, I thought, the practical and the theoretical were your babies.

We parted rather gravely. I did not invite her in. On the one hand, as the night wore on, mathematical disaster seemed a hairline away, and I hoped to God to make it through the night; and on the other, an elusive professional happiness finally within sight cautioned me not to move at cross-purposes. Cousin Enid's nifty white Honda blew away like a comet. I looked up over Brooklyn and saw the Secaucus moon without its bow, but not without its scars.

Michael and Deirdre are missing: Bonnie and Clyde packing a copy of the Old Testament. Two outlaws gone religious. Or so Marilyn tells me. The call comes just as I am ready for sleep.

"Barry, come clean. Tell me what you know. All of it."

"What do you mean, they're missing? Where *are* they?"

"They supposedly went to a twilight rock concert near the water. But I haven't seen them since. Barry, what do you know that you're not saying? *You bastard, where's Michael?*"

"How should I know? Please! Talk rationally. This is as much a shock to me as to you."

"Well, they're gone. I had a call from across the street. Deirdre's missing and so is her Bible. She always keeps it near her bed, the new Jewish version she just bought. You should've heard their tone. As if this was all my doing! Especially the Jewish Bible! Barry, *do* something."

"Have you called the police?"

"No. The Hoddesons said to wait. They know for a fact that the two of them came back from the concert, took the Bible and whatever else they had stashed, including some baby-sitting money Deirdre always kept in her top drawer. The money is gone."

"How much?"

"How do I know how much."

"If we can hang on for a few more hours, maybe they'll be back."

"What are you *doing* in Brooklyn? Where the hell are you, Barry, when we need you?"

"I need a few minutes."

"You're im*poss*ible!"

"I need to think this through. I'll call you back."

The room has been an oven all night. Now that summer is here I crank the windows open and keep an electric fan turning in one of them. Under my pillow I store a shirt cardboard from the laundry to fan my face during the night. Such makeshift air conditioning was the way my mother managed our sleepless summer nights on Kossuth Street. We were a family of summer insomniacs, waving cardboards in our sweaty beds as the Bronx street lamps shone in on our palely moving wrists. The inexorable heat of this attic room will kill, if alarm and guilt don't do it first. Michael, thirteen and a half, she, fourteen by now—how do the police ignore two kids padding around America by themselves? Where is decency? Civic accountability? Who is answerable? Beautiful, soft-looking Deirdre might pass for sixteen, but Michael? I can see his boyish American figure, barely 5' 3", smooth-as-a-baby chin, thin hands, thin shoulders, his small Eastern Mountain pack slung between them, though brittle-tongued, rasping out opinions, exchanging advice with Deirdre in a way that makes no mistake that theirs is a partnership. Bonnie and Clyde. Surely I will hear it from Ed Hoddeson. After all, why *should* Deirdre leave the bosom of a lively household, both parents at home, four brothers and sisters, popular, pretty? Why indeed? He'll blame it all on Michael, make him into some kind of Jewish Merlin bewitching the virgin Deirdre into this criminal escape. I dread times like these when anti-Semitism doggedly pops up. He'll be out there chopping wood, viciously pretending each log a Glassman: whack, Michael Glassman! whack, Barry Glassman! WHACK, the state of Israel! sweat pouring off his thick fireman's neck. I boil water for Nescafé and notice on the milk carton the faces of two missing children, their eyes stealing accusingly through me as though I were a South American dictator in designer eyeglasses who had "disappeared" them for political purposes. I swallow gulps of Nescafé. I read their vital statistics: one five, the other eight; 3′2″ and 3′11″. Out among the lost children of America, Michael and Deirdre are giants.

And then, unavoidably, I am obsessed by the case study of Harris Mintz, 6′4″, vanished twenty years ago without a trace, without a phone call, except once from the mysterious Georgina, who was after a quick-fix blackmail. In America! Sorrow flows like sand out of my heart for Harris's beleaguered parents, who had to die without ever locating their missing child. My blood thumps back and forth in my empty heart like a kid walking on an empty sandbox.

Spring had been a war against a nagging jealousy, a suddenly rising cholesterol, and dubious X rays, but Dr. Scarf at last declared my lungs free of shadow and, as I was buttoning my shirt collar, delivered a tight-lipped lecture on caring for one's body after forty. My weight was coming down. I promised to persevere, but already the dog days of summer were here, the casual desultoriness of July giving way to Coca-Cola and the serious eye-blurring heat of August. "The first thing to do," he said (I expected a second lecture on my cholesterol) "is to look after your boy. He's sarcastic, and his pulse is fast."

His advice snapped at me like an attack dog. I wanted to get what I came for, but I left his premises immediately. Even though I understood that my errors in dealing with Michael since the separation (these days I speak the word easily) were not random but determined by external causes (my coughing seizures, for example, render me in his eyes temporarily unfit as a father), and in spite of a restful holiday mood awaiting my restored health, a slab of guilt stood over my body as if marking a living grave.

But I have no time to act upon Dr. Scarf's warning; by six this morning, a female voice is already on my phone assuring me that she and Michael are about to board a bus out of the Port Authority.

"Is that Deirdre Hoddeson?" I ask, my husky voice jolted out of sleeplessness.

"Is that Barry?" she retorts. I can't remember having talked with the girl beyond mumbled greetings, and I am struck by her nerve. She uses our first names, though on suburban Fifty-first Avenue it has always been Mr. and Mrs. Hoddeson, Mr. and Mrs. Glassman. "Please call my parents. Say that you heard from us and that we'll call from time to time. Barry, Michael says not to call his mother. He'll take care of Marilyn himself."

"Put Michael on," I say sternly.

But Deirdre is giggling. "Not yet, Barry."

"What about the orthodontist? What about school?"

"What about them?"

"Aren't you both entering the senior high school in September? Aren't there papers to sign? Don't you need to be vaccinated?"

"Nonsense," she says. Then she repeats, "As soon as you hang up, call Bev and Ed. Uh, I wouldn't want them to send the fire department after me." A click severs the connection.

Now I wish I *had* invited Enid in. I need more of a base between us so I can share this new heartache with her. What an asshole I was not to ask her in after the mosquitoes. I want advice, and no one to talk to! I reach for the phone. A full four minutes later I dial.

It is the middle of the night. A morbid civility has invaded her voice. She says she has been expecting this call for years.

"This has nothing to do with Harris," I bellow. "It's Barry. I need help!"

She cannot believe I haven't called Marilyn back.

"But they said—"

"And you listened?" The formality shifts; she begins to sound authoritative—like her old self.

"The hell with—"

"We're wasting time. You've got to act fast. Think, Barry. Where might they be heading?"

"How should I know? It's a big country."

"Would they head out to San Diego? Doesn't your sister live——?"

"She and Michael don't see eye to eye— Besides, Frannie would call."

"*You* didn't call a soul for hours!"

"Enid, stop harassing me."

"Barry! You're whimpering!"

"I can't help it—"

"Call the police. Call the principal of his school. Call your rabbi. Call the parents of his friends. Above all, call Marilyn and Deirdre's parents. You've got to get organized."

"Okay. O*k*ay!"

"Barry, listen, listen carefully. This is not the same as Harris. They *want* you to find them."

Marilyn and Donahue have begun without me: called the police, called the Hoddesons, called school and synagogue, and accepted the advice to stay near the phone. Meanwhile, the police have broadcast a description of the two kids to bus terminals within two days' journey of New York. I am also instructed to sit by my Brooklyn phone. At 9 A.M. Feliz is jumpy, since Santina is ready to give birth at any moment, but he is in the shop and willing to take calls.

CHAPTER 15

My primary consolation is knowledge, and my secondary, Enid Moscow, who has agreed to sit by the phone on Saturday so that I can attend to affairs in the shop. She appears in surprisingly scanty attire and smelling of baby powder—flowered shorts and a pink halter, each naked knob of shoulder carefully dusted, a metal clasp pulling the coarse bob of her hair up off the perspiring nape of neck. She has brought her briefcase and a bag of fruit, and sets about rinsing plums, grapes, and peaches for storage in the refrigerator. I watch her at work at the sink, the back of her thighs long, her silky spine, banded by the pink bra, aggressively naked and a little fleshy.

As I am preparing to leave, she is glancing compulsively around at the open volumes scattered about the apartment. One by one every title is read, and bending closer to study a page here, a paragraph there, she brings her knees together in concentration, her thighs pressed like twin loaves of the whitest bread. "I thought it was all optics—" she says in amazement. "I have so many questions to ask." She begins to comprehend that my readings are philosophic, broadly metaphysical and narrowly ontological. "Barry! Who in the world still reads Spinoza?"

"Well, I couldn't sleep. The best I could do was sit by the phone and study. He's an old favorite of mine."

She glides closer to me, a pamphlet copy of *On the Improvement of the Understanding* in her hands. As she approaches, reading, I see a flicker of argumentativeness in her eyes. But she extends a conciliatory hand, a trickle of perspiration sliding down her throat and into the cleavage of her breasts, their roundness spilling over the fabric of the pink halter. God, it is warm! She kicks off her sandals and walks barefoot across my bare floors. Her conciliatory hand falls to her side, leaving in its place a question, unasked, in midair.

How to be friends, cousins, scientists while Enid Moscow's female body is in the way?

And a hot, embarrassed anguish follows as I remember Michael and Deirdre lurching cross-country at this very moment on a Greyhound, acting as if they owned the world. The fundamentalist father of a U.S. victim of terrorism put it in a way that ached with religious sorrow: We know that God is great; what we don't know is the power of Satan.

Enid slips to the back of the room, out of my way, as if my need for philosophy has created a truce between us while she recoups her forces. Across the room, in a quick effort to compensate, her eyes pore over the text and a tinge of color creeps up her neck into her cheeks. She opens her mouth as if to criticize, the booklet pressed to her breasts. She is an enigma to me. Who the hell does she think she is, making this ill-timed comeback into my life, grilling me like a school examiner instead of a loving and consoling relative?

The phone rings. I hear Feliz's excited voice on the other end. "Santina is in the hospital. Barry, are you *coming*?"

"Twenty minutes," I say. "Go ahead and leave, Feliz. Linda can manage for a short while without you. And Feliz?"

"Yes, Barry?"

"I'm happy for you, kid. This is a great moment," I say huskily. At my show of emotion, Enid's eyes linger on me instead of on the book.

I have to tell myself over and over, as I flee down the steps past Bernard Messenger's door, that the greatest good in life is attained through the intellect, pursued as I am by the image of Professor Winning wagging my B+ final exam on *The Ethics* before my nose. "The last essay a muddle," he had said without a trace of consolation. "Mere sentiment and turbulence."

By the time we close the shop, Santina has given birth to a baby girl. Linda Kemp comes away from the call pale and silent. She plants a big kiss on my forehead and hugs me in her skinny arms. But she is gloomy. "By this time tomorrow," she finally says, "you'll have your boy back, mark my words."

I feel revived, as much by the air conditioning in the shop as by the good Algarve news. "So Feliz is a father," I say in wonder. "He'll be a very good one." Sentiment catches in my throat, and I decide to present the couple with a substantial check as a baby gift. Half an hour later, after the alarm is set, the door slammed, and Linda and I are walking along Eighth Avenue, I notice how leaden she is. Her thin cheeks pale under their rouge. Her forehead, perspiration pouring off it, goes white. She can hardly walk. "What is it?" I ask as we prepare to part ways on the corner of Eighth Avenue and Thirty-seventh Street. "Linda, are you sick?"

"It's nothing," she says. "You've got your own problems."

I have, but she is quivering. We stop in front of an Orange Julius. "Come in here, let's get you a drink," I say, my mind torn between a desire to dash back to the Brooklyn phone and Enid, and the necessity to administer orange juice to a perspiring Linda Kemp.

"I'll be all right," she says, forcing a smile. "It's a reaction."

"To a drug?" I ask with alarm.

She shakes her head.

Leaning against the brick wall of a building, she says softly, "I'm so jealous, I could die." I can barely hear her voice. "Barry, I'm, like, thirty-eight years old, and I thought I didn't want kids—"

The haze of the humid afternoon burns my eyes. Linda Kemp removes her big, stylish eyeglasses and wipes her tears with my handkerchief, then blows her nose. "They're so happy about their baby. I can't get them out of my mind. And you—you're frantic about *your* kid— Everywhere I turn—"

"One thing has nothing to do with the other," I hear myself saying. A lie, of course. God is free, not because he is *not* tied into the world, but because he *is*, because he is always actualized. Santina has shaken Linda's resolve. These women hardly know each other, but I may never again think of one without the other. "You're a neat guy," Linda Kemp says, trying to speak more loudly, traffic snarling in the street before us. A taxi driver, his hair in a long blond braid, is standing in the road behind a line of trucks, leaning into the window of his cab, blasting his horn. She screams over to him, "Gimme a break!" Then she composes herself. "Some of these dudes . . . no manners. Law school," she is saying, ". . . die rather than go back . . . so sick of it . . . fucked over by this law student . . . nobody has manners . . . just a kid, overworked, overcompetitive . . . I'm too stupid to act my age. In the name of God, I've made up my mind!" She is clinging to me, running the tips of her fingers up and down my arm. "You're such a sweetheart! I can't begin to tell you—" Then she presses my hands to her thin, hard breasts, whispers, "I've got to make a class—" and breaks away, looping along Eighth Avenue and onto a waiting bus.

For the first time in my life, my living is secure. The mind can continue to reflect while my hands do their work. The bucks roll in. I have the satisfaction of an ally in Feliz; and Linda Kemp's shrieking admission on the corner of Eighth and Thirty-seventh reminds me of the enduring good of the universe. To be virtuous is to live in accordance with the laws of nature. Though failure may be my fate—disease, pain, dismay, desertion by wife and child—I am blameless.

But wasn't I an ass to let Linda Kemp get away! Too late I realize that approval of the soul, even by a virtual stranger, alleviates grief. I should have taken her hard, sweaty body directly to an air-conditioned room at the Sheraton, patiently putting my no-risk cock into her as she reluctantly extolled the virtues of childlessness. Now I am going home, erect and agitated.

The second I turn the key in the downstairs door, Enid is rushing to the top of the steps. "You just missed his call," she shouts. "Not to worry, he says they're fine. I had to explain who I was. But he remembered that I drove Nathan to his bar mitzvah."

"Oh, *nuts*," I say. "Linda Kemp—" I take the steps two at a time. Enid, clasping my hands, leads me inside. "He's okay, Barry. Having a ball, in fact. I could hear them giggling, and I heard singing in the background. Something from the synagogue."

"Are you sure?"

Enid has done well. Pours a glass of cold Perrier, removes an ice-cube tray from the freezer, bangs the tray on the edge of the sink. Two crackling cubes finally slip free of the tray into the sink. Scoops them out and pops them into the glass.

"Drink this," she says. Helps herself to a peach. "And buy yourself an air conditioner, mister. There's no need to suffer like this."

Men are blameless, but they suffer just the same. "Where the hell are they?"

"He said they're safe. 'We're not traveling anymore,' he said. 'Tell Dad we're safe. We're with friends.'"

"Friends! What else did he say?"

She is relishing the peach, sticking her ass out behind her and her lips out in front as the peach drips juice into a paper napkin.

"I asked him when he'd be coming home."

"Yes?"

"No dice. But lots of giggling. His girlfriend took the phone and asked you to call her parents again. She apparently doesn't want to risk talking to them herself. *Very* womanly, by the way, for fourteen."

"Enid, for God's sake, try to remember. How'd he sound? Who was singing? What was the song?"

"I don't know one of those songs from the other," she says, sucking the peach pit one last time before tossing it into the sink. Suddenly her eyes brighten. "'Ain Kelohenu' maybe? Say, do you know it? Sing it for me."

I do.

She laughs. "Well, I haven't been in a synagogue in years. I couldn't say."

I drop into the chair near the window, unbutton my shirt, and take off my shoes and socks. I stretch out my legs, pinching the crease of my pants to air my ankles. In the heat, my briefs stick to my testicles.

"Sing me another song."

"No."

"Come on, Barry. You've *got* to."

"It's too hot."

She pouts.

"Well, all right. Was it 'Adon Olom'?"

"Sing it, Barry. Sing it."

> Adon olom
> Asher molach
> B'terem kol . . .
>
> Lord of the world
> The king supreme
> Ere aught was formed . . .

"Ere aught was formed—" Substance implies existence. It never does not exist.

She shrugs. "They're pretty songs," she says. "You'd make a terrific cantor."

"No more," I say, covering my ears, as if I had just heard the din of killer bees.

My singing amuses her.

"At least he's alive," I say bitterly.

"You're overreacting," Enid says, barely able to control herself. The woman dismisses me with the same patronizing cruelty she and Messenger exhibited in his apartment on that midnight months ago. And I resent it! Why must the tragedy of her life trivialize everything I do, everything I feel?

"He's more than alive. He's fine. He's a devilish kid toying with problems he'd rather not face."

"Don't be pitiless," I say, but the fact is, her good humor, her confidence, her tough little laugh at my expense give me new strength.

"Keep your cool, Barry. Michael and his lady will be home in a matter of days. Meanwhile, teach me about Substance. I want to learn about monism." She is perched contentedly on the arm of my chair, waving her hand at the open books, her pink bosom at the height of my nose.

"Okay. What do you want to know?" I ask weakly, sniffing baby powder.

"How do I know what I want to know?"

"The kid sounded okay, hnh?"

"Very okay." She reaches for my Perrier and takes a sip. My brain is spinning. She bends over and kisses my bare chest, pressing her pink bosom along my arm and neck, squeezing herself against me. "I owed you that," she says, very quietly, the sweat under her nose glistening.

"Let's go buy an air conditioner," I whisper.

Enid Moscow figures out the installation diagrams of the small casement model air conditioner. The pleasures of knowledge are limitless. Together we hoist the unit into the window and adjust the sliding panels for an airtight fit, she holding the machine while I adjust the metal clamps. Within minutes Enid Moscow's cool body has mounted mine, and my lips are hushing her questions about Substance, and she is stroking and stroking the insides of my thighs, and everything is fitting marvelously into place.

CHAPTER 16

(1) I forget about Bernard Messenger while Enid Moscow and I make love. For I have studied "The Origins and Nature of the Emotions," and I know that if I were to recollect him and contemplate him even for an instant, my body would be affected in the same torpid way as if he were present. Besides, I'm sick of looking at that arrogant, blind mug, which never fails to engender pity in me no matter how vigilantly my intellect battles it. (Later, as Enid and I smolder in our smug happiness, I imagine Dunkirk, New York, the site of a pernicious air current that distorts the flight patterns of passing craft. I assign Messenger, on his flight back from Toronto, the same fiery fate as the angelic optometrical contingent and, in so elevating him, reduce the remorse of my malevolence.)

(2) A movie marquee on Kings Highway reads for all the world to see

GENEROUS AND EXUBERANT LOVER

STARRING ENID MOSCOW

FOUR STAGES IN THE CROWDED HIGH-RISER

FEATURING THE BRIGHT PLAYFUL ARDOR OF BARRY GLASSMAN

(3) I forget about Michael and Deirdre while Enid Moscow and I make love. Being father and lover at the same time is trying to have it both ways. You can't! As we are slipping out of Stage One (cousinship) into Stage Two (a playful sibling antagonism), the phone rings. Parted mouths, spurts of

kissing, long gentle caresses, rising, rising into Stage Three on the high-riser, the Glassman high riser high and nimble, we let it ring.

(3a) The erotic career of Marilyn and Barry passes meanwhile before him like a peepshow. He has not made love to a woman in ten months. He uses his recollections of a sexually brimming Marilyn to egg him on. (He *can* love a woman.)

(4) Over and over I bring Enid to the brink of pleasure (Stage Three), coaxing and thrilling her, ever narrowing the terrain, joining in the depth of her trembling until our bodies (Stage Four) leap as one, shivering, over the border into freedom.

(5) Having been so long in bondage, is there a life in the new land for Anatoly Glassman?

CHAPTER 17

We decide not to phone in advance, but simply to burst in on them.

Dolores drives—a glowing, dust-free navy blue Buick, Marilyn rigid in the passenger seat next to her, I, taking plenty to think about, in the rear. The rabbi has a theory: Michael had been bringing Deirdre to services (or perhaps it is the other way around, the rabbi suggests). Since the call came on Saturday at about sundown, the mysterious song was part of a *havdalah* service they were attending—somewhere, recited by Orthodox Jews on Saturday evening to separate the sacred Sabbath from the profane week. Marilyn conveyed his conclusion that the song was "Alaynu."

What could I do but sing a bit of it to Enid, who listened, urging more, more. Reluctantly, I croaked out another line, for in spite of my irreverence I felt a twinge of sacrilege in this profane rendering. "That's it!" she cried, relying on an ear developed through ten years of piano lessons. "I'm sure of it."

But since Mayberg still avoids my part of Brooklyn, the *presidentka* is entrusted with the name and address of where we are heading. So I have to surrender my craving to spend all of Sunday enfolding Enid in my arms, our new air conditioner puffing cool breezes over us as we munch plums and grapes, peaches and nectarines, and go through the first propositions of the *Ethics*. We would have started with the Definition of God. *I. By cause of it-*

self, I understand that, whose essence involves existence; or that, whose nature
cannot be conceived unless existing.

How I long to entice her to my metaphysic and watch her keen mind leap
into phase with the durable, nylon thought waves of Spinoza's system. First
God; then Substance; next, Enid my brainy love, the marvelous idea of the
attributes as that which the intellect perceives of Substance—we in our limited reason know only two: thought and extension; and the modes—the af-
fections of Substance—what men and women, you and I, recognize as individual things taken to be our world.

Yet, when it was understood that she had to leave, that they were coming
here to collect me, the mischance of her exit faded and gradually turned to
relief. Each point of the philosophy, after all, was like a shard of glass, which,
if handled carelessly and without respect, might cut, injure, or be lost in the
premature comparison with an opposing system. I knew Enid's shameless
habit of opposition (both shamelessness and opposition are strong in her), a
skepticism gathering since yesterday like snow.

"How can you be so naive?" she had said on our way to buy the air conditioner. "Who can adhere to an implacable system that is static, where time
disappears and history is insignificant? What about the Holocaust and Viet-
nam? How can you ignore quantum theory and the force of accident in the
physical universe? Haven't you heard of the Uncertainty Principle?"

I am not ahistorical, and lately I have been too poetic a witness to my own
erratic history to accept my beloved philosophy as absolute. After my worries about Michael, it keeps me company when I am awake at night. I'll argue my position when I have to, but because I am never 100 percent certain,
I do not enjoy argument. I quickly changed the subject to air conditioners.
But she certainly had put a lot of Spinoza under her belt!

For everything comes from God. That is my great consistency. Weren't
Enid's inconsistencies a sign of her skepticism? See the physicist in flowered
shorts and halter lugging the bulging briefcase full of Grumman data. Yes,
she had gotten through most of it in Saturday's heat; but also through a few
of my books, scattered across the tiny, suffocating apartment, competing for
her attention—or are they the comic relief? Am I the comic relief for her
serious work with Messenger? Who can mistake the fun in her eyes this
morning as she continues to pummel me with questions? First, I think I am
having the time of my life. Now, I am not so sure.

She leaves my room shortly before Marilyn and Dolores arrive, our cool delicious morning ended, the skimpy high-riser shut down, as lifeless as the Flatbush Avenue appliance store at closing time, the final customers out, the two of us loading our air conditioner onto her Honda at a quarter past ten at night, both of us alluringly romantic. But at Enid's reminder, I had first to telephone Marilyn from a phone booth on the street and tell her about Michael's call. "Yeah, he was exuberant, they giggled a lot, they sang a Jewish song." And this morning Marilyn reaches me in bed, the enigmatic Enid, slightly subdued, already slipping on her glasses and rereading *On the Improvement of the Understanding*, her smiling breasts cool against my chest; she lays the book aside every once in a while to ponder what she's read, her finger absently circling one hard little nipple of my chest (several times Marilyn snarls into the phone, *Barry, are you listening?*, as, aroused, I peer across to admire the depth of Enid's interest and note which particular passage has broken through her skepticism), and finally I have to get out of bed, for I have *Marilyn's* voice in my ear, *Marilyn's* terse imprecations not to be a fool, this may be our last chance to see Michael alive.

Enid, of course, understood; I prepared her a cup of Nescafé; she showered, climbed into her brief attire, and kissed me good-bye, briefcase in hand, face beautiful under the doubt (could I be certain it was doubt?) that hung between us, momentarily, as she departed.

Dolores Gutman chatters endlessly as we head up I-95, though Marilyn scarcely replies. I am assigning yet another meaning to *separated*, for the fearful, trusting Bronx girl who joined me in a sacred Jewish marriage at the catering hall of the Twin Cantors has become this gutsy, exasperating middle-aged woman on a mission, physically nearer to me than she's been since those stupid attempts at reconciliation in my basement workshop, months ago. Marilyn sits formally erect, of course, while I am jelly with the private trifle of just this night having taken Cousin Enid Moscow as my munificent lover. If only Marilyn could know (the one person in the world I yearn to tell)! The alternating relief and anxiety of last night, however, leave me no happier than Marilyn appears to be. Self-righteous, self-congratulatory, self-obsessed, I am as solitary and preoccupied as Spinoza himself, though in my tumultuous heart, Enid's affectionate bedtime choreography is its own ethic and leaves room for little more.

Mad with worry about Michael, Marilyn had taken it upon herself to discourage Bev and Ed Hoddeson from coming along with us for fear of overpopulating the rescue: but this is no Entebbe. Dolores, shoulders bent, big sunglasses on, grips the wheel with both hands. Marilyn's trendy new hairdo is bunched severely behind by a rubber band. She has things on her mind. She was always pressed for time and, though locked in a moving car, shows her habitual impatience by glancing repeatedly at her watch. "Philosophy takes time," I used to tell her as she rushed me to the bank or the post office before they closed, bending her wrist in front of my nose to flash the time. Maps of Long Island and Connecticut are strewn on the front seat and across her lap. Every now and then she puts on her reading glasses, which hang across her chest on a black cord. I offer no advice. The women blunder along, missing exits, arguing with single words, "Left," "Right," like pick-axes, circling back onto the highway, exiting again later, and passing through the Gothic canyons of a heat wave at Yale University as the carillon strikes the hour, not knowing where the hell they are, taking directions from a perspiring female student, bundled in sweatshirt and sweatpants in the 95 degree heat and stopped on her bicycle for an ice cream.

From the back seat, I detect that Marilyn is on the brink of emotion, glasses off, on, off, but her effort is superhuman, checking every impulse to sigh, to scream, to talk, avoiding my eyes by rotating her head forward one-quarter arc toward the sizzling windshield whenever she senses that I am moving mine in her direction. Dolores's muttering drones on. Marilyn utters not a word about Donahue, the repairs to the downstairs bathroom, the unpaid temple bills. She is balancing fear, determination, even (can it be?) humiliation. In her way, she is a damn good acrobat, her facial muscles set in a laconic reserve. What she says about Michael's recent bitterness is astute and brief: "He lives on potato chips, and he stays in his room."

As I detect all of this, I am fighting off a wave of nostalgia for home, for I feel suddenly as dubious as a tourist at the end of a long trip, and I hold to the memory of Marilyn as to the most vivid souvenir of the first country visited.

The four-storied house on Lawrence Street is typical of houses we have seen all over New Haven. The scrabby lawn needs cutting; the privet hedge is overgrown and irregular, sheets of punched-out computer paper caught in its branches. A cluster of mailboxes outside signals that this once commodious house has been split into a nest of student apartments. A few neglected tomato plants gawk on the front lawn around a red metal art construction shaped like a huge X. When we step into the hall to ring the bell, a baby is crying.

A man's strong voice answers.

Dolores takes charge. "I am here from the synagogue." Not exactly a lie. The baby is wailing forlornly.

"Which synagogue?" Then the crying ceases, and an intense, curly-haired young man, bearded and bare-chested, a crocheted yarmulke clamped to his hair with a bobby pin, opens the door. A toddler with the same dark intensity, in a diaper, is anchored on his hip, curious.

We succeed in wedging the door open without rushing in. "Are you Jerry Zapolski? Do you teach in Bayside? Are you a student at the Yale Drama School?" Dolores's fusillade of questions is terrifyingly inept. Zapolski moves swiftly to slam the door, but Marilyn has taken hold of the baby's hand.

"Don't," she shrieks. "You'll hurt the baby!"

My blood is pulsing inside of my knees. Pushing Dolores aside, I assume a reassuring voice, like that of an old friend. "Jerry," I say calmly, "it's much too warm—" when I hear Michael's voice, singing at the top of his lungs, "*Da-veed, me-lech yis-ro-el* . . ." David, King of Israel . . . The wife, an animated woman with a swaddled infant in one arm, rushes to the door.

"Jerry," she says, "they're his parents. You mustn't." A sulking Dolores, meanwhile, elbows her way back into the center of things. "Look," she says, "Rabbi Mayberg asked *me* to speak to you."

But the wife has imposed herself between husband and visitors. A tall, impressive young woman, she speaks in a full-throated, theatrical voice. "Michael, leave Hannah-le and come here. Deirdre, you too." By this time, we have made our way inside. An air conditioner is humming loudly, a mechanical baby swing stands in the middle of the room, empty, but still swinging. Shades are drawn. The walls, covered with Israeli art posters and Arabic calligraphy, are nonetheless baking in the sun. Jerry backs his wife into a corner. "Isabel, we promised!"

"Have they done a job on you! You're a *father*. How would you feel—"

Michael stops mid-dance, unbelieving, as though we have located him on a desert island, pressing his lower lip against his upper in the way he has. He is not unhappy, faintly smiling, and holding the hand of a dark-haired three-year-old in white cotton panties. Marilyn rushes him, flinging her arms around him. "You must never—" and begins to cry.

"Hey, kid," I say quietly.

"Hey, Dad," he says back.

I now find that I am being carefully examined, as if the next move were mine, Michael standing by like the king on a chessboard, holding the game, but restricted in his moves. I am in no hurry. Marilyn and Dolores, inert themselves, have also turned to me, their scheming zeal insufficient to the unexpectedly tender moment. Marilyn's body has aged; she is harder than I remember her. Remembering Enid, I feel catapulted into youth, ten years more fortunate, ten years softer. Michael is in a state of repose. Jerry Zapolski stands by, his wife vanished into a bedroom to attend to their infant. I feel a connection to everyone in the room. Difficult decisions are expected of me, and conduct I am unaccustomed to. I have interrupted a glorious and godly occasion. Even the babies conserve their being (it is absolutely impossible that they not so endeavor). I haven't seen Michael as calm in a couple of years. God himself is creating His divinity—at that moment, in the inescapable yellow sunlight of that weakly air-conditioned room in New Haven. And Deirdre? tall and tense, in a knit cocoon of a dress that shows her nipples, hanging onto Michael's hand as though each finger held an eternal truth.

Which is that Michael's face, just flowering into the soft hairs of manhood, is the most beautiful thing in that room. I am too timorous to kiss it, for I also know that a father's kiss is elastic and must endure for a lifetime.

"Why are you looking at him that way?" Deirdre says to me, and Michael says, "He always looks at me like that. Now let's go home," running his fingers in and out of Deirdre's, checking out her melancholy face with his sly, metallic eyes.

Jerry Zapolski, the toddler still astride his hip, wraps Michael and Deirdre in a one-armed bear hug, as the beautiful Isabel apologizes to Marilyn, sweetly, candidly. "We didn't want them to split. They were unbelievable with the kids, especially Deirdre. Frankly, it's the first bit of rest we've had since Shimon was born." She is struggling in this heat to be cordial; but Marilyn will have none of it; she never did take the heat well.

Marilyn glares at me in blame, spacy, icy. She is a queen, ruling vast galactic regions. We are all earthlings, and Isabel's endearing effort to be civil is an alien language, or a capacity she has never seen before, or a phenomenal change in sound. She has that "I will never understand the likes of you" look, and disappears into the bathroom. I know exactly what she is doing in there, exactly how she is indulging her aloofness, pampering her anger. How many times I used to stand by and watch her go through her overreactions to something I said, or didn't say, or should have said, and here it is again, her famous polar-bear act, willing things to be *thus* and freezing her emotions while the change takes place, waiting in the john until I, her ignored husband, compromised by external causes, call her name. Now despite the heat, she is a sheet of glass, at this moment transfixed on the edge of the tub, transparent, doing nothing.

Isabel is alarmed. "Is your wife all right?" she asks.

For Isabel's sake, I pretend that I too am concerned. "It's the heat." And I keep an eye on the bathroom door, but I do not knock, I do not call her name. She is in there what seems like an eternity, and when she emerges she glides past me without an eyelid of acknowledgment, though I admit her cheeks are sunken and she looks half-dead. Oh, I am through with that iceberg I think confidently, enjoying the sting of sweat in my eyes.

She presents herself to Isabel, who continues as if nothing had intervened.

"We had a lovely Shabbat together," Isabel says, turning to Deirdre. "Didn't we?"

Deirdre, at the edge of hysteria, buries her face behind her pocketbook. A heavy-lidded glance passes from her to Michael, who leads her out to the car, and as they pass I get a whiff of her perfume.

"We do a traditional Sabbath," Isabel is saying. "No lights, no car, no TV—just reading, good food, feeding the babies, napping—on Shabbat we talk until we fall asleep. They're both interesting kids; Michael's quite a Platonist in his own way. You've done a great job with him. He's *thoughtful*. And Deirdre, well, *she* could general an army." I nod absently, astonished by the idea that a son of mine is a Platonist and at the same time has capitulated to the heavy-lidded style of fireman Ed Hoddeson's daughter.

"That mystic Mayberg—sometimes he pulls things right out of the air!" Jerry Zapolski surmises the truth.

I offer to drive, but Dolores, determined to complete her presidential service, tries to manipulate the seating so that Marilyn and I are thrown together in the back seat; failed in her plan and ruthless about driving, she plunges down I-95 toward New York, Marilyn and the kids pitching about in the back, I traveling up front. Dolores's T-shirt is damp, the long slit up the side of her skirt is taut at the seam. The muscle in her bare, tanned thigh twitches as she presses and releases the accelerator.

The car rolls along like a cage filled with animals: Gutman deadly and silent, not breathing a word about the rabbi; Deirdre moaning, Marilyn's distractions preventing her from any thought of comforting the girl; each one glaring restlessly through opposite windows. Every once in a while Marilyn shifts her position contentiously.

I decide to test Dolores. "Did the rabbi tell you about our scene?"

"The rabbi has been on vacation," Dolores says, "in the Amish country."

"We had an incident several months back—after a funeral. Didn't he *tell* you?"

"Rabbi never breaks a confidence."

"He's keeping things from you, Dolores."

In the back seat, Marilyn is the old self-absorbed Marilyn, unflagging in her desire that I cure her of yet another problem. "Leave her out of this. Talk to *me*. I have things to discuss with you, Barry. Come back with us tonight, and we'll talk."

But Dolores is interested. "Well, what *was* it? A religious decision? A rabbinical decision?"

"More like a boxing decision." I choose to ignore Marilyn and her moods. When I tell the whole story, Dolores's face turns purple. Her teeth flash. I might have expected disbelief, but rage?

"We don't need you and your *meshuganeh* letters," she shouts, "you don't pay your bills, you're critical of everything we do, you intimidate the rabbi, you invent lies—" Billboards are whizzing by.

"Hey. You want to kill us all? Slow down, Dolores!"

"Ignore him, Dolores. He is an eccentric."

But Dolores is furious. "Now there are factions who don't want to renew when the rabbi's contract comes up. This congregation is out to hang him by the neck because he's too simple, too spiritual. You can thank Steinman and that clever trick about the sermons. And rabbi's been unaware! thinks everyone is his friend. They want a Park Avenue rabbi, somebody who drives a nice car. I'll just bet—" She turns away from the road intermittently to give me the eye.

"Who? Me? How can you *say* that?"

"You're not to be trusted." She affects a hoarse whisper. "You got to Za-polski only because of the rabbi's intuition. Where would you *be* without him?"

"I'm *fond* of Mordecai, and I believe he's fond—"

She is bewildered. "He would like to get rid of you. We all would. You're in everybody's hair, Barry Glassman. This congregation has enough prob-lems of its own."

From the rear seat, Marilyn lurches forward and screams. "Why don't you just drive and shut *up*."

Deirdre's moaning turns to anger; she swings her shoulder bag and bops me on the head. As I lurch to the left, the car swerves.

I grab hold of the wheel. "*Do* something, Michael. Take that bag away from her."

"I can't *see*!" Dolores wails, shoving at me with her right shoulder.

"Dolores, pull into that McDonald's."

But she is doing seventy, and she misses the exit for McDonald's. "Strength of mind" is the desire by which a person uses reason alone to pre-serve his own being. I know that on reason alone I will never make it home tonight alive. The philosophic life is rolling, like an eye, off the face of the earth, with the blurred billboards, the sun-spotted hulks of cars, the dou-bled exit ramps oversped by distracted motorists. Narrowly I switch places with Dolores, who is mumbling bitterly about a blind spot; we are out on the anonymous strip of highway one hundred yards beyond McDonald's, the noxious fumes of cars blasting by us within an inch of our lives. My sense of the present moment is severe, a perilous, headlong, exhilarating flight from philosophy into action. Michael, at the edge of his seat, is restraining his mother with his knee. The Stoic ideal of equanimity through reason doesn't work when the wheel is in the hands of a grievously offended driver. I take over. The *amor intellectualis dei* is too heady for the ironies of a child's day-to-day love. Certainty in God and ethical practice? They begin to give way like quirky memories in the earth, at first a small percentage on a scale, until the rage in the car is momentous and the white line is turning into an earth-quake and someone has to keep us from cracking up. I give no thought to Bernard Messenger, to Enid or Marilyn, to Dolores Gutman, or to Spinoza. Deirdre, satisfied, is dabbing her earlobes with perfume; only Michael's iron eyes hold any promise of deliverance.

"Everybody sit back and no funny business," I bark.

CHAPTER 18

I drive straight to the synagogue on Utopia Parkway, bounce the keys on Dolores Gutman's tightly skirted lap, and run for the bus, then down into the subway, grabbing the first blazing "F" train for Prospect Park and home.

A handful of Sunday riders—four black men and one white woman—are my fellow passengers, though none are near me, and I stretch my throbbing knees, shut my eyes, and try to regain my composure by contemplating how a man steeped in God would apply his faith to the study of the sun's light in drops of falling rain, how the archbishop of Spalato, for example, an expert in optics in the seventeenth century, obtained scientific judgments on the passage of light, for the quality of the light he saw interests me: did ordinary light merge with religious radiance, light that billows, sprays, and pulses, unstoppable light that builds slowly and magnificently, like a good fuck?

I am nodding and lurching, lifting one lid every now and then to safeguard my presence, but I am not asleep. The roar of the subway seems to repeat SpalatoSpalatoSpalato as the car heaves from station to station. The woman passenger is in a white nurse's uniform. Her legs, opposite and to the right of my lowered eyes, are a silky distraction, the white glitter at the calves curving to neat white ankles, white feet into white gumsoled shoes. The black man nearest, reading a small Bible, is in clerical vestments, black suit and vest and a clerical collar. He seems very black, she very white. The other men are dozing. We are all on our own in the hot, windy subway. Overhead fans are rotating. The windows are open, and warm air is smacking me across the eyes. I try to dwell on the archbishop and his dialogue with the scientific academy of Spalato, imagining their skepticism, his conviction, their doubt, his fervor; but I am exhausted, and Dolores Gutman's shrill condemnation repeats in the heavy rattle of the train. "You're in everybody's hair, Barry Glassman. We would like to get rid of you."

And now the rabbi, too. Getridofhimgetridofhimgetridofhim.

Is she saying they expected more of me? They wanted me to bust my balls for them, was that it? But how? Why? For Bayside? My head bobs with the motion of the ride. I am busting my intelligence for them; isn't that enough? (The best thing about Enid is that she expects nothing of me. She satisfies her own expectations. She is a new woman, who never quotes ideology except for "the geography of her pleasure." She is scientific, matriarchal, slightly abrasive, not overly neat, with "sex organs everywhere.")

But Dolores's revelations work like pernicious enzymes in my gut; the thought of Bayside sours my digestion. What the subways need are waiters, a vodka martini (also Alka-Seltzer would do it) and a movie. For God's sake, this ride takes as long as La Guardia to Buffalo, maybe longer. The passengers are ghosts; Michael is considerably more vivid to me, in the act of restraining his mother, than the strangers before my eyes.

Who else expects nothing of me? Michael. Stuck his own knee out to pull Marilyn back, held her with the cap of his own bent knee, kept her at his side.

What is a moment? It passes.

One cannot dispose of the slurs, however. They stay. You cannot take a tweezer to them, as to insulting eyebrows, for they flourish inside. And if I die, who will shave the insult of my life off the face of the earth? No family. No rabbi. No kaddish. Anyone who believes in one substance has got to tough it out, so fuck off, Glassman, you're beginning to sound like Uncle Nathan.

In a time before cremation, the threat of no burial in the community cemetery often brought the excommunicated back to the synagogue to beg forgiveness of the community and repent; yet even then, responses varied. Be-

tween the years 1622 and 1683 thirty-six men were excommunicated, some
for a day, others for four days, a week, three years, some forever; and a hundred ordinances were passed in the Jewish community of Amsterdam gov-
erning excommunication—that dread decree, the merciless *herem*. What
were the transgressions and who the transgressors? Insults against the authority of the *parnassim*. Attempts to establish a dissenting group of ten men
for prayers. And adultery. And secret marriages without consenting parents
or rabbi. A bridegroom who stood on the platform in the center of the synagogue at the side of his bride and at the last instant, as his foot rose to shatter
the wineglass, quietly lowered his foot and refused to marry her. (Anathematized!) A wife-beater, an ox of a man, the wife (no longer young), hidden
under a gray shawl, pointing one arthritic finger: *"Behemah!"* (Anathematized!) And circulating derogatory statements about the Jews of the community. And offenses against the holy Torah, public criticism of traditional
Judaism. (No hereafter! No immortality!) And circumcising a gentile. And
fraudulent burial. (One man, Herbon Italiano, buried a dead infant in Ouderkerk and falsely claimed it was his child. For this ungodly heresy, excommunicated!) *Herem*. Dread word. Jews never spoke the word lightly. From
the Middle Ages excommunication was an important disciplinary measure:
they called it "prison without bars," "iron fetters the eye cannot see." On the
12th of Sivan 5404 (1644), the officers of the Jewish community of Amsterdam passed an ordinance requiring travelers to Spain and Portugal, who
had to pass themselves off as Christians, to beg forgiveness of the whole
Amsterdam community upon their return; they could not be called to the
Torah for three years. In April 1656 (three months before Spinoza's ordeal)
the community punished Abraham Gabay Mendez for not worshiping
with other Jews in a minyan while in London, although Jews had resumed
the right to pray there openly. Mayberg would have called Mendez a "marginal" Jew who never paid his contributions and who made no strict obser-
vance of the *mitzvot*. Because he had plenty of non-Jewish Dutch friends,
excommunication had a trivial effect. Transgressors were commonplace.
Excommunication was a widely accepted form of punishment. The *parnassim* imposed order.

My grandfather and my grandmother went to synagogue. My mother,
however, equivocated—"forgive my restlessness," she said—detouring her
discontented soul through Eastern mysticism, theosophy, and scientism.

Frannie's model was Mama (the high priests of California psychology and human relations sitting in for Madame Blavatsky). Mama, searching and searching, visualizing (I'm embarrassed to contemplate the objects of her visualization), ransacking the literature of Mary Baker Eddy one day and luxuriating in astrology the next, only to begin in desperation again on the third, ransacking the Veda this time, or the early feminist wisdom of Mary Shelley, not knowing why they appealed to her. By contrast, I married conformity—Marilyn's father went to shul, Marilyn's mother lit sabbath candles, everybody used doctors, and impulsive, phobic Marilyn believed she was a Jew until death. And *they* married *me*; they kidded my universalist trust in reason and tried to replace it with a resigned, regular, weekly, and dutiful connection to Judaism—Temple, a challah at the Saturday meal, a rabbi, unfailing notice of *yahrzeit* in the mail, and bar mitzvah—Michael's bar mitzvah recalling my own like chickens coming home to pray. Mayberg is something of a bonus—he gets under my skin—and those murderous fists!—but he is no liar and he believes in God. There is an old Yiddish proverb: A liar is worse than a murderer.

"You're in everybody's hair, Barry Glassman. We want to get rid of you."

Enid's hands grope through my hair; she thrashes on top of me; ten months of my life incommensurable with one kiss, her tongue quickening my need, in tiny places where the arm folds, where the crease of the groin begins as the pubic hair grows sparse; I flower into something extravagant. Spinoza, you could be wrong! Here is faith, hard and individual, the evasion of the universal is necessary, the hardened, headlong individual is everything.

On the 27th of July in 1656, the 6th day of Ab, 5416, in the Hebrew calendar, Baruch Spinoza's impatience for truth met its reward.

The train lunges out of the station with a deafening whistle, high and piercing. Before the Ark, the shofar wails. Black wax candles are lit and held upside down, the spectators of the community caught up in their expectation of a blood-filled vessel, though none was used, for Mr. Spinoza had not blasphemed. Mr. Spinoza was tried for a lesser infraction, a breakdown of reverence for Moses and the law. In June of 1656, Spinoza had been ordered to appear before a court of rabbis. A list of his heresies was recited in Spanish, and Spinoza, in Portuguese, launched an explication of his philosophic position. He was excommunicated for a month. The rabbis expected repentance; but repentance never came.

By the 27th of July word flew in a hush from house to house in the Jewish community of Amsterdam that the *herem* would be pronounced this day against him. The *parnassim* and not the rabbis pronounced the anathema— the businessmen of the town, importers and exporters who had a stake in the Amsterdam municipality. Against you, Baruch Spinoza—. For wrongheadedness. Irreverence. Retrograde and unavengeable insults. For the sin of separation the sufferance of irreversible separation. Unless. Unless, of course, there is repentance, from the springs of the heart before this brethren, this community, this surviving band of relocated Spanish and Portuguese Jews who dealt with one another only as bitterly as they had been dealt with by their oppressors.

Some thought Baruch sought it, and when it came, his position was clear and untrammeled, that he belonged no longer to the God of Israel, but to the universe.

I am not sleeping. I am holding an imaginary mirror to history. For time is unreal. Necessity is eternal. The figure I see is that of Marilyn Glassman; the flame on the black wax candle glitters in her eyes. She speaks Dolores Gutman's curse, a communal, female curse, ritual and sacralizing, a dominating assertion of power:

"The Board of the B'nai Chesed Temple (Sons of Kindness!) on Utopia Parkway in the Borough of Queens hereby declare to all of you that, having long had knowledge of the evil opinions and reproductive inadequacies of Barry Baruch Glassman, they did try to bring him back to the path of righteousness by every means and promise. Unable to set him right and each day reading his *meshuganeh* letters and learning of the new and terrible heresies that he perpetrated and taught and the abominable sperm he put forth, they summoned many trustworthy witnesses (Peres-Pritzker, Gutman, Steinman, Mayberg) who spoke and gave their testimony in the presence of the said Glassman, by which he was convicted. When all this was explained in the presence of the rabbi (Mordecai! *You* again? Once wasn't enough?), it was decided that the said Glassman should be accursed and exiled from the people of Israel, which they do by this *herem*, the *herem* that follows:

"By the sentences of the angels, by the decree of the saints, we anathematize, cut off, curse and execrate Baruch Glassman, philosopher, doctor of optometry, son of the exacting Leah Glassman, father of Michael Glassman, lover of Dr. Enid Moscow, student of Professor Immanuel Winning, international specialist in Spinoza and the Stoics, with the six hundred and thirteen precepts that are written therein, with the anathema wherewith Joshua anathematized Jericho; with the cursing wherewith Elisha cursed the children; and with all the cursings that are written in the book of the law.

"Cursed be he by day and cursed by night; cursed when he lieth down, and cursed when he riseth up; cursed when he goeth out and cursed when he cometh in;

"the Lord pardon him never—

"There shall be no person speak to him, no person write to him, no person show him any kindness, no man or woman stay under the same roof with him, none shall ride the 'F' train with him, nor come within a city block of him, no man do surrogate deeds for him, no woman take him to the New York Public Sperm Bank, or to the New York Public Library, and none shall read anything written by him.

"the Lord pardon him Never—"

None read anything written by him! cursed be the pen and the wielder of the pen! I left the subway car in a burning house, a knife in my back, the heart plucked out of my belly, the engine of my downfall rolling deeper into Brooklyn.

A week after this event I am told by Michael that Rabbi Mayberg's contract has not been renewed. As I write my sorrow to him, the curse of the anathema—like a cloud lined with radioactive carbons—has drifted directly over Mayberg's head.

CHAPTER *19*

Dear *Mordecai,*

While it's true I didn't show up at the congregational war dance to speak up for you as I've done in the past, I'm stricken by the outcome and regret the loss of your beloved presence in my life. Believe me, I didn't have the strength to attend. In the end, you have been anathematized, not I, though let me tell you about a strange experience I had.

I was in the subway. I fell asleep. We have both heard the wrath of the Bayside community, haven't we? Well, they bellowed the excommunication against me. Later I recalled the account of Uriel D'Acosta, twice anathematized, twice repentant: "I had to strip and was lashed thirty-nine times with leather thongs. Spectators sang a psalm during my whipping. Then I was absolved from my excommunication, dressed at the door of the synagogue, and prostrated myself while the doorkeeper held up my head. All, both old and young, passed over me, stepping with one foot on the lower part of my legs, and behaving with ridiculous and foolish gestures, more like monkeys than human creatures." Some critics claim this account to be an anti-Semitic forgery, but they were crackpots. As everyone knows, in 1640 D'Acosta was a suicide.

Do I need to point out that our fellow congregants, mine as well as yours, have stepped on us for the last time, rabbi?

As with Spinoza, excommunication has set me free. I write, then, as a free man to forgive your slugging me outside of the coffee shop. It was unprecedented in the history of rabbi-congregant relations. It happened. So let's forget it. But since you are banished from Bayside and not I, there's an ironic justice at work here. You've got to admit we both went about our inner life with a vision of high seriousness, while at the same time glasses slipped down our noses; in the outer life we squinted, sleepwalked. It's possible that while I was squinting through my marriage, you were sleepwalking through the Temple.

We can't help but know. Believe me when I tell you that that is not our limitation but our power. I am often wracked by doubts, rabbi, but I am just as sure we can't help but know more today than we knew last week. Still, I urge you to remember that adequate knowledge of personal events is hopeless if we consider them isolated from all of nature, to which they belong. To Pascal, every whole is a part of a more comprehensive whole. I'm confident, given our previous discussions, that you and I will keep our poignant Bayside histories in perspective.

My love to you and Dvora for the years ahead. Let me keep in touch.

Barry Glassman

And to Dolores, three sentences:

Dear Dolores:

I am heartsick that the rabbi's contract has not been renewed. As a gardener, I fully understand the Talmudic saying "Immorality in the house is like a worm on vegetables." If I can be of help to you or to the rabbi's family, please let me know how.

Barry Glassman

CHAPTER **20**

"But I'm *not* perfect," Uncle Nathan says when I tell him that our confusion is part of our perfection. "The ride out here is reasonable. You're trying to make a point. The Long Island Railroad is not far, the LIE is not far, I can smell the ocean, but it's not for me, Barry." He speaks respectfully, a porpoise trapped in a wheelchair. "I'll get Anya to do it, I'll pay her. Maybe Enid Moscow will help. I know you're a softie, Barry. It's okay, Barra-le. Don't give it another thought."

With Uncle Nathan waiting, I stand at the flat rubbly grave site next to my father's neatly mounded grave, not believing that it exists until I pull up a few weeds and place a pebble on my father's headstone. The pebble is for her, too, I think, with only the memory of her stubborn chin and elevated eyes and not a flake of ash in sight. Then I roll Nathan's chair back to the car, treat him to fish and chips at a drive-in fish house near Bayshore, and begin the drive back to Brooklyn.

I've been trying to occupy my time. So I see Nathan one Sunday, and on the next, Michael, who, following Frannie's advice to lie low during a storm, surfaces long enough to let me take him to dinner and a movie; but he is distracted. At first he says the rabbi's departure has saddened him. Having lost his contract, Mayberg packed, hired a mover, swept the congregation's house broom clean, and immediately after the 7:30 A.M. minyan on a Thursday morning, got into his loaded car with Dvora and set out for Cleveland, where they came from. It bothers Michael that Mayberg left like a thief, when he was a good guy, too good for the idiots in Bayside! But something else is tormenting Michael. School? No. Deirdre? Uh, no, she's okay. Just before the movie begins he blurts it out: Marilyn and Donahue have split. Did I know? No, I did not. Well, knowing, what did I think?

"Michael, I don't know what to think."

"I thought thinking was your specialty."

"There are many issues, Michael. The bottom line is the necessity to follow your own nature. Your mother has a way of forcing me against my nature. That's compulsion, not necessity."

"So let's see the movie," Michael says forlornly as the house darkens and music throbs like blood pressure in the background. A funny offbeat flick set in New Orleans about an Italian immigrant who lands in jail with two Southern ne'er-do-wells. We sit through it, laughing, munching popcorn from the same container; otherwise, miles apart. Michael is growing up, however; after the movie, as I coast up to the house on Fifty-first Avenue, he sits awhile, greatly composed, trying to bring me to a reconsideration.

"Mom's changed," he says, "since New Haven."

But I do not ask in what way.

"I'll tell you in what way," he says. "She's willing to sit back and let things happen. Passive, you might say."

Marilyn passive? I say nothing.

"And Dad?"

"Yes?"

"Donahue really wasn't such a schmuck." Michael is looking straight at me. "He cried for his friends who died in the crash. He couldn't stop crying. He was upset for weeks."

"Am I supposed to be impressed?" The free man doesn't dwell on death.

"You're supposed to be fair."

"Michael, what's *fair*, for Chrissake? *Fair* is never more than fragmentary. Human beings don't know enough to be *fair*."

"Dad, you're making me crazy. Just answer the question, okay? *Okay?* Are you ever coming home?"

My unbudging heart cannot deal with his yearning. He is trying his damnedest. "Michael, sweetheart. I wish I could say what you want to hear."

His fingers are pushing the doorlock up and down. "You sure don't say much!"

I allow a long silence. "Did you have a garden this year?" I ask finally.

He puts his lips between his two hands and blows in disgust.

"I miss the garden," I say.

But he rallies. "You prefer living in the pits in Brooklyn to being with us!" It's a statement, requiring no reply.

A pause.

"How is Deirdre?"

"Good," he says through his teeth. Then, reluctantly, "She's thinking of converting."

I almost believe he's making it up.

"I told her without Rabbi Mayberg here, she'd better wait. You never know what kind of an asshole may turn up in Bayside next."

"What do her parents think?"

"How should I know?"

"Doesn't she tell you?"

"She's not living with them anymore."

"Since when?"

"Since she went back up to the Zapolskis. She's going to school there. She sort of helps with the kids after school."

"My God!"

"What's so terrible? She wants to be Jewish."

"Well it's a shock." I try to imagine Ed Hoddeson coping.

"It's like living together before you get married. She's trying it out," Michael says.

"Were you as taken with the Zapolskis as Deirdre?"

"Don't get me wrong. They're the best. But I miss Rabbi Mayberg. He's more practical."

"Listen, I'll drive you up there next weekend. Maybe you can talk her out of it."

"Come home for Yom Kippur, Dad. Try it out."

When a light shimmers across the street, I see Ed Hoddeson's face at his bedroom window, peering into the suburban night like a Klansman. Is that the butt of a rifle projecting from the window or one of Ed's cleverly angled rain gutters? "Better go now, Mike," I say, sorrowing for Hoddeson, not daring to look again at the house that a Jewish fate has struck. I kiss Michael on the cheek and crush him to my chest. Then I open the door and push him out.

Frannie marries a total stranger named Cyril Magill, after a quickie divorce from the recuperating Alan, on the beach at Santa Barbara, in the middle of a dazzling September, shortly before Rosh Hashanah. I fly out for a week to attend the wedding. The beach club is sumptuous; the marriage takes place in a Mediterranean villa, blue and green mosaics bordering a gorgeous round pool; green islands are visible across the channel. Before the ceremony, I have an urge to call Enid, but I keep getting a busy signal, and the ceremony is about to begin. Fran has written an emotional service asking those present to visualize the chambers of the heart as they do their work, though I confess I miss the connection she makes to a new steadfastness. Hearts, farts. To me the successive marriages are more like footballs hurled back and forth in defensive play. The suave Canadian Magill, owner of a chain of sporting goods stores, sprained his ankle on the golf course, and Frannie insists he sit through the ceremony. From the waist up, and with his pince-nez glasses and cigarette holder, Magill looks a lot like FDR marrying my sister Frannie. The girls seem fairly sedate, Karen in a long pink cotton sundress, and Larisa gorgeously Polynesian in a tunic and pants of orange silk and gardenias in her hair—but bored. They have been through this before. The air is as fine as the champagne; the palms are swaying. Behind the cigarette holder, Magill is broad and garrulous and wears a western-style belt with a silver Navajo buckle. I hardly know the man, but he seems solid, like a good sleek horse. Frannie—bride, hostess, and Esalen lecturer all rolled into one—stands alone after the ceremony at the shoreline, her skin and dress the same pale ivory, water glistening against her bare feet in the morning sun, hugging each guest as reverently as if they had just emerged together from a long spiritual retreat. The groom cheerfully hobbles back and forth to the bar, insisting to the circle of people surrounding him that he plans to keep a golf date tomorrow. She says repeatedly, "Barry, I have to tell you about Cyril—" and though I believe she means it, she hasn't a minute. I leave on standby on Sunday, a day earlier than I had scheduled. My face, which always burned more easily than Frannie's, has had too much sun.

I swept in from California half asleep on the tail end of a storm and never noticed the taxi parked outside or the branches of trees down on the sidewalk. Were they there when I left? Ever since Bernard's return from Toronto, I have been avoiding him, and now after the flight I am too played out to take up with Bernard's eloquence. There is a message for me from Bernard on a large sheet of notebook paper, the handwriting huge and erratic. He has evidently climbed upstairs or sent someone up to slip it under my door. He says he must ask for my help with the house. He has engaged an agent to rent the downstairs, since he is entering the New York–Cornell Home for the Blind on Tuesday. On the back of the paper he has scrawled: "These shadows will pass. You have my gratitude. With great affection, Bernard."

I try to nap for half an hour, but Bernard's decision fills me with shame. I toss and turn and finally go down. The door is opened by a sandy-haired young fellow in aviator sunglasses and a sweatshirt, flashing a smile in my direction.

"Bernard!" he yells inside. "Is someone at door for you."

Behind him exists a state of disorder, curtains down, living-room rug rolled. Cartons, sealed and unsealed, some full of dishes and pots, line the entry hall. Two valises, half-filled, are flopped open on the floor. Shoes, pants, shirts, some still on hangers, lie across them. Bernard appears, and the young man steps through the maze of suitcases, grips Bernard under the arm, and steers him to the door.

Bernard stumbles along unhappily. "Enid?" he says, extending both hands.

"How you say your name is?" the fellow asks. He sounds a lot like Anya.

"Bernard—" I interrupt, "I got your note. I see you've really made up your mind—"

"Barry! I was expecting Enid. The phones have been dead since the storm. Grigory here said Enid was coming." He forcibly extricates himself from Grigory's iron grip, shuddering. "If she doesn't, I swear he will kill me. He has no sense of how to clear the way for me. He's an imbecile!"

Grigory is patient. "I am nephew to Anya." He sticks out a hand.

"That your cab out front?"

He nods. "I promise to make packing for Bernard, but here is like packing a museum. Now I have to go. You know, from Russia I come with whole life in one suitcase." It is a serious reflection. "We almost finish. Tuesday I come back and drive him to hospital."

"It's not a hospital, Grigory. I *told* you the difference."

Grigory's intelligent eyes flash at me. He pulls on a jacket and pauses at the door. "Enid is coming soon. You will stay?" Bernard is bending down for the nearest boxes and shoves them full force against the wall, clearing his own path.

"Go out and drive your cab," Bernard yells at Grigory, "and don't come back!"

"He is strong man," Grigory whispers to me. Then at one temple he describes a circle with his forefinger and rolls his eyes. "We finish on Tuesday." And he is gone. I hear the taxi sputter off.

Bernard is almost reduced to tears. "Ghastly Grigory," he mutters, as I lead him to his chair. Greatly dejected he sinks his head back. "It would be superfluous for me to admit that I am terrified," he says. "Barry, you mustn't say a word of this brouhaha to Enid. She hired Grigory with the best of intentions to help me, but a more insensitive imbecile I never want to meet. How do the boxes look to you? Are they full? Are any of them taped? Have I cleared a path for myself? I want them all to be stored in the back hall and in my mother's closet. The agent will have to come to an agreement with the tenant. I refuse to rush into getting rid of everything."

Bernard throws forward a hand and I take it. He grips my fingers tightly. "It's the best home in the city. My cousin Arthur in Toronto made the connections for me, but this opening came up unexpectedly. If we let this one go, another spot might not open for a year. The truth is I was ready, until Grigory told me about his blind Russian grandfather who took the wrong medication in a Leningrad institution. In five minutes he went into convulsions and died on the spot. Barry, do you want the downstairs apartment?" The question is abrupt. "I want you to have first crack at it."

My eyes roam over the meanness and clutter of the apartment. If I were to move, I would move to a place where mind and body had the convenience of harmony—a leafy space, a garden. "Thanks," I say, "but no thanks. I'll just stay in the attic. It suits my need for aloofness."

He pats my hand and smiles. "I can't tell you how unused I am to strangers."

"He's still young—"

"Too young to be separated from his mother. God, what our mothers do to us—" He drops my hand. "But I'm tough. I'll take their rehab and mobility program and maybe then I can come home again. Or maybe I'll meet a woman. Or write a book. Or love being pampered . . ."

"I wish I could persuade you not to—"

"No dice."

"No—I meant I wish I could persuade you not to give up your interests."

He looks disappointed. "No one ever treated me like dirt," he says proudly, "and they're not about to. Some people don't know I am blind. I'll be all right."

I set about sealing up a few more of his boxes, stacking them in the back hall. I fill a few more, find a pile of books and letters (they are his father's), and neatly pack them in a small carton, seal it, and load it with the rest. Into another I layer his mother's nightgowns, all of them reduced to a loathsome grayish pink. I do not enjoy handling them. Bernard sits motionless, dreaming the dreams of the blind, his eyes wide open.

Just as I am about to move a heavy box of linens, Enid clatters through the front door. Does not ring since she has the key in her hand. Stands there, bag and baggage, the ubiquitous Grigory alongside, carrying in a tall plant that he bends to place in the middle of the cleared floor.

"Not there!" I quickly say, picking up Bernard's tone. "In the corner out of the way. You want him to kill himself?"

Bernard sits bolt upright. "Is he back? Get him out of here. I don't want him in my house!"

Enid rushes to Bernard's chair and embraces him. "He's doing the best he can," she says sternly. "Be patient. He's not a fool. He has a degree in botany. Anyway, I have a surprise for you!"

Bernard takes her face in his hands. They lapse into a reverential moment, the two of them, their cheeks glowing, their fingers zealously groping each other's temples in reassurance. The scene is epic in its silence, and I hang back as Grigory carries in a few more tote bags containing Enid's books and papers. He examines the plant, pinches off a few drying stems; then he leaves.

"I'm moving in." Enid's voice is a whisper. "I have enough with me for several weeks, Bernard. I don't want you to feel roped into anything. You'll have time to think through your decision. If you'll let me stay, I can teach you. It's only a matter of learning *how* to be blind. You *can* learn! And I'll see that you do! There's plenty of room here. And Bernard?"

But Bernard is sunk in exhaustion. The late afternoon light from the living-room alcove is lost on him, though he vaguely gestures at his lids as if his eyes are hurting and he is shielding them from light. He stares autocratically off, his features set in a feverish intelligence, unapproachable, and unmanageable.

"Barry—" he says suddenly.

I am beginning to sweat, and I step in closer to them, smelling Enid's sweet-scentedness, adjusting to the extravagance of her generosity, and at the same time exasperated by her habitual amateurishness. She is lovelier than I have ever seen her, but still gauche, still unaware of my peculiar presence between them.

What do Enid and Bernard expect?

"Barry," he repeats.

"Yes, Bernard?"

"Help me." He turns, and in the way he has, looks just past me into nothingness. "Tell her that it's no use. Tell her I've made up my mind."

"It's his relatives," she says. "They've convinced him to do this. Not one of them offered to—"

"Not so! Arthur invited me to live with him," Bernard says, "but I'd rather live at the bottom of Sheepshead Bay." He laughs. "Arthur is a prick!"

"Barry, tell him I mean to stay. Tell him I mean to see him through this—"

And again, each one in turn implores me to tell the other, to plead with the other. Barry, I am counting on your intelligence, I am seeking your intervention, set his (her) thinking straight, Barry, please, tell her (him). Please.

And what is my position? I have many personal answers crowding my tongue, but I withhold them as some durable memory of disaster forces me to slow down and bow out of these particulars as gracefully as I can. Men and women are profitable to one another, they serve one another in their search for true knowledge. They are part of the eternal and will find they are commensurate with the power they seek to understand. But where will Enid's decision leave me? I beg her with an unspoken gesture to step outside and talk to me. But she has something more important to say.

"I want you to take your essay back. I don't want to lose it in all this chaos. It's almost October. Deadlines have a way of coming round." She puts on her glasses, reaches into one of the tote bags and rescues my manuscript from a bag full of papers. Most of the pages have been retyped on paper bearing the Grumman logo across the bottom.

She has not had time to work on it, she says, during the week I was in California. She hands it over.

"But Enid, time is very short. Why don't you—"

"Because I haven't the time to give it, Barry. I can't seem to work late at night any more. The conclusions on the gases don't work—they don't jibe with the refraction figures. I can't put my name to it, Barry, not in this condition." She is thrusting the papers into my hands.

Bernard, meanwhile, has tactfully felt his way into the bathroom. A common impulse drives Enid and me to look away from each other, as if eyes that do not see pain will bear it more resolutely. "The work is murky," she says, looking away. "I had someone else read it." She shakes her head.

I wish fervently that she not show any sign of affection to me, but she does, her two hands reaching for my face in a gesture I have come to despise as pity, her lips forming the words, "I'm sorry," my hands struggling with her fingers.

"What's this all about? Enid, what in hell's going on?" I ask softly, lowering her hands forcefully.

"You and I have a lot going between us," Enid says. "Old family ties, optics that may or may not work out. I don't regret any of it."

The manuscript in my hand might be papyrus, a dead paper from another civilization. "Regret it?" I say. "You mean it's over?" The possibility drains the blood out of my knees.

"Well, we *could* continue—"

"You're about to move in with this guy—!"

"You're both exceptional men."

"How long do you plan—"

"To stay? My life is not simply you and Bernard! I'm not giving up my apartment. I'm not quitting my job." Again she extends her fingers to my cheek. I lift them away. "Cheer *up*," she says. "Don't oversimplify. Think about it."

"And the rainbows?"

"Your work in the observations section is good, but the conclusions are too fussy. Maybe you can get somebody else . . . somebody in ophthalmology or another physicist."

"With four weeks to go?" ·

"You can revolutionize physics in four weeks!"

She is being catty. I fling the essay across the room and the pages fall all over the open cartons and valises. She stoops to the floor and methodically collects them, takes a stapler from one of her tote bags and bangs a staple into the corner. She drops the essay on my knees. "Don't *do* that again," she says. "It's not worthless. It just needs work."

"What will you do if Bernard says no?"

"He won't," she says, reaching into her suitcase and pulling out my father's blue and gold plaid scarf, looping the ends, then pressing it into my hands. But the present is everything, her stapler, her magnanimity, her unpredictable eyes. It is impossible to remember winter days in the Bronx.

As Bernard makes his way back in among us, she is already unpacking her bag. "I'll hang my things in your mother's room," she says quietly.

Bernard reseats himself. Here beyond a doubt is a decision that shows how active the mind is, that it is not a blank tablet as Locke and Bacon would have it, but an activity that initiates ideas. Existence is not a property of God, it *is* God. Bernard and Enid have allowed the dispute to slip away. I have heard it said that the human body is up to its neck in experience.

CHAPTER **21**

I take advantage of Rosh Hashanah to pull myself to-
gether, for the Sunday/Monday holiday will not be put aside. It still disso-
ciates itself from the rest of the week, and I take the opportunity early Sunday evening to be Mr. Nice Guy and descend with a bottle of Manischewitz
wine.

"A toast for the Jewish new year?" I suggest as Enid lets me in.

"All *right*," she says, calling, "Ber*nard*, Barry is here to wish us a happy
new year."

Bernard makes his way into the living room. I hear water sloshing in the
background. "Ah! We have been reduced to doing laundry on Rosh Hashanah," he says. "But I see you still distinguish the holidays."

"Something in me loves the holidays," I say.

"Something in *me* loves the wine," Enid says, producing a tray with
glasses.

We raise our glasses. Enid and I reach across to clink Bernard's glass, then
each other's. We drink, but he scarcely sips, muttering something about sug-
aring the grape and gilding the lily. (Is he such a connoisseur that kosher
wine is intolerable to him?)

Enid and I enjoy ours, pour a second, a third. The apartment has a fresh-
ened air about it, furniture in the same old places, cartons flanking the walls
or out of sight, though Enid's books are piled on the end tables and her in-

door/outdoor thermometer is hooked up in the far window. The sofa has her bright red Guatemalan blanket and a pillow thrown across one end. Her sweater hangs crookedly on the back of a chair. (Has she moved into the mother's bedroom or Bernard's, or does she sleep here?) Cooking smells come from the kitchen, and a piano plays quietly on the stereo. Enid's huge plant, spikier than ever, stands out of the way near the window. Grigory, she says, has been treating it like a baby.

Bernard's head tips back against the top of his green easy chair, one hand clutching the arm rest, the other holding his barely touched glass of wine. His eyes are shut. Enid, twirling the stem of her wineglass, is on the couch. I am in the chair on which her sweater hangs, opposite the TV, but it is an upright, uncomfortable chair, and soon the hardness of the seat has sent a radiating pain into my left knee. Bernard begins to reminisce. He is talking about selling the winter line of blouses with his father in the heat of August and then setting aside the Jewish holidays for an outing with mother and father to Jones Beach. They passed the lovely September days loafing, picnicking, hopeful parents taking along the blind daughter of a neighbor's friend. But she was silly and dull. He is vexed as he speaks, the memory of the girl still bitter; soon he is in a time so distant and real that blindness doesn't exist. "I was about eight and my bedroom was filled with light. It was the morning of Rosh Hashanah, no school, the smells of holiday cooking in the kitchen. My neck was strange, I couldn't move it, and my favorite toy milk truck was stuck at my side. I had built it out of an erector set. It had smooth wooden bottles that I loved to roll between my fingers, but I could no longer remove and replace them. I remember that I dumped the wooden bottles under the blanket and they were hurting me, pressing into my flesh, until my mother made a clean sweep of everything with her arm, gruffly, brushing my leg; then she shrieked for my father. 'He's burning up!' she said. The doctor came and the stiffness became excruciating and that funny word was repeated and repeated: *meningitis*. A taxi took me to the hospital; white walls, white nuns, sheets and coverlet white as geese, my mother's sad smiles, my father's tears, pain, fever, gray, shadowy nuns like gray snow; the optic nerve infected, someone said; rarely affects both eyes, someone said; but after a curtain shut down the right, the left began to gray, barely admitting shadow and light. The doctors were frantic. In a week I was sightless, and my knees and joints swollen in pain, and my ears swollen shut, though the deafness was intermittent, and now I would not sleep, didn't sleep for days, leaning with exhaustion against the pillows, a mere boy willing his remaining senses to survive. I was eight. And totally blind. But I could hear, so I knew I wasn't dead, and I could make decisions. 'I am not dead.'" He tells us he screamed it out loud for hours.

When he pauses, Enid slides into his chair to comfort him. But Bernard is serene, his face as rosy as a peony. My knee is moving in a museum of pain. I kick out my leg, and when Bernard has finished I must stand and walk a bit.

"What is it?" Enid asks.

My back aches. I walk unhappily and flex my knee. Bernard's history has merged with my own.

"What is it?" Bernard repeats.

"The old kink-in-the-knee problem," I reply, "and a new lower backache to keep it company."

Bernard says, "I know just the thing. But you have to be willing—"

He whispers something into Enid's ear, and she nods. "Bernard is an excellent masseur," she says quietly.

"Please," Bernard says, as Enid stands, allowing him to rise out of the chair. "Come into the bedroom and I will massage your back and leg. I have a high rate of success. Only you have to want it, of course."

Enid runs into the kitchen. Bernard stands in place. It is up to me.

I am expecting Michael to call to wish me a happy new year. And Frannie's annual custom is to do the same. A massage? I would miss my calls, I think hurriedly, I must go upstairs, and why did Bernard offer this? Oh, the touch of him, I think, finally allowing the thought its due, the touch of him, could I bear it? *Should* I bear it? A perversion. The amazing river of pleasure branching into sinister regions. Pain shakes the muscle of my thigh. I catch my breath and my muscle convulses, but briefly. He has a high success rate, he says, and I'll bet he does.

Why not? I shift my weight with great care. What have I got to lose?

Bernard's bedroom has no sign of Enid; a fast peek into the mother's bedroom shows twisted sheets, a notebook flung open across the pillow, Enid's pocketbook, a pink robe hanging from the foot of the bed. But I also spot his white stick, leaning against the nightstand like a wand.

I lie on my stomach in shorts and T-shirt across his carelessly blanketed bed, face down. Bernard bends over me. A bottle of witch hazel is on his chest of drawers. He finds it, unscrews the top, wets his hands, and returns. His touch is icy, the chill trailing up and down my leg and torso as he begins to pat my flesh, working up and down, stopping to oil my spine and the flesh in the lower back, kneading it, rubbing the knee, inside, outside, along the hairy lower thigh; he raises the leg to massage and massage the kneecap itself. His hands are deft, his hands are delicate; he cuffs the thigh with a stiffened palm, reciting cheerily, "Happy new year, happy new year," with each stroke, the fingers rubbing down the length of the leg, the calf, the ankle, and finally the feet and toes, bending them securely in his whole hand, rousing them to new sensations. I am tingling with pain. "Happy new year, happy new year, next year who knows where?" he sings under his breath as his hands swoop under my T-shirt, stroking into the basin of the small of the back and down to the buttocks. "Barry, relax," he says, "loosen up."

Enid peers in. "Relax," she calls out. "The whole thing is a charade unless you relax."

As I hear her voice, my ass stiffens, but I try, I *try* to relax, damn it, stretching fingertips, fingers, letting hands go limp, arms, thighs, each cheek of my buttocks. "Breathe in." "Exhale." "In." "Exhale." Messenger instructs; and waits until I comply. The exhaling and inhaling exercise my intestines. My bowel tells me intestines and existence are one. I exist. The bastard has done it, legs and ass aching, but alive.

I stand up, pull on my trousers and shirt. "Where'd you learn all that?" I ask Bernard mournfully.

"You may be sore for a couple of days," he says.

But already I feel the difference. I understand that he has a knowledge of anatomy. He has "adequate ideas of the properties of things," which is *knowledge*.

"Happy new year," Bernard says, smiling, waiting for my response.

"Yes," I say, but I am defeated beyond words by the power of the man's knowledge converted into such physical cunning, such action that I am unable to say back what is expected of me, to him, or to Enid, who looks a little wan, the triumph of his physical strength implying that true equality between *them* may not exist after all.

He is too strong for her.

I don't leave immediately, though I desire to, for I fear the cowardice of such a departure would run counter to the intent of my visit:

to wish them well with a bottle of wine

to test the air between them

to see Enid and tell her *perhaps*

to draw her out a bit further on the essay (isn't there a chance?)

to estimate how long their dubious arrangement might go on.

I accomplish only the first of these purposes. But my body is muscular again and cool, as if I have had a good swim or a long hot bath.

Only Uncle Nathan calls to say happy new year, and at the same time that someone—the guy wouldn't leave his name—wants to get in touch with Enid. "Where *is* Enid?" Nathan inquires. "I've been trying and trying her number. What do I do?"

Anya takes over the phone to say, "Man is wanting to talk to her. I ask, 'You are friend? relative?' 'Relative,' he say. 'Maybe relative.'"

I supply Nathan with Messenger's number and explain Enid's arrangement.

"Ho, ho!" he says effusively. "Good for him! You know how I admire that blind man."

"I *know*."

"Listen, Barry, don't hang up. I'm an old man. You got to do me a favor," Nathan says before I can say good-bye. "I'd like to get my $15,000 back from the Cremation Society. You think it's too late? And please, find out whether Messenger wants to be cremated. I gotta know." Then he hangs up. I phone downstairs to tell Enid to expect a call.

A week later Enid phones in a frenzy. "Barry," she says, "I'm back in my apartment. I want you to pick up your article and bring it over."

"Is Bernard alone?"

"Don't worry. I've made excellent arrangements. Can you come?"

"Who called you? Was it Detective Burke?"

"Detective Burke?" She is incredulous. "I want you to meet someone."

I expect on the other side of the door, a tall, skinny, bearded, hippylike phantom of the sixties, maybe homeless, lugging a cardboard suitcase or pushing a shopping cart. When the door opens, Enid is smiling and next to her is a short, bald man in an open-collared white sport shirt, tufts of graying hair sprouting from the ears and at his chest. He wears wire-rimmed glasses and has vivid, wide-set blue eyes. He extends his hand.

"Barry, this is Lutz Moscow, my once and future husband."

I put out my hand. For a short man, he has a large, comfortable hand-shake. King Arthur he is not, I think as he says "How do you do," his accent slightly European or Israeli, hard to tell which. The two are in excellent spirits.

"Come on *in*," Enid says. *In* of course means her disorganized version of home. Many of the essentials are still in Messenger's apartment.

But the true essentials are here, husband and wife, two talented physicists, chatting confidently over cups of tea. "Lutz says he can help you with your calculations. He's been brooding about them."

"I've been in New York teaching for several months." A foolish smile appears on his face. "I behaved badly when we were married, but that's a long time ago. There has never been anyone else."

He has a very candid way of looking at me, but I do not speak to him. "Enid," I say. "My God, what next?"

She tosses her stiff hair about with a whoop of laughter. "I must seem totally cuckoo," she says, leaning across to me. "We want to have a baby." She turns, and Lutz pulls her to him with a huge tender kiss.

I do some rapid trips back and forth over our lovemaking during the last couple of months. Is she pregnant now? Could a baby be mine? Glassman! No contraceptives and no kids in thirteen years! And what about Messenger?

Brilliant cousin Enid, you could be in big trouble.

But she is coasting like a beautiful cruiser being pulled into safe harbor by three tugs.

"Lutz understands the whole situation. I know what's on your mind, Barry. This is not going to be a teenage pregnancy. I know what I'm doing!"

Lutz Moscow quietly sips his tea, glancing into my eyes with amusement. I like him.

"I know how you feel," he says. "She's a tiger to keep up with."

For the record, I want to ask her about screwing Bernard, but decency keeps me from firing off that cannonball. Moscow is a reasonable chap! He picks up the article on the rainbow, which has been lying on the kitchen table. "How much time do we have?" he asks.

"Until October thirty-first," I say.

"If I can do what I think has to be done, I will be delighted to share the authorship with you."

"Glassman and Moscow?"

"Glassman, Moscow, and Moscow. We both have to sign it with you," he is apologetic, a trace of irony in the repeated name, "because the outcomes, as I understand it, were a collaboration, and they need to be recalculated. Besides, it is an auspicious collaboration. No promises, Glassman," he says, seriously now, professionally. "I have three days to devote to it. But if you're still willing—"

"Don't be a fool, Barry," Enid says. "Let him. He's on the faculty of the Technion—. He's *good* at what he does."

I am undecided. Haven't I had enough of Enid Moscow? Must I take on Lutz Moscow as well? They are a formidable pair. I've ended up a loser before with smart-aleck professors.

"Barry! We leave for Israel in two weeks. It's now or never."

"For good?"

"To size things up. I'm not at all sure I want to risk living there. Anyway, I'm hungry! Let's get some food."

I have little to say.

"We'll try it for six months. Then we'll decide."

"And you've given Grumman notice?"

"Lutz thinks I'll be able to find something at the Technion."

Enid calls a Chinese take-out place and begins to order dinner. "None for me," I say. "I've got to be going."

Lutz raises the essay in his hand. "You've been very kind to Enid—"

"Think of it as a three-way ticket on the lottery," Enid says. "You know, three street cleaners with a million dollar ticket."

"So, all right." I extend my hand. "If you need me, try me at the store during the day or in Brooklyn at night."

Shakes my hand. "I'll do my best." Walks to the bedroom to put the article with his possessions.

Alone at the door, Enid and I fall quiet. "Aren't you going to ask about Bernard?" she says finally.

"I thought it might be a delicate issue."

She nods. "Most delicate," she says, "but Bernard is willing to make one last attempt."

"He knows?"

Her nod confirms that I am the last to know.

"Anya's nephew is moving in with Bernard. He's really a decent fellow. Bernard is much more confident. I worked on him like an Olympic coach, but I'm not the best organizer. I think he'll get the hang of it. Frankly," she whispers to me, "if I don't become pregnant—at my age you never know—I'll come back to all of you. I feel *safe* here. Do you know what I mean?"

"And Lutz?"

"Lutz, remember, is not an American. He seems to do well in Israel. He has something to love and to criticize—like a true Israeli. And he hasn't exactly been sitting on his hands." She giggles. "He's sure he's fertile."

If ever a man sensed another's fertility, I sensed Lutz Moscow's.

"Anyway," her eyes turn sharply to mine, "I'm not going to marry him before I conceive."

This information strikes my heart like a trophy—an absurd keepsake that ought to bring a divinely blissful satisfaction, but now merely worsens the receiver's responsibility. I feel mine both worsened and quickened by her admission.

"Besides, he's brilliant. His mind is like a light bulb. So, I'm going to put my life on hold for a while and go. Oh, Barry, can you blame me?" She puts her arms around me and holds me.

"I wish you luck," I say feebly, "Cousin Enid. There always was an eccentric strain in the family." Already, I can feel the softness of her future like a snowstorm in my eyes. Who can make plans on a howling night?

"One favor?" she asks, pulling back.

But she has taken my breath away. My tongue weeps. I nod.

"Can I give your name to Detective Burke as a next of kin? You know. Just in case."

I nod again.

"One more favor. In case Grigory doesn't work out—" she breaks off.

"Yes?"

"But you'll know what to do. Lutz is adorable, isn't he?"

CHAPTER 22

And now I face the loss of Enid, in whose womb somebody's child is about to float; I drive the knowing unflappable blue-eyed Israeli Professor Lutz Moscow and the rumply sexy gritty take-charge take-a-chance Brooklyn intellectual Enid Moscow to JFK for their flight to Israel, he in a khaki safari suit, she in jeans and her old tweed jacket, bullying him to move a little faster, looking like a hundred other travelers, each shoulder loaded down with a blue nylon duffel bag stuffed to bulging. They are as nervous as two goats, blaming the elaborate security check at El Al and the long lead time required before an El Al flight. As part of the security measures, I have to say good-bye at the detection gate.

"We're family," Lutz says. "Come to Haifa!"

Enid purses her mouth in a distant kiss, glancing ahead of her, already anticipating the next lap, perspiring, chattering about her landlord, Grumman, the revised essay that Lutz has just handed me, semi-attentive, unable to get close to me because of the huge bags hanging from her shoulders. "Here I am talking your ear off," she says, breaking into her monologue. "Good luck," she adds benignly, "with, well, you know—life, philosophy, the essay, *all* of it." But she shifts the weight of one bag fiercely onto her back and slips in close to me, embracing me in a not so cousinly farewell; I can feel her lips brushing my ear. "Barry, shut the books and come to Haifa. *Do* something. It's tough to be a philosopher," and she is already on her way, turning one more time, "Good-bye to Bernard!" waving! waving! and they are loading their carry-on bags onto the X-ray conveyor and walking through the metal detectors one behind the other and into the teeth of Israeli security.

I was not much older than Michael when I understood what it cost to live with an exceptional woman like Enid. My mother's exuberance struck me around then as an all-out effort to belong to no one but herself, to snap the cords that tied her to her parents' generation and to all the generations before. That is not to say that Frannie and I were always taken in by her schemes—truths of every fragrance, and the ever-shifting expectations she had for us. God knows she was fun, but we were forever vigilant for signs that a new game with unlearnable rules had already begun. Her excitement came through in the emphatic way she lectured us and in the distracted way she threw dinner together—forgetting to bread the veal chops, no knives on the table, dropping slices of meat loaf, raw in the center, burnt at the edges, onto our grapefruit plates (how we gobbled it! it was the only fare we knew), and at the same time drilling us that this week at school we must focus on forgiving our enemies, that the exemplary Buddhist child wears rags but is the friend of all. We were very confused. We trudged off as young Buddhists to school and then at three o'clock, switching religions in the late Bronx afternoon, to Hebrew school (for Hebrew school meant learning and supporting the Jewish state, and she was reckless for learning and a passionate Zionist), telling no one there what our own Jewish mother dared purge us of. Her efforts to understand the infinite were on her own grand scale. Spinoza says: "Only those who have broken away from the maxims of their childhood can attain to the knowledge of truth, for one must make extraordinary efforts in order to overcome the impressions of custom and in order to efface the false ideas with which the minds of men are filled before they are able to judge about things for themselves." Still, she couldn't *quite* sever the ties. Diligence notwithstanding, she remained in her straying and dissatisfied heart a Jewish lady from the Bronx.

Judge for yourself, Barry. Espouse no party. The two commonest human faults are indolence and presumption. My mother had neither.

Of course, she had other faults (as Enid has), but that is Glassman history:

the virtues, the vices, the freethinker herself and all the outrageous conse-
quences, vanished. Since my mother left no instructions about what to do
with her ashes (the truth was she was terrified of dying, but stonewalled to
the end), I secretly drove out to the cemetery one winter afternoon, the blue
New York sky already casting hard shadows.

I was alone among the graves. Our family plot was well in from the road
in a secluded section marked by tall stone monuments. I held the urn of
ashes in a plastic bag and with frozen hands reached in for fistfuls of my
mother's ashes. For lack of anything more appropriate, I kept mumbling
the kaddish and scattered them over the space next to my father's grave with
a broad sweeping gesture as I had once seen in a movie done over the Grand
Canyon. But this was no Grand Canyon: it was vacant ground reserved next
to my father's two-by-four-foot grave plot in Farmingdale, stony, a stubborn crop of weeds blowing on it; the ash blanketed it as lightly as snow. I
thought I would get away with an emotion-free afternoon—just dump the
ash and get going—but I couldn't get going. I've heard it said that the dead
refuse to leave us and we won't leave the dead. I leaned against my father's
granite marker, numb fingers in my pockets, and wept cold tears at the ash-
strewn rectangle next to his where my mother should have lain, the space I
had since offered to Nathan. I now realize that I need not have been so generous, since I may need that space for myself. My mother tricked my father
out of companionship not only during a lifetime of group meetings and
spiritualist pursuits, but out of eternity as well. Dad, you are alone for eternity in a double bed. Now, without Enid, without Marilyn or Michael, without a compulsory partner in life, I may want to slide in next to him. That day,
I knew I had never really cried before in my life; I cried for my father's un-
deserved loneliness and for mine, until a rabbi, in beard and sidecurls, shovel
in hand, appeared out of nowhere to say didn't I know the gravediggers
were on strike and they would be locking the gates fifteen minutes early. I
placed a pebble on my father's gravestone and ran.

I agree the episode smacks of romance and superstition, but where in the
world other than with my father could I have deposited my mother's ashes?

Which is exactly Michael's—any child's—problem: how to keep father
and mother together through eternity? And although Enid is flying to Israel at the side of Lutz Moscow, I have trouble creeping back to Marilyn:

(1) I attribute my marriage to Marilyn to an error of the imagination.

(2) A free man living among the unenlightened tries to refuse their benefits.

(3) On the other hand, Marilyn claims she can still make me happy. "I can put a smile back on your face, Barry," Marilyn says, and I want to believe her. So I agree to be a guest on Fifty-first Avenue for Yom Kippur. Spinoza's two key interests are a rational explanation of the universe and a system of ethics. What, after all, is the purpose of human life? The end of the search is the attainment of happiness through wisdom. Happiness in *this* world is a Jewish ideal.

(4) *It is tough to be a philosopher and live without getting any happier.*

(5) Enid and Lutz, their marriage in doubt, are meanwhile returning to their old scientific-erotic pleasures. I will not give up my studies on the rainbow. Goethe says the discovery that the earth moves around the sun is the most sublime discovery of the human mind. His devotion to science is the central clue to his character.

Marilyn prepares a feast on Yom Kippur eve. All our favorite holiday dishes plus a little nosh of sushi. She has always longed to be chic, and though upscale Bob Donahue is gone, she retains the unshakable residue of class—hours at the pool, a Hermès scarf tied loosely around her neck, and raw fish, pink and sparkling. While Michael is dressing, we sit with our chopsticks, dipping the fish and rice into the tangy horseradish soy mixture and into our mouths. Michael won't eat it, so we have it all to ourselves. Marilyn is quiet. Her compliance suggests the time has come to set things right.

It is only 4:30 in the afternoon; we won't need to be at the Temple until 6:00, through with dinner, ready to begin the fast. Michael begged me to be prompt. It was the least I could do, but now time is hanging over me like a dentist.

"Michael is tickled you're here," she begins. "But it's okay to talk a little without him."

Old disappointments rankle. "So let's talk," I say as a start, despite the bitter knowledge that we are already playing roles memorized long ago, she always initiating discussion, I avowing reason. This time I take the lead. "For starters, what happened between you and Donahue? Unless it's private."

"Let's just say he's interested in material things, and sex is one of them."

"And you? What about the pretty clothes, the spontaneity?"

"I don't need Bob Donahue for them."

"Let me say that *I'm* not different than I was a year ago."

"But I am."

Is she already one-upping me, forgetting that restraint is a sign of caring, all dolled up for the holidays, looking strikingly athletic in an ice blue wool suit that is tailored and smart? A starched yellow apron is tied about her waist.

"Can you itemize?"

"Well," she says, amused at the word we use for inventorying the items in the shop, "I left the Vision Centre. I'm available, Barry."

"Feliz is a partner now. Have you heard about our renovations?"

"I heard you're expanding."

"It was time."

"Well, in case you're hiring— I'm also enrolling in a course in the great books. We start with the *Poetics*."

"And Aristotle is supposed to bring us into step again?"

"I never appreciated your powers of concentration. I saw your studying as stubbornness. Unwillingness to do the things I wanted. Even our sex—"

"What is it exactly that you wanted?"

"You know. I'm still working on myself. I don't need to go over all of that, do I?"

"You were getting to our sex—"

"It was never *bad*, Barry. Do you think it was bad?"

It's not easy for me to talk about sex in the abstract. But I am not a first-time offender in this regard.

My silence about sex disturbs her, as I expected it would. She tosses another piece of fish into her mouth. "We might still be lucky," she says finally.

I am beginning to see! Without Donahue, she hasn't a moment to lose. "If all you want is another—"

"Every day there are new techniques. We've never tried artificial insemination."

"Well, what am I to think?"

"It's not *only* that. You still have the same problems, don't you? But we *owe* it to ourselves—"

"Christ, Marilyn."

I had been hoping to get a message that Enid is pregnant, already two months, and then in another letter, one of his Thomas Mann specials, an elaborately beautiful confession that Lutz is willing to do the right thing and turn her over to me. As if Enid were anybody's property! How would I be related to my own child, third cousin, second cousin once removed? Oh, if only I were a month older, I would know.

"Michael has three more years of high school. In the meantime, he's shaving, Barry! He needs you."

"If you're thinking Michael is some kind of crazy glue that can keep us together—"

Unwilling to admit that we are getting nowhere, she calls in to Michael that dinner is ready. He is shined and sparkling in his navy blue bar mitzvah suit. Marilyn serves chopped liver, mushroom and barley soup, roasted chicken with braised celery and rice, tea, ruggelach, and orange slices to cleanse our palates before the fast. Michael packs away enough for a month. We arrive at the Temple just as the Kol Nidre is beginning. The sanctuary is luminous. The congregation is standing, praying that all vows they are about to make be canceled for the year ahead. It is one prayer that I admire for its legalistic good sense. Michael wanders to the side of the synagogue where the young people sit. Marilyn is radiating the excitement of the day, the hurry to get through with dinner, to stand with other Jews and pray.

"Our marriage hasn't been perfect," she whispers as we take our places, "but it's the best we've got. Read the prayer, Barry. Jews don't feel bound by foolish promises. All the more reason to make them."

"I miss Mayberg," I say, looking about.

She smiles at our neighbors in the pew, people I don't even know.

"Happy new year," they say.

"Happy new year," we reply. To Marilyn I add, "Ending what was imperfect is more bitter than ending what was perfect."

"For God's sake, it's Yom Kippur," she says. "Don't be mean!"

The Yom Kippur day services are conducted by a visiting rabbinical student from the seminary, a red-cheeked fiery twenty-three-year-old who preaches on an Iranian folk proverb: "If you see a blind man, kick him, lest you be kinder than God." The irony of the sermon is brilliant, and though I hear people around me puzzling aloud and asking who brought this yeshiva-boy lunatic to Bayside (kicking a blind man!), I am heavy-hearted with the mysteries of blindness and Bernard's unparalleled suffering, and thoughts of Enid, not as lost cousin but as lost lover. How can I endure not knowing whether the child she will have is mine? Or Bernard's? In a month, the possibility will have passed—. Meanwhile, I put another sleepless secret to bed in my heart. Bernard, my philosophic friend, am I playing at being meaner than God? Am I? Let me be your friend. Let's get together, out of friendship for the greatest *E* of them all—Enid Moscow.

Mordecai's conspicuous absence as the congregation sings one of his favorite hymns finally undoes me, and I tell Marilyn and Michael that I am in need of air. I've stayed long enough for a fellow who doesn't believe in sin and therefore has nothing to atone for on this Day of Atonement; but I am sad. On the way out, stopped by Professor Gene Peres-Pritzker (St. John's University, Department of Physics), I ask him if he will read my essay before I submit it. "You don't need an illiterate like me," he says, attaching very little importance to what I'm saying. But visibly uncomfortable at my silence, he is forced to ramble on, "A new government contract just came through. Have to keep my graduate students busy. Sorry, Glassman. Can't possibly." And he heads back into the singing congregation, the low deep rumble of male voices vaguely off key without Mayberg at the lead. As the door opens and closes I catch a glimpse of Marilyn, slumped in prayer, the seat to the right of her empty.

I return to the house for the essay I have brought, seal its manila envelope, and drop it off at the Bayside post office.

The Yom Kippur experiment fails. I know down to my socks that I must throw my things together and clear out of this house. Marilyn is not at all passive, but mannered, a highly stylized version of Marilyn. She ends by proving to me that her love for her child is the only reality in her life, which she is desperate to repeat. Somehow she has come out of the Bronx more genteel than I remembered, but keyed up, with her own fixed agenda, and striving to impress me with how young and successful she is, as if she and I were meeting at a class reunion after twenty years.

I pick up my suit and overnight bag, and as I reach my car, Michael is running toward me. I reach my arms out to him as I used to when he was learning to walk; he skids to a halt just short of my reach.

Now, at thirteen, post–bar mitzvah, Michael has been fasting for the first time. He pulls at his tie and loosens it.

"You look pretty wiped out," I say.

"Where are you going?" He is out of breath.

"Wanna come?"

"Tell me where," he repeats.

"Wherever. Wanna come?"

"Don't kid around!"

"Okay. Maybe to look for some land."

"Land?"

"You know. A couple of acres, Michael, upstate in the country."

"Now? It's the middle of Yom Kippur."

"So it is. Tell you what. If you want to come, I'll wait. We'll go next weekend. Together."

He hesitates. "You going to move upstate?"

"Maybe."

The sun is warm, and Michael slides off his jacket and slings it across his back, his shoulders broader under the white shirt than I remembered. He winces.

"Mike, can I persuade you?"

A stone, kicked clear down the street, glances off the hubcap of a car parked at the curb.

"Come on, Mike. Follow me." I take his arm and lead him around the side of the house and into the backyard. The old ground where the vegetable garden had been shows rows of ancient corn husks. Tatters of the black plastic mulch that I used around my plants still cling to large rocks that anchor it in place. The herb garden has some life in it, a bush of tarragon, thick clusters of thyme and rosemary, the gray-green spears of sage still redolent despite a year of neglect. I bend down and, using my fingers, happily rake around the sage, clearing out the hay caught at the roots, freeing the cool, damp dirt. I smell the earth. I sift it through my fingers. I find a stick, poke it in the ground and prop the tarragon against it. Then I set the rocks in a straight line at the border of the garden, pulling away fragments of black plastic and depositing the shreds in the garbage cans at the side door, whipping along into the garage where I grab a handful of garden tools, throw them into the trunk of my car, and slam the trunk lid before I can be sure what I have taken.

"Mike, I want to find a piece of ground. I can't seem to *do* much in Brooklyn. I want to clear some land. Grow melons."

"What about the shop?"

"Shop's doing fine. And I have another one in the works. Theresa Gluck has let me know she wants to sell me Herm's practice. I'm going to buy it. So if you don't decide to run away again, I'll treat you to four years of college, and I'll still have enough to pay off this house, and a piece of land— Look, Mike, I'm not asking for blood. I'm not telling you to leave your mother— but a ride in the country?"

I don't expect Michael to come. I don't expect him to leave Marilyn. I don't expect him to talk about it.

And I am right. He is now mindlessly trailing his jacket in the dirt, inhaling gently, shaking his head. His soft cheeks are pale.

"Deirdre's coming home tonight. I want to be around."

"For good?"

"Looks that way."

"She didn't convert?"

"Her parents got on her case . . . well, I don't know the whole story." He grins at me. "But I want to make sure she hasn't weirded out. I hope you find something, Dad. You want a lot of trees?"

"Not too many. Plants need sun."

I grin back and give him a hug. "What are you going to do now, Mike?"

"Go back to the synagogue. Finish up the fast with Mom."

"Good idea."

Then I drive away. In half an hour I am pounding at Bernard's door, prevailing upon him to join me. He is suspicious, but I plead with him.

"A ride in the country," I say, pity for him filling my eyes and impeding the life I want to live, for he is blinder than I remember, and I have kicked this blind man enough. Behind him the living room is scarcely a triumph of order. While it is true the map is the same, and he moves about with ease, the surfaces are aclutter with an assortment of daily artifacts—spoons, cups, Scotch tape, a pocket calculator thrown down on the coffee table, a moldy piece of bread leaning against the table lamp, a new row of tiny potted plants on the window will. Grigory is not at home, though I spot a pair of his cowboy boots standing on top of the TV next to a glitzy doll of the kind won in a shooting gallery. Grigory has mastered the art of keeping the floor free of obstacles; Bernard asks me in as he shuts off the record player, returns the milk to the refrigerator, and moves his lunch dishes to the sink. I congratulate him on his efficiency, though I am on the brink of more pity at his living here amid such disorder. But when he pulls his coat out of the closet and pulls it on, he is vastly confident; though he buttons it deftly, it goes askew. His fingers pause over the bottom buttonhole; there is nothing to fill it with. He ignores it, ignores the crookedness, ignores the Scotch tape and moldy bread, and, like the rest of us, ignores what he cannot see, as though things everywhere are a mix of invisible irregularities and tiny mismatches, all rather silly in the scheme of things. I make no offer to set him straight. He takes my arm expertly. It is warm in Brooklyn. The humidity breathes on our necks, and a slight breeze seems to come from the direction of Queens. I allow his crooked buttoning to stand between us as a sign.

Soon we are high over the Hudson on the span of the George Washington Bridge and heading north toward Orange County. The severity of Yom Kippur has been like vodka in my veins, as I sat in shul, mailed my essay, and talked to Michael. I hadn't felt it then, but the day now throws me into the air. I am pleasantly enervated, but no longer hungry. And here we are, two solitary men on the Palisades Parkway at the peak of afternoon; the road is the entire universe galloping from one slow foothill to the next.

"Bernard," I say, knowing that the mind can suffer great changes, "on the left we are coming to a magnificent stand of trees, swamp maple I think, a mass of flat golden orange leaves, and on the right the green countryside is falling away. Down below I can see the river, the same color as the sky. The truth is that it all exists, side by side, seamlessly."

" 'Features of the same face,' " Bernard says. "Wordsworth," he adds quietly, pinning his fastidious memory to what I see.

"And now, coming up on the right—Bernard, you'd love this—"

"Do you miss Enid?" he asks suddenly. "Do you think he's made her happy? Do you think he's changed her?"

"Her happiness doesn't depend on him. Her happiness is not to choose whether to be Enid, but to *be* Enid."

"Well, go on, Barry. You're doing beautifully—"

"Oak or pin oak, I'm not so hot at trees, but the scarlet of the leaves stands out, is flung right out over the road. Behind it, nothing. A few clouds. We can't conceive of Enid not exercising her power."

"You make her sound like God," Bernard says. "Far from it!" He wipes his lips with a hand.

I am driving slowly, for not eating all day has slowed my arms and legs, but Bernard is fast in thought and so private that I have surrendered all danger of pitying him. Pity requires impotence, Godlessness, and I am a man with a gene for God! Nor do I pity myself, for I know in my knees I shall have to hunt for a piece of land, something in the mountains, about an hour, an hour and a half from either store. It may take Sunday after Sunday, all my free time. I may get sick of looking, but I am willing. This is a beginning, though perhaps banal, and I talk banally to Bernard, who sits at my right, blithely accompanying me as my heart yearns for acreage, land, nothing a human being can provide. For once he misses the influence of my heart, and believes he is a source of power for me, his hair as black as ever, his zeal as mysterious, his talk as anguished and as glorious.

We go over a bump in the road, and a loud rattling and banging come from the trunk. "What was *that*?" Bernard asks. "What's *in* there?"

"A few shovels and a couple of rakes."

"Digging is better than thinking about digging," he says.

In the next fifty yards I spot a deer standing motionless off to the right in a clearing before a clump of white birch, and I don't mention it to Bernard, I don't breathe a word of how ferociously his ears are pointing into the mountains, how his hearing must be everything. There are silent things in this world a blind man will never know.

"When I die," Bernard says, but he is needle-sharp, sensing that I have left a blank in his enduring vision, "I'd want my ashes scattered right here on the Palisades in the autumn—in this broad space."

We settle peaceably into the cool breeze rising to the car from the river below. As the road ahead is concealed by the half-wild hills, I turn on the radio. Bernard hums along, while I vaguely consider not phoning Uncle Nathan with Bernard's answer.

ACKNOWLEDGMENTS

The author is indebted to many individuals and institutions for their advice and instruction on Spinoza and optics. I wish especially to thank Professor Harvey Burstein, Department of Philosophy, Queens College; Dr. A. K. Offenberg, Bibliotheca Rosenthaliana, Universiteits Bibliotheek, Amsterdam; Cantor Solomon Vaz Diaz of the Portuguese Synagogue in Amsterdam; the Amsterdam Municipal Archives; Dr. F. J. Hoogewoud, Secretary, Spinoza Society, Amsterdam, and Mr. van Dam for opening the Spinoza House in Rijnsburg; Mrs. Charlotte van Oeffel, for opening the Spinoza House and Museum in The Hague; Ms. Dina Abramowicz, YIVO; exhibit on optics, Science Museum, The Hague; the Joods Historisch Museum, Amsterdam; the staff of the Portuguese-Israelitische Cemetery in Ouderkerk. I am grateful to Dr. Mark Sverdlin and Mr. Oscar Ehrlich for introducing me to current optometrical procedures. My special thanks to the staffs of the British Library, the Columbia University Library, the Queens College Library, and the New York Public Library for their assistance.

Spinoza Selections—"On the Improvement of the Understanding," "Short Treatise on God, Man, and His Well-Being," "Ethics," and "Letters of Certain Learned Men to Spinoza and his Replies"—edited by John Wild (New York: Scribner's, 1930) and *The Chief Works of Spinoza*, translated by R. H. M. Elwes (New York: Dover, 1951) formed my primary texts. While I consulted many other books and documents, I relied heavily on the published work of the following Spinoza scholars, editors, and biographers: Hannah Arendt, Lewis Browne, Marjorie Grene, J. Alexander Gunn, Stuart Hampshire, S. Paul Kashap, Karl Jaspers, Dan Levin, Adolph S. Oko, Frederick Pollock, Bertrand Russell, A. E. Taylor, Roger Scruton, Leo Strauss, W. G. van der Tak, Theo van der Werf, A. M. Vaz Diaz, and A. Wolf.

I referred most usefully for background in optics and the rainbow to the following works: Carl B. Boyer, *The Rainbow: From Myth to Mathematics* (New York: Thomas Yoseloff, 1959); Francis A. Jenkins and Harvey E. White, *Fundamentals of Optics*, 4th ed. (New York: McGraw-Hill, 1957); Sir Isaac Newton, *Opticks*, repr. from 4th ed., foreword by Albert Einstein (New York: McGraw-Hill, 1931).

All of the above have my profound gratitude.

Design by David Bullen
Typeset in Mergenthaler Granjon
with Gill Sans display
by Wilsted & Taylor
Printed by Maple-Vail
on acid-free paper